TEED UP
FOR
TERROR

TED MULCAHEY

Book layout by ebooklaunch.com

Teed Up for Terror is a work of fiction. The places are mostly real, the people not so much. While some folks have similar or the same names, rest assured that any similarities to those in this book are coincidental. Any mistakes, omissions or screwups are my fault and not my wife's. She had the burden of reading the first draft and was helpful in more ways than she knows.

CHAPTER 1

It was called Glow Ball. It was a popular summer evening event at many of the private country clubs in the Pacific Northwest—for that matter, throughout the country. It went something like this:

Start drinking at six o'clock. About sevenish, dinner was served; something with a theme. Could be Mexican food, Italian food, burgers and beans, anything solid and with enough carbs to soak up the booze. Of course, it was essential that wine was served with the dinner; it would be a shame to dampen the buzz too much. It started to get dark around nine or nine thirty in this part of the country, so cordials and more wine had to be consumed until it was time to head out to the golfers' assigned holes. It was very important that it be dark.

Each group had eight golfers— four couples; it was a social event, after all. The golf balls were translucent and had a small hole through the center in which a glow stick was inserted, thus creating a "glow ball." Each couple was a team, and the format was alternate shots by each team. In each group of eight, there were four balls in play, and the number of holes played was only six. Four slightly inebriated couples swinging golf clubs in the dark over hilly fairways, sand traps, and creeks was almost always a recipe for a trip to the ER. If it wasn't a sprained ankle, it could easily be a sand wedge to the shin; maybe a torn ACL from falling off the tee box or a broken arm from falling out of a golf cart. Multiple injuries were possible, even probable. On this particular night, however, the thirty-two contestants escaped serious injury—well … thirty-one of them did.

It wasn't uncommon at these events to come across a wayward golf cart, either deep in the rough or on one of the holes not in use, that looked to be rocking from side to side more rhythmically than

1

expected. They were members, of course, and it *was* their club. These discoveries were almost always overlooked and made for great locker room gossip.

Jenne (pronounced Jenny) and Kevin O'Malley were two of the evening's contestants. They had finished up on the third hole, the farthest from the clubhouse, and were now headed down the ninth fairway, which adjoined the fourth, toward the clubhouse. The clear sky and tiny slice of moon created enough light to see where they were going as long as they stayed on the fairway, out from under the cover of the firs and cedars in the rough areas. It was July in Washington State, when it seldom rained and where the air smelled fresher than any place they had ever visited. It had turned out to be a spectacular evening and they were certain their two over par score would be a winner—maybe even a sleeve of balls.

The ninth was a dogleg to the left, and as they headed toward the lights of the clubhouse, they noticed one of the electric carts parked behind the huge western red cedar that penalized any golfer straying into the rough on their second shot to the green. It was a little surprising, but not unheard of, to see one of the members with a new honey, off recreating while the married couples called it a night. What was disturbing was the stationary nature of the vehicle and the sense that the cart had been abandoned.

"What do you think, Jenne? Is it someone just getting lucky?"

"Well, if they are, they're awfully quiet about it. Maybe they just left it there, or it broke down and they walked in."

"We're only a couple hundred yards from the pro shop. If it was just ditched there, I'll take it in for them." This fleet of carts was not equipped with headlights, since they were just for day use here at Kelsey Creek Country Club. "Just pull over there, Jenne. I'll see if it's drivable."

Kevin hopped out and gingerly stepped around the very dark cedar to the driver's side of the abandoned cart. He paused for a moment, then approached the buggy even more slowly. "Someone's slumped over the wheel. Maybe he's just passed out. I'll see if I can wake him up."

Kevin moved in a little closer and gently shook the golfer's shoulder. "Hey, buddy, wake up. Whoaaa, *holy shit*!" The driver of the cart slumped to the left and fell over onto the ground. Jenne had never heard that a yell that shrill from Kevin.

"Who is it? What's wrong?"

"Stay there, honey. It's Jerry Johnson. I'm pretty sure he's not just passed out. It looks like someone took a sand wedge to his head, maybe even a sixty-degree lob wedge. It's not a pretty sight."

There was still revelry going on at the club when the O'Malleys pulled up to the bar entrance. Lots of laughing, reliving good shots, making fun of the bad ones; all in attendance were enjoying themselves. They immediately sought out the general manager, who was doing his best to make certain anyone absorbing a little too much alcohol had a sober ride home. Many nights there were more than a few cars left in the parking lot.

"There he is, Jenne. Vincent, Vince, please come here for a sec." Kevin couldn't see the sense in creating an uproar among the partiers.

"Hey, you two, having fun?"

"Vince, we just came in from the ninth hole. There's a cart in the rough and JJ's lying on the ground beside it. I got an up-close look and I'm fairly certain he's dead. We need to call the police right away."

"Is this a joke? He dropped his wife off about thirty minutes ago—said he lost one of his clubs and went back to see if he could find it. I told him somebody would turn it in tomorrow, but he seemed preoccupied and told me no, he'd get it tonight."

Kevin thought the story a bit strange. No one went out at midnight to look for a golf club. "I don't know what he went out there for, but he sure as hell isn't coming back. Call the cops—now!"

Most of the members were gone when the police arrived. Vince Walker, the club's manager, was a wreck. Normally affable and politically astute, as any club manager with any tenure must be, he was struggling to calm Jerry Johnson's wife of only three years. Fortunately, one of the officers was a woman. Unfortunately for her, she had been delegated to break the news to the newly widowed Mrs. Debi Johnson, which she did as delicately as possible. Now Vince was trying to calm her, having already instructed Bret, the bartender, to contact her daughter to come and take her home.

The City of Bellevue, an affluent bedroom community of Seattle, had grown to a population of over 150,000, a 50 percent increase over the last twenty years. The wealthy residents, many Microsofties, Amazonians, and Starbuckians among them, provided a tax base that afforded wonderful schools, parks, and roads and a first-class police force. As such, murder by sand wedge was not a frequent occurrence, and the detectives had their hands full.

About the time the sun began peeking over the Cascades, the crime scene investigators were just wrapping things up. The body had been removed, the golf cart processed for evidence, and activities began to return to a sense of normalcy. Scuttlebutt in country club communities spreads like wildfire. The entire greens crew was now aware of the "Glow Ball Massacre," as it was being called. Dedicated as they were, though, nothing prevented them from preparing the course for the first tee at eight o'clock. Greens were mowed, sand traps raked, fairways and roughs trimmed perfectly. Kelsey Creek was famous for its lightning-fast greens, and today they were at twelve on the Stimp meter.

Thursday was ladies' day. Most clubs had finally given in to equal rights, allowing both sexes the freedom to play at any time, but a few still reserved Thursday mornings for women and Wednesday afternoons for men. Kelsey Creek was among the latter.

The club's origins went back to the 1950s. At that time, the wealthy blue-blood private clubs thought it inappropriate to allow Jews in as members. In the Seattle area there were many Jews who enjoyed the game, loved the camaraderie, and insisted on a game of gin rummy after golf. They were also pissed about not having a club of their own and not being allowed to join the snotty places. So, they said *screw it* and started their own private club. And so was born Kelsey Creek. Over the years it had morphed from entirely Jewish to mostly Jewish to slightly Jewish. Even today when the name came up it was, "Oh, you mean that Jewish club?" People were just plain weird.

The O'Malleys very much enjoyed the game of golf; they had both been raised with it. Their interior design firm had been growing nicely over the past several years, and they had looked at several private clubs before joining "the Creek." While a few of the area clubs had nice facilities, they came across as stuffy and exclusive. The members, and even the staff at Kelsey Creek, treated everyone the same. No one was more special than anyone else; the staff was treated like family. They had made a number of close friends here and felt very much at home. Sure, there were still little cliques and frequent gossip, but for the most part they enjoyed it immensely. Not so much last night, though.

By the time the weekend arrived, the club and the entire city were abuzz with the story of the demise of Jerry Johnson—JJ to his friends. A jeweler who owned a small manufacturing shop in the SODO area of Seattle, his sixty years of age and forty-four-inch waist belied his level of success with the ladies. The shop produced custom-designed jewelry that he wholesaled to various retail stores across the West Coast and Canada.

Debi was Jerry's fourth wife and had recently sold her hair salon in order to focus completely on her golf game. JJ was a low-handicap golfer, after all, and had been runner up in last year's senior club championship. It was important for her not to embarrass her husband in the mixed club events, hence her new dedication to improvement. Of course, now it didn't seem that important.

JJ, a member of the club for almost twenty-five years, was part of a group of six who played at least five times a week, weather permitting. Depending on who showed up on any given day, it was two threesomes, a foursome, or a fivesome. The group was known as the "A" Train, primarily because they were the heaviest bettors at the Creek. On a good day the big winner could take home five or six hundred dollars. Conversely, if it was a day of three-putts and double bogeys, it could cost upwards of seven or eight hundred bucks. For most of the golfers at the club, regardless of their millions, it was out of their comfort zone. Apparently, it was nothing to gamble tens of thousands on the rise and fall of the S&P, but a few hundred bucks on the links, well, that was a bridge too far.

The "A" Train had been together for a dozen years. Occasionally one of the six would leave and a newer member would join. Sometimes the group dwindled to only four, but mostly it held at five or six. Kevin

O'Malley was now the newest member of the Train, having joined the group shortly after becoming a club member. The stakes at first seemed a little steep. The opportunity to play with a group of single-digit handicaps was enticing, though. After a few months of playing with them, two things became obvious. One, nobody cheated on their handicap; every score was posted religiously after the round. Should someone fail to do so, the rest of the group would issue stern reminders. And two, since all the handicaps were accurate, the money never stayed in anyone's pocket for long.

In fact, over the past ten months that Kevin had been playing with them, he was maybe a hundred up. He knew this for certain because Jeff, an accountant and a five handicap, kept track of the wins and losses of every member of the Train. The man loved numbers and finally started keeping track because of the frequent bitching about who was the biggest loser. The ledger for the past ten years—nine before Kevin—revealed the obvious. The money was just passed around. One or two of the guys won for a few weeks while they were playing well. Once their handicaps dropped, they became losers. That was the beauty of the handicap system. Kevin realized that he might win, or he might lose, but mostly he would just have fun and do it with little risk. The rest of the club thought the "A" Train were big gamblers, but that was far from the truth. They *were* big bettors, but at the end of the year, there was very little difference in their individual outcomes.

At breakfast on Saturday only Kevin and Jeff showed. Normally JJ would have joined them, and the rest would meet on the driving range. Gone was the usual banter and lighthearted conversation. Jerry's absence was palpable and cast a pall over the grille.

"Hard to believe, huh, Kev?"

"Yeah, I feel that way for sure, and I'm the one who found him. That's something I won't soon forget."

"I never asked; what did it look like?"

"It looked like someone took a sand wedge and smashed his head in. Good thing it was dark and I didn't see it too clearly."

"I know this sounds silly, but how do you know it was a sand wedge, not a nine or an eight iron?" Jeff's sarcasm was always in a nip-and-tuck race with that of Kevin. His ability to see even the tiniest light of humor in the darkest of subjects was appreciated only by a select few.

"Don't be a dick. Didn't I tell you they found the thing under the cart?"

"Uh, no, you didn't, otherwise I wouldn't have asked."

"Well, they did, when they moved it after they took the body away. Just in case you're wondering, it was a Vokey, sixty-two degrees with eight degrees of bounce." Kevin figured he'd throw in some useless crap as well.

"Sixty-two? That sure as shit wasn't JJ's. He may be—sorry, may have *been*—a five handicap, but the man had the hands of a blacksmith. No offense to blacksmiths everywhere, but no way could he have hit that thing."

Maryanne arrived with their bacon-and-egg sandwiches, so they dialed back the dialog until she was gone.

"The cops asked me if I thought it was his and I told them the same thing. His clubs were still on the cart, though, and none of them were missing. It's not like there are murderers hiding in the woods here, waiting for prey. I can't imagine who or why anyone would do that."

"Wait a minute, I thought he told Vince he went out looking for one of his clubs. If they were all in his bag, then he went back out there for something else, right?"

"Seems like it, but I'm sure they'll figure things out. Good thing Bellevue's finest are on it and it's not up to us to solve it."

CHAPTER 2

Jerry Johnson's funeral was the next week with a reception at the club immediately afterwards. The turnout was modest considering his tenure at the club. The man lived for the competition and, unlike the other "A" Trainers, he was known to frequent the bookies and the track. While betting on the links was one thing, other forms of gambling, save for the stock market, were not favored by the balance of the group.

JJ's jewelry business had been in his family for fifty years. His dad had built it up over time and developed a solid portfolio of clients, supplying them with bespoke designs and quality merchandise. When Jerry took over the company, he initially made a consistent effort to maintain those clients while attempting to expand his sales with new ones. As often happens with inherited businesses, Jerry grew comfortable with the steady cash flow; as a result, his efforts at expanding soon diminished. Getting his kicks by risking his not-so-hard-earned dollars at games of chance and with sports bookies occupied much of his time.

A gregarious sort, Jerry was always quick with a joke or a pun. Despite his proclivity for pissing away his inheritance, he was still fun to have around. His fourth wife proved no hindrance to his frequenting the "singles for seniors" bars and taverns in the area. His broad smile and open wallet endeared him to sugar daddy seekers and piano players alike. The drinking spots were sure to take a hit upon his passing off to the first tee at the Golden Gate club where St. Peter manned the starter's booth. His short stature, florid drinker's complexion, and wide girth would be sorely missed by the "A" Train. Debi, maybe, would get over him a little sooner.

With his heavy nightlife schedule, it was understandable that Johnson Jewelers would start to leak oil. First, the established clientele started noticing late deliveries and shoddy work. The quality of the diamonds and other precious stones deteriorated. The new customers discovered that Johnson's slowly upped their pricing beyond a reasonable markup, leaving them feeling like suckers. This distressing trend encouraged a steady decline in sales, resulting in a walloping 30 percent decline over the recent five-year period. JJ began laying off his most dependable employees and craftsmen, further amplifying his poor production standards. At the time of his death, he had downsized his place of business to a 500-square-foot office with one employee. It was not going to be a pretty sight when Debi was presented with the pittance of her inheritance.

Nothing seemed to stop the man, though. He drank the same amount, caroused equally, and more than held up his social contract to the "A" Train on the golf course. In spite of his failings—and there were many—Jerry was a likable fellow. Perhaps dying before the creditors came to collect was a fitting conclusion to a man who exemplified carpe diem.

After several weeks, the shock of the murder of a well-known club member slowly leaked away. There would always be the funny stories, of course, and the Train would continue to miss him for some time. Even in their small group, though, life inexorably plowed forward. They were down to five now, so there was only one tee time needed; at least the pro shop would be happy about that.

It was Wednesday afternoon and the foursome consisted of Kevin, Jeff Williams, Chris Connally, and Danny Driggs. The fifth player, Mani Darzi, was out of town visiting family but promised to be back for Saturday's game. The handicaps were fairly close today: two fives, a seven, and a nine. As always, the higher handicap was teamed with the lowest to minimize the stroke differential. Today it was the seven, Kevin, with Jeff, and Danny, a nine, with Chris, the other five. The betting games were many. One team against the other, individual bets with the two members of the opposite team, and skins, which was every man for himself. There was also a "snake" game in which the player who three-putted owed each of the others five bucks. To the novice it seemed complicated, and if anyone joined the crew as a guest, the common refrain was, "Yeah, sounds good. Just let me know what I owe when we're done."

Truth was, if a player shot to his handicap or better, he almost always came out on top. Since that only happened 25 percent of the time, it was usually a spirited contest. The only thing to avoid was finishing dead last.

It only took until the approach to the first green before Jeff popped off, "So have the cops figured out what happened with JJ yet?"

"Yeah, Kev, any news?" Danny, too, wanted the scoop.

"You're probably aware that they don't consult with me with their findings."

"We know that; we just thought that because you found the body and everything, you might hear something before it became public," Chris chimed in as he lined up his thirty-footer for a bird. It was a hard left to right breaker, downhill. The yellow Titleist rolled by on the high side, settling six feet past the hole.

The familiar "snaky wakie" chirps sounded as the very real possibility of Chris losing fifteen bucks on a three-putt loomed. In most groups the joy of an excellent shot was shared by the participants. In this one, probably because the handicaps were lower, the laughs and guffaws after a terrible shot far outpaced the accolades given to a superb one. It was something the occasional player in the group never understood or got used to. Maybe that was why the camaraderie was so strong; they relished being misunderstood.

Chris stepped up to his six-footer and promptly pulled it, not coming close to the hole. "Shit! You'd think you guys could cut me a little slack. I'm still upset over JJ."

The other three looked at each other, and Danny spoke first. "You're right, Chris. So are we. That'll be five bucks for each of us, thank you." The Train gave no quarter and expected none.

It was overcast. This time of year, it usually started out that way and burned off by noon. The temperature was comfortable, though, and the level of play was a notch above their usual. Chris and Danny were within a few shots of par as they turned to the back nine and were up at least 150. As they climbed the hill to the tenth tee, Jeff asked, "Really, Kev? You haven't heard anything?"

"Nope. I really don't expect to, Jeff. I'm surprised that we haven't, though. It's been almost three weeks and I think they usually have a pretty good idea about suspects right off the bat. Jerry was a good guy and well liked, even though he caroused a bit. I just can't imagine why anyone would kill him."

"Nor can I. He had his issues for sure, but I kinda miss the guy."

"Me too. I don't know why I should hear anything before anyone else, but if I do, I'll let you know. In the meantime, unless you get your ass in gear, these two are gonna force us to hit the ATM when we finish."

O'Malley and Associates occupied the first floor of a former firehouse on Main Street in Old Bellevue. The entire surrounding area had become "gentrified," meaning lots of condos and mixed-use high-rises that exhibited zero redeeming architectural qualities. Kevin had owned the building for over thirty years, first as his residence, now as their office and *former* residence. Their business was still young—less than four years old—and their marriage even younger—less than two. They felt like they'd known each other forever, though, and time spent with each other was far more preferable than any alternative.

Until a few months ago, the upper floor of their office building had been their home. Their recent Vancouver Island adventures had brought them closer to nature, while their new friends from that experience had taught them the value of tranquility and its soothing effects on the soul. The O'Malleys were now the proud owners of a five-acre parcel of property, the entire southwest corner of which was bisected by Bear Creek. The thirty-minute drive to their studio from their new home in Woodinville was a small price to pay for the peaceful seclusion they enjoyed while away from their business. At 1,500 square feet, the A-frame dwelling wasn't much, but for the two of them, it was plenty. It was a common occurrence to see all manner of wildlife slaking their thirst at the creek's edge. Deer, bobcats, even the occasional black bear would pay a visit to their slice of paradise. Kevin's travails with bears notwithstanding, they loved the place.

"You know what this means, don't you?"

"Um, no. What does what mean?" They had just finished a glass of sauvignon blanc while sitting on the deck overlooking the creek. The gentle zephyr accompanying the still-warm six o'clock sun was enough to encourage a melting of the pressures of the day. Kevin was still trying to figure out what was causing him to pull the three-foot right-to-left breaking putts, while Jenne was apparently on another wavelength.

"Now that we have all this property, we need a dog."

"Huh, what? Sounds like you've been thinking about this for a while." Both of them were animal lovers, but their former downtown loft had been no place for a pet.

"I have been. And, you know, we've always said if we had the room, we would just *have* to get a dog."

"Yes, we did. We do have the room, but what about during the day? What would we do then?"

"Easy. He or she comes to the office. When we're out on a job, Ilene and Valerie can watch the dog. They both like animals, and I'm certain none of our clients would care. If they do, screw 'em. I wouldn't want to work for them anyway." Jenne was easygoing about many things, but her patience with folks who weren't animal lovers was nonexistent.

"Okay, so how do you really feel? Have you given any thought to what kind of dog you're going to get for me?"

"It's for us, smartass, and yes, I have. Since we have some land here, I was thinking a big dog. I've always wanted a German Shepherd."

"Really? That's news to me. Have you been keeping this a secret?"

"Kevin, don't you remember talking about this when we were having dinner at the club last week? There were six of us at the table— Jeff and Anne, and Danny and Sally. We were all talking about our favorite dogs."

"Sorry, hon, must've missed that part. I was probably occupied with golf talk."

"You probably were. Anyway, that's what we're getting. There's this place up in Maltby that breeds the little guys. Let's go up there Saturday and—don't say it, I know; after golf."

Kevin knew when Jenne had her mind made up. Truth be told, he'd always wondered about those dogs and what they were really like. They seemed both fierce and regal at the same time, and their loyalty was unquestionable. "Sounds wonderful, dear. I can't wait."

The workload for O'Malley and Associates had grown steadily. Over his fifty-three years, Kevin had filled a variety of sales and marketing positions with manufacturers of interior furnishings. His experience working with the design community and his frustration at the ever-increasing interference from folks up the ladder who didn't know any better provided the catalyst for him to resign from his position and look for another direction. The gods were smiling on him when his and Jenne's paths crossed during an industry function. Since both were coming from difficult breakups, a new entanglement was the furthest thing from their minds. And yet it happened, very suddenly. They were stunned by how easy and natural it felt being together.

Jenne, too, had been at a crossroads. An accomplished interior designer with a number of published projects both in the US and abroad, she held the position of Director of Interior Design at one of the top Seattle architectural firms. Her dissatisfaction with the glass ceiling at the firm had given her the impetus to look in another direction as well. After dating for a week, the two became inseparable, and three months later, they started O'Malley and Associates. Kevin had encouraged her to name it after herself, Browne and Associates, but Jenne had made a strong case for the Irish surname. "Here's the deal," she'd said. "I really like the name O'Malley, and we'll probably get married anyway, so let's go with that."

She was difficult to argue with, and even at this early stage, Kevin was certain that this was the person he'd be spending the rest of his life alongside. The last four years had been wonderful. Business was challenging but fun, plus they'd been incredibly fortunate with their two employees, whom they considered family. Joining Kelsey Creek was mostly a result of their love for golf, although the flurry of new business as a result of their social connections there, while unexpected, was certainly welcome. The only bump in the road—more of a crater, actually—had been the Tofino Inn and Spa project. Things had worked out marvelously in the end, but they would not easily forget the ordeal.

CHAPTER 3

It was Saturday, after golf, and the designing duo was headed to Maltby to look at German Shepherds. But Jenne's mind was elsewhere. "Kev, you remember yesterday when we shut the office down early and I played nine at the club?"

"Yup."

"Well, I ended up playing with this woman—her name is Shelly Chesnick. She said her husband is named Bernie. Do you know him?"

"I think I ended up with him as a teammate in one of the opening day events. He was kinda loud—a tad obnoxious, as I recall. He was also very shitty. He sported a twenty-eight handicap and couldn't come close to playing to it. How was the wife?"

"She was actually pleasant—maybe a little too impressed with their money, though. She just had to tell me about their ski place in Jackson Hole and their winter home in Palm Springs."

"Yeah, well, must be nice. Where do they live here?"

"That's just it. She said they're renting a place in Clyde Hill while they finish building their new home in Medina."

"Yikes, big bucks building there."

"I know. She made a point of telling me that Bill Gates's place was just down the road from theirs. What I wanted to tell you, though, was that she fired their interior designer and wanted me to take a look and see if we could finish up the project for them."

Picking up the pieces in the middle of a project *after* someone has fired their original designer is a minefield fraught with danger. Firing a designer while the project is under construction is always a red flag. There are some designers who aren't on the top shelf. Still, most know what they're doing, and if the clients followed their direction, the end result would be at the worst pleasing, at the best spectacular. The challenge is to deliver what the client says they're looking to achieve—the "feel" of the place—and, often, doing it *in spite* of the client. Professionals know what goes with what. They understand that a little of some colors goes a long way and that early American dining room sets don't belong in mid-century homes. The interior designer's number one goal is to gain the client's trust, for he or she to accept that all the pieces of the puzzle will eventually deliver the desired product. Each square of tile or yard of pillow fabric isn't critical, but one finish poorly selected can make for a disaster. The folks who are paid to do this work usually know how the puzzle pieces fit if given enough room to do it. Personality conflicts are usually at the root of a dismissal.

"Jenne, you know how I feel about starting in the middle of things. Hell, you feel the same way."

"I know, but the architect is the son of a Wright protégé. He's doing clean modern lines but still incorporating some of Wright's principles. I thought we should at least take a look." They had just taken the turnoff to Maltby, and Kevin glanced over at his wife. Every time he saw those big hazel eyes and prominent cheekbones juxtaposed with her auburn hair and olive complexion his heart melted just a little. He knew she loved contemporary design elements and had always wanted to work with this architect.

"Tell you what, hon, let's meet with Shelly the first of the week if you're certain she's the one calling the shots. If it's that Bernie guy, we should probably take a pass."

"Okay, I'll email her when we get back home. Hey, take a left here. There's the sign."

They turned into the gravel road that meandered up a gentle hill, driving past the modest sign that announced "Maltby GSDs." A newly painted red barn marked the end of the drive and the kennel office. When Kevin turned the engine off and opened his door, a cacophony of barks and howls greeted him. "Well, I suppose there's no way we're sneaking up on anyone here. Sheesh!"

Several dozen individual kennels were spread in a semicircle on the west side of the barn, all of them occupied by German Shepherds of various sizes. A twenty-something gal with a friendly smile came out of the barn. With her slender build and short wispy hair, she looked more like a Starbucks barista than a kennel manager and German Shepherd breeder. "Hi, you must be Jenne. I'm Erin. Welcome." The sound of the dogs made it difficult to hear her.

She said, "Excuse me" and turned toward the dogs with her arm raised. "Halt!" she commanded. There was immediate silence. The O'Malleys looked at each other, impressed.

"Wow, that was something. Do they do everything you tell them?" Kevin was seriously paying attention now.

"They are all at different levels of training, but as you can see, it's important to get them to shut up every now and then. These animals are not ordinary dogs. They come from Germany, from strong working breeding lines. They are extremely intelligent, so much so that if you think you'll be getting a nice pet you can leave at home during the day, you are sadly mistaken. In fact, if that is what you'd like, you should get some other dog." Apparently, Erin cared more about finding suitable homes for her dogs than making money.

"These dogs need to work. They need exercise and training. They are *pack* dogs, which means you two will be her pack mates. He or she will never leave your side. Are you looking for protection?"

"I guess we never thought about that. I've always loved this breed, how regal they are. I knew they were intelligent, but that was about it." Jenne appreciated Erin's frankness.

"If you get one of our dogs for whatever reason, you need to know two things. First, you'll need to spend lots of time with them. Their intelligence requires it. They get bored easily and they need lots of exercise. Secondly, the protection thing, that's pretty much built into the animal. Their loyalty to the pack—that's you two—takes priority over everything else. If you understand that and you are committed to your partnership with your dog, you will never have a more rewarding experience.

"That's my spiel and I mean every word of it. My dad started this place and now I run it and do it the same way he did. We get too many folks who come here thinking these animals are like plants or goldfish. They're not, and they're not like other dogs. They're special. They'll be more a part of your family than you can ever imagine."

"Geez, Erin, you make it sound like they're people."

"No, they're not people, but they are more trustworthy. If you get one and work with it, you'll understand."

Kevin wasn't impressed easily, but he was now. "Okay if we look around?"

"Of course. Take your time. My two-year-old is inside with our own dogs. I need to check on him."

Jenne was curious. "You left him in the barn with two Shepherds? Is that safe?"

Erin looked at Jenne like she was daft. "Come here," she ordered with a crooked finger. "Take a look for yourself."

The O'Malleys gingerly opened the door and peeked into the barn. The young tyke was rolling on the floor with two tan-and-black German Shepherds, each well over a hundred pounds, their father sitting at a desk several feet away. That was until the squeak of the door warned the dogs, who immediately alerted and barked furiously, stampeding toward the door.

"Halt!" There was Erin with the command again. Both dogs instantly stopped and sat, waiting for instructions.

"Well, I can see your son is much safer than we are with his two pals here." Jenne had never seen such a display of discipline.

"They wouldn't hurt you unless you tried something with Tyler. Their barking and aggressive behavior is usually enough to discourage anyone. Once I introduce you to them, they'll be friendly to you. The thing to remember is the *pack* element. They only have one pack, and if you're not part of it, they aren't interested. They aren't mean or vicious; they just don't like anyone screwing with their family. Why don't you go out and look around? If you see an animal that interests you, I'll be in here with my pack."

The O'Malleys made the rounds of the kennels. There were youngsters from ten weeks old to three months old, their huge floppy ears waiting until their bodies caught up.

"What do you think, Kev? Are we up for this?"

"I thought you always wanted one."

"Well, I did, but I don't know about the training and all."

"Erin said that every Saturday they offer a training class, Shepherds only and Maltby dogs only. Maybe that's one way we could do it. Most of the other stuff I think is just common sense. You know, you—I mean, we—have to be the boss. We walk him, not him or her walking us. I'm pretty sure with Erin's help we can pull it off."

"Kevin, look over there." Jenne pointed with her chin to one of the kennels with a somewhat older dog in it.

"Looks like a she; the sign says her name's Emma." Kevin clucked his tongue several times and the dog met his eyes. "Hey, Emma, hey, sweetie, how ya doin'? What's it like being in this cage?"

Jenne was surprised at the tenderness in her husband's voice, but one look at the animal told her why. She was a beautiful animal with sweet eyes and an incredibly perceptive face. "Geez, she's gorgeous. Let's see if Erin can tell us about her."

After an hour of walking and playing with Emma, there was no separating her from the O'Malleys. They discovered she was six months old and had arrived from Germany about a month ago. All of the dogs at Maltby were bred from the same original German stock, and training was begun as soon as they were weaned.

"I think we'd like to take this girl, Erin. What do you need from us?"

They were given all the paperwork, including her registrations both from Germany and from the AKC. She had been chipped already and all shots were up to date. Even though he'd heard GSDs from excellent breeders were expensive, Kevin still received a little sticker shock when he came to pay Erin. He'd never thought the day would come when he'd fork out over four grand for a dog. When his mild suggestion of protest brought a stern look from Jenne, he knew they now had a new member of the family.

"Don't forget she's still a little unsure of herself after her trip here. Please remember to be patient with her and take this with you."

"What's this? I don't think I can read it." Kevin suspected he was looking at something in another language.

"Those are German commands," Erin explained. "She's *from* Germany, remember? That's what she knows; you'll have to learn them. After a while she'll learn English, but you'll need to use those for now. You're going to love this animal, and please call me if you have any questions or concerns. And don't forget class on Saturdays."

Kevin had the feeling that Erin could handle anything that came her way. No wonder she was so good with this breed. "Emma, you hop up here in the back. Jenne, you can ride up front with me."

"Think again, Mister. I'm riding in the back here with my girl." And so began the formation of the O'Malley *pack*.

Although wary of the pitfalls of attempting to pick up the pieces while construction was under way, Jenne arranged a meeting with Shelly for Monday afternoon. She and Kevin spent the entire day Sunday getting Emma acclimatized to her new home. That she was still somewhat confused was obvious, but they were both convinced that they had acquired a new family member. They left her at the office with Ilene while they went about their day.

"Did you find out if we're meeting with just Shelly or is her husband going to be there?" Kevin asked as they pulled into the driveway of the Clyde Hill rambler that the Chesnicks were renting.

"I got the impression this was her baby. I guess we'll see when we get in there."

Shelly opened the door before they had a chance to ring the bell. "I'm really glad you could make it. You must be Kevin. Bernie told me that you play in the 'A' Train and that you're a very good golfer."

"I'm not sure how good I am, but yes, I do play with those thieves. Should we sit and take a look at your plans?"

They perused the construction drawings while making small talk. Jenne, knowing it was critical to establish a direct line of communication with the decision-maker, addressed the question head on. "Will your husband be making any choices regarding the furnishings or finishes?"

"Nope, this is all mine. We've been married twenty-eight years, but only ten of them to each other." She smiled, proud of her cleverness. "When he told me we were going to build in Medina, I told him that it was fine with me, but I get to choose the architect and the interior designer, and he has no say in any of the decisions."

Kevin was slightly taken aback. "And he's fine with this arrangement?"

"Bernie has eighteen stores up and down the West Coast. He spends all his time on them—when he's not playing golf, that is. I'm sure you've seen his ads on TV. The damn things are on all the time."

"What ads? What kind of stores are they?" Jenne was curious.

"Cascade Creations, a name you can trust, when love is calling, a visit's a must." Shelly's rendition of the familiar jingle, sung to the tune of "Rockabye Baby," immediately conjured up the omnipresent ads of lovers holding hands, young men proposing to starry-eyed sweethearts, and recently, just to show how progressive they were, a gay man proposing to his partner. It seemed they were on the TV every ten minutes. Sporting events, movies, and cop shows, it made no difference; the freaking things were even more annoying than the insurance commercials.

"Your husband owns those jewelry stores?"

"Yup, he does. He started with one, in Seattle, just after we got married, and now they're in Portland, San Fran, LA, several in Arizona, and a bunch more in Southern California. He does more TV advertising than anyone in the business, and it's paid off. Sales are off the charts, and that's why we're spending six million dollars on a 5,500-square-foot house. Course, that doesn't count the lot; that was another three million. He tells me the house is gonna be too small but screw him. I told him any bigger and we'd be wasting resources. I'm very concerned about the planet."

Kevin was unsure if reducing the size of the Chesnicks' palace to *only* 5,500 square feet would have much of an impact on the earth's resources. He did know with absolutely certainty that there was no person in the entire western US who was unaware of the Cascade jingle. The conversation with Jenne after their meeting was gonna be fun, but back to the task at hand.

"Shelly, it's unusual for one interior design firm to take over after another, especially when you've just started construction. Can you tell us why you let the other outfit go?"

"Sure. They were assholes. I just couldn't stand them anymore. They treated me like I was stupid just because I used to be a house cleaner. I still do three houses a week. They were always meeting with the architect—you know, that Huber Group. Tom Kronin is the guy I picked cuz he's done some stuff I really like. He's slightly aloof, but at least he treats me with respect. Those two at Liz Thomas Interiors … sorry, I just couldn't do it anymore."

Jenne couldn't help herself. "Did you say you still clean houses? Really?"

"Sure. I like it. The three I do have been clients since I met Bernie. He's on the road all the time, so I'm alone a lot and it gets me out of the house. On the days I don't play golf, I see my friends and clean their houses."

Jenne knew of the other firm. They had only been in town less than a year, yet rumor had it they had already ruffled a few feathers. With newfound respect, she inquired about what services Shelly would like or expect from O'Malley and Associates.

"I'm happy with all the architectural elements of the house. They poured the footings and concrete walls yesterday, so we won't be making any changes there. I'd like you to review the entire finish schedule to see what you think. If you feel something needs changing, then let me know and we can review. We still have some time before we get to the kitchen and bathrooms, so I'd like you to take a look at all the tile and stone selections. I'd expect you to pull together a furnishings spreadsheet as well. I need selections and suggestions for all the rooms. Since it's a mid-century look, I'd think many of the Knoll Studio pieces would be appropriate, but you bring me what you think makes sense and we'll talk about it. How does that sound?"

Kevin's Irish face looked as surprised as Jenne's. "What it sounds like is you've either done a lot of homework or this isn't your first rodeo."

"I used to clean lots of homes, both rich people and not so much. I notice things, and I've seen stuff I like and stuff I absolutely hate. I've read books on furniture and those who design it; I've read up on how to deal with contractors, architects, and interior designers. I also talk to lots of people about who's good and who isn't. They say you two are good. More importantly, they say you can be trusted to speak the truth whether I want to hear it or not. That's what I need, not some dipshit decorator telling me I don't know anything."

"Shelly, I think we can help you. In fact, I think we're looking forward to working with you. We'll take a copy of these plans and the finish schedules to review, then we'll hook up with Tom and let him know we're on the team. We will probably want to meet with him just to clear the air, and you should plan on being there. Does this make sense?"

Shelly's bright smile, framed by her stylish gray-streaked dark hair, was enough of an acknowledgment. "Perfect sense. This should be the fun I was looking for when I started this project. Thank you very much."

CHAPTER 4

The first hints of fall crept into this early September afternoon on the twelfth hole at Kelsey Creek Country Club. The low angle of the sun, that golden hue against the vibrant green of the fairway, bordered by the yellow-green leaves of the tall cottonwoods and the red-turning ones of the maples, all contributed to the slight sadness that these, the best days of the year, were on the wane. In another month these magnificent days in the northwest would succumb to the relentless drizzle and darkness that marked the winter months. While the temperatures rarely got below freezing, the gloominess at times got to even the most fervent advocates of this Queen City metropolis. Thank god for the always mild temperatures, which allowed for the occasional golf outing in between the raindrops.

Today, though, was one of the special ones, spectacular, and the entire "A" Train was together. The banter had been spirited and the betting large. Even though there were several games going on concurrently, it wasn't uncommon to bet on individual shots. Closest to the hole, from the fairway, the trap, or the rough, it made no difference. If two golfers were in a similar position, it was common practice to offer a wager on who could get the shot closest to the pin. Jeff's second shot to the par five had ended up in the right greenside bunker, while Kevin's sand wedge from ninety-five yards out skipped off the front right hump on the fringe and ended up three feet to the left of Jeff's ball.

"Okay, Kev, give me two to one and I'll put five on closest to."

"You're fucking nuts. I wouldn't give my mother two to one, and why would you think I would?"

"You know you're better out of the sand. I'm just trying to equal the playing field." Jeff was correct; Kevin was an excellent trap player, while Jeff's distance off the tee was superior.

"Tell you what I'll do. I'll give you three feet. You on?" Kevin's offer was that wherever Jeff's ball ended up, he would get an additional three feet closer to the hole—for betting purposes only, not for permanent position on the green.

"You're on. I'll go first." Jeff splashed it out nicely, the ball rolling twenty feet and settling six feet past the hole. "There you go, pal. See if you can get it inside three feet."

Kevin's turn. He was a handsy, feely type of player with more of a manufactured caddie's swing. It made for great touch around the greens, but unless his timing was precise, he fell victim to the random push or hook off the tee. He settled his feet into the sand, making sure he wouldn't slip during his swing. A sixty-degree wedge with very little bounce was the tool he selected, and rather than run it to the hole, he decided to loft it as close as possible, then spin it to a stop. The ball flew over the edge of the green, five feet past the hole, and spun back to within a foot and a half.

"Everybody hates a fucking showoff, Kevin. I told you I needed the two to one."

"Hah, that'll teach you to make stupid bets." And so, the rest of the round continued, each member of the Train taking his turn as the butt of jokes, scams, and wagers. It was a wonderful afternoon.

After changing in the locker room, Kevin ran into Vince on his way to the bar. "Kevin, glad I saw you. I'm sure you've heard the police aren't having much success in finding JJ's killer. They were just here this afternoon going over some details again. The lead detective, Bill Owens, said he'd like to interview you again to see if maybe there was something you'd forgotten about finding the body."

"Vince, if there's one thing I'm certain of it's that I couldn't forget anything even if I wanted to."

"I know. I told him that, but he said he'd still like to talk to you, maybe something would come up that you hadn't thought of before. I think they're grasping at straws because they're not getting anywhere; I told him I'd have you give him a call when you came in from your round."

"Sure, I'll be happy to."

Kevin would have been much happier playing gin with his pals than talking to the cops. Owens, though, seemed to want to talk right away, and he agreed to come back to the club to have a chat. They found an empty conference room, and Kevin grabbed a beer to sustain him through the conversation.

"Kevin, I know we chatted at the crime scene and then later on that week. We've met with some difficulties on this case and I thought if we could just talk over things one more time, maybe something new would come up. Not that you purposefully omitted anything, it's just that every so often after time passes and a scene is mentally revisited, something new pops up. Just take your time and tell me again what happened."

"Thing is, Detective, there really isn't much to say. We were driving down the ninth fairway. We were in the middle of it because the moon offered some light and the roughs were very dark. We were about a hundred fifty yards from the green, where that huge cedar tree is, when Jenne saw a cart just on the far side of the tree. I think she noticed the white roof on the thing."

"Even when it was on the other side of the tree?" Owens was playing the investigator now.

"I don't know how she noticed it. You'd have to ask her." Kevin was somewhat annoyed at the interruption. "Anyway, I pulled over to the rough, but not too close just in case it was a couple doing the deed, you know? I'd *really* hate to walk up on that. I do remember that it was very, very quiet. That's when I was pretty sure there was no hanky panky going on."

"Did you go around the front of the tree or the back of it?"

Kevin looked up and to the right, thinking for a moment. "Almost certain … yes, I'm sure it wasn't the golf green side of the tree, it was behind it."

"Then what? Tell me exactly how you approached the cart and what you did."

Kevin took his time, picturing in his mind his every step. "I was driving the cart we were in. I pulled it just into the rough, put the brake on, and got out while Jenne stayed in the cart. It was seriously dark, so I walked slowly and was careful not to trip on any roots or any limbs that might have fallen. When I got to JJ's cart, I noticed he was slumped over the steering wheel. I thought someone was drunk or something, so I said 'Hey, buddy' or words to that effect and shook his shoulder. That's when he fell out of the cart and I saw that gash in his face. Jenne tells me I screamed or yelled. I believe her; it was not a pretty sight. Then we came right into the clubhouse and told Vince."

"Did you go back to the scene after that?"

"No way. We both stayed here until the police arrived. Once was enough."

"Did you see the murder weapon—the wedge we found?"

"No, but I wasn't looking for anything. After Jerry fell out of the cart, we got the hell out of there."

"The reason I ask is, the crime scene techs tell me the club was only halfway under the cart. When they finally moved the body, they saw the club. Mr. Johnson had fallen over the thing. When you were there, it would have been sticking out a foot or two, the grip under the cart and the head outside. Seems like you would have seen it or stepped on it or something."

Kevin squinted like he was trying to recall some lost vision. "I can tell you I did *not* see anything, but if it had been there, I probably would have stepped on it. Could someone have come back and put it there? There had to be twenty minutes between the time we left and when the cops arrived."

"If you didn't see it or step on it, then I suppose it's possible that someone came back and placed it there. Thing is, I can't figure out why. It was wiped clean of prints. There was also very little blood on it, but what there was matched that of the deceased, and the shape of the wound fit as well."

"Did Vince tell you JJ dropped his wife off and then went back out to look for his club?"

"He did, but we know that was bullshit because he had all his clubs in his bag. He obviously went out there to meet someone for something and it ended badly for him. Thing is, we've looked at all his connections, both personal and business, and we got nothing. The guy loved the ladies and pissed away his share of money gambling, but we can't turn up anyone he owes or anyone he's even pissed off. We're stuck. We'll keep at it, though, and thanks for taking the time away from your friends. Maybe you can sneak in a hand or two of gin. If we need to talk again, which I doubt, we'll give you a call."

Cascade Creations had just signed a lease for the 5,000-square-foot street-side corner space in the new Lakeside Towers high-rise on the corner of 104th and Main Street in Bellevue. The building had been completed for six months, but the asking price for the prominent space was exorbitant. One hundred dollars per square foot had frightened even the most aggressive retailers, but Bernie craved attention, and this would give it to him. The rent didn't bother him in the least and the lack of parking was only a minor inconvenience; there was always valet parking, after all.

Bernie plowed ahead with his dream of being the most profitable jeweler in the country. He didn't care about the number of stores or the quality of his work or the satisfaction of his customers. What he really wanted was to be the richest individual in the business. With money came recognition and that led to fame. As the child of a second-generation Italian mother and a first-generation Greek father, his lifelong habits were shaped by a very noisy household. That he was the only youngster in the house in no way toned down the sound level of his childhood.

Sure, the food was fabulous and the attention even better. His mom was the stereotypical Italian mother: feed everyone all the time, never put up with any shit from anybody, including your stupid husband, and always give your son lots of hugs. His dad, a regional sales manager for a costume jewelry distributor, was home only intermittently. Since his territory included the entire West Coast all the way to Denver, he spent four happy nights a week on the road. When he returned home, the bickering commenced immediately and with great volume.

"HOW WAS YOUR TRIP?"

"WHADDA YOU CARE? WHAT'S FOR DINNER?"

"THAT'S ALL YOU CARE ABOUT. BERNIE MISSED YOU."

"I'M SURE HE DID. CAN WE EAT NOW? I'VE GOT PAPERWORK TO DO. GODDAMN EXPENSE REPORTS, SALES REPORTS, THESE FUCKERS WANT EVERYTHING RIGHT AWAY. DUMB BASTARDS, COULDN'T SELL ICE TO PEOPLE IN HELL, AND THEY'RE TRYIN' TO TELL ME HOW THE FUCK TO DO THINGS."

"THEO, DON'T USE THAT KINDA LANGUAGE IN FRONT OF THE BOY."

"HE'S THIRTEEN YEARS OLD, I'M SURE HE HEARS THIS SHIT IN SCHOOL ALL THE TIME. RIGHT, BERNIE?"

"Um, yes, I do."

"CAN'T HEAR YOU, BOY."

"YES, I SURE AS FUCK DO."

"THERE YOU GO, CARLA. BOY'S A NATURAL."

And so, Bernie learned the ways of the world, or at least *his* world. He became the loudest boy in his class. If he attempted a whisper, it was heard as a normal-for-anyone-else speaking voice. His home life experiences combined with a constant diet of pasta and Coke produced the expected: a chubby, tall for his age, loud, obnoxious individual with few friends and shunned by most. He had inherited the olive complexion of his parents, the bulbous nose of his father, and the wide sensuous lips of his mother. He would not be a candidate for the centerfold spread in *Cosmopolitan* magazine.

As he grew into manhood, he focused on the best way to get attention in spite of his less than impressive physique and his annoyingly loud discourse. Throughout his college years he made money by placing small ads for jewelry in magazines for triple retail prices, then showing the ads to fellow students, explaining that they could buy the same stuff from him at 30 percent off. With the frequent and steady turnover of girlfriends by college men, his enterprise provided plenty of cash with which to impress certain members of the opposite sex. These certain members enjoyed the expensive restaurants and outings once or twice, but putting up with Bernie's unbearable and annoying habits proved a bridge too far. His college years provided lots of cash and sales experience but very little in the way of romantic encounters.

Upon graduation, he hired on with the same company his father worked for, Wholesale Jewelers, Inc., while expanding his magazine scam, now with internet assistance. Bernie Chesnick became flush with cash, but he still seemed destined for one-night stands with the ladies.

One evening, while at a Seattle watering hole famous for steaks, chops, and single women, he stumbled upon Bernice Bostwick. The bar was nothing but concrete and glass, making for a notable increase in the decibel level. Perhaps Bernice—Bernie to her friends—was impressed that she could hear Bernie among the din. Either that or she was slightly deaf, which was probably the case, since she was able to weather the storm of the very loud, unattractive, overweight man who showered her with cash. She ended up marrying the putz.

Bernie's sales ability was remarkable. Perhaps prospective buyers agreed to his proposals just to get the annoying douchebag out of their office. He moved up in the company over the years while still maintaining his side gig. His wife, however, was growing increasingly tired of him. It was okay when he was on the road and she had money to spend, but when he was home, she could no longer stand him. The sex was awful. The only saving grace was that he got his rocks off immediately, so she could roll over and feign sleep until he started snoring. She started hoping that if he wasn't already fucking around when he was on the road, he'd start. Maybe he'd get some poor girl pregnant and leave her. They talked about children early on, but after a few years with him, she decided she couldn't do that to a child and did what needed to be done to prevent any accidental pregnancies.

A decade into their wedded disaster, she threw in the towel. Ms. Bostwick may have been a little slow on the draw and slightly deaf, but she was nobody's fool. She was done with this turkey. Bernie couldn't have cared less about the divorce and they reached an amicable settlement quickly. Bernie got the house and Bernie moved into one of the new high-rise lofts in Seattle's Regrade area, his brand spanking new bachelor pad.

As time went on, even Bernie's excellent sales numbers couldn't keep him in good stead with his superiors. His habit of loudly talking over anyone within earshot and beyond had worn thin. His customers now ignored his calls and phoned in their orders, while it slowly dawned on him that his tenure at Wholesale Jewelers, Inc. was in jeopardy. Finally, it became apparent that only by being the boss would he be able to call all the shots with no interference from above.

Since his only experience in business was in jewelry, the choice was obvious. He leased a 400-square-foot cubby hole on the lower level of Pike Place Market. Tucked away between a vintage comic book retailer and a "Gypsy" fortune teller, he began promoting his custom designs at well below retail prices. He was quick to hire a pleasant young woman who could interact with the customers, because, strangely enough, Bernie, at least on some level, knew he annoyed people and that it was best if he ran things from behind the curtain.

He expanded his wares to include loose diamonds and other precious stones, which were presented to prospective customers, who selected the stone first and then the setting in which to place it. A one-man Vietnamese workshop in the SODO area did the assembly work for him quickly and expertly. His reputation grew, and the soon-to-be-wed flocked to the basement jeweler.

After a year of hunkering down in his basement store, he'd saved enough to move to a 1,500-square-foot space on Sixth Avenue, just down the street from the Four Seasons. Leslie, his one employee in the Market, was promoted to store manager and then tasked with staffing it. He wisely spent his time advertising, advertising, and advertising. He hired a firm to come up with a jingle for Cascade Creations and then promptly fired them. The thing was awful. Who the hell wanted a tagline to the tune of "Rockabye Baby"? Because he had already purchased radio time when the imminent release of the jingle was apparent, he just sucked it up and let them play it. He'd pull it as soon as he could.

He was correct; it was awful. In fact, it was so awful that seemingly all the radio stations made fun of it, and the more they made fun of it, the more it was played. The old adage that there's no such thing as bad publicity had worked spectacularly. Even ten years and eighteen, soon to be nineteen, stores later, the annoying little ditty had endured.

Leslie was on the floor of Cascade Creations one afternoon when an attractive young woman walked in. At five feet, four inches, her dark-brown hair and perky nose gave the impression of Meg Ryan in *Sleepless in Seattle*, sans the blonde hair.

The manager put on her most engaging smile. "Hi there. Welcome to Cascade Creations. May I help you?"

"You sure can. One of my clients bought a ring from you guys when you had that tiny place in the Market. The damn diamond keeps falling out of the setting and she's afraid she's gonna lose it. Can you fix it?"

"I think so. Mr. Chesnick's in the back office; let me go ask him."

On his way to the restroom when the customer entered, Bernie had caught a glimpse of the attractive woman through the open hallway. Upon his return he was surprised to see her still at the counter and more so to see Leslie when he entered his office. "WHAT'S UP?" boomed his blaring voice.

"Sorry to bug you, Bernie, but this lady says her client bought this at our other store and now the setting's come loose. Can we get it fixed?"

"Well, we were using Quan Tang down in SODO when we sold that, but now we're using Johnson's for fabrication. I'm sure they can fix it, though. Let me see that."

Since his divorce, Bernie mistakenly fancied himself prime poontang material. While he hadn't hit any home runs yet, he always held out hope. Many women were impressed by the trappings of wealth; he just needed to find one who could tolerate a rich loudmouth who thought he knew everything and posted a two on a scale of one to ten in the "handsome" sweepstakes. Hope sprang eternal in the Chesnick fantasy world.

Bernie promptly walked up to the customer side of the counter and introduced himself. "Hi. I'm Bernie Chesnick, the owner. I can see your ring has sustained a little damage on the corner here." Since Bernie always knew everything, he hadn't paid attention to Leslie when she'd explained that it was the lady's *client's* ring.

"Well, actually it's my client's ring, but yes, I can see that. Can you fix it?"

"Your client, oh, are you an attorney or something?"

"No. I'm her house cleaner and sometimes I run errands for her. *Can* you fix it?"

She's a goddamn house cleaner, Bernie thought, but she sure was a hottie. Maybe he stood a chance with this one. "Of course, we can, Miss … I'm sorry, I didn't catch your name."

"That's cuz I didn't give it to you. It's Shelly. Shelly Thornton. How long and how much will it take?"

This gal is a bit of a firecracker, thought Bernie. Maybe he stood a chance if he could just turn the asshole dial down to simmer for a while. "Tell you what, Shelly, I'll take care of this myself. I'm going down to our manufacturer shortly. If you can make it back before five this afternoon, I'll have it ready for you."

Leslie looked over at Bernie, wondering if the man had suffered a stroke. She had never heard him speak in such a calm, measured tone. She'd have to watch him.

Shelly's sparkling eyes brightened considerably. "Why, thanks, Bernie. That would be terrific. I'll just do a little shopping and stop back at the end of the day. How much? My client needs to know."

"Usually we just charge whatever time the fabricator takes, but in this case, we'll just absorb the cost. We can't have you looking bad in your client's eyes, can we?"

Bernie's stupid grin and patronizing comments had pushed the dial up to medium high, but apparently Shelly either hadn't heard or she was used to dealing with dipshits.

"Geez, thanks, Bernie. I'll see *you* later."

Of course, Bernie took this personally, like maybe the lady actually liked him. He felt his face flush and his armpits start to run. He really needed to get down to Johnson's and get back here in time for her return.

Upon Shelly's reappearance, Bernie once again was able to scale back his more obnoxious tendencies. A very understated suggestion for a cocktail at the Garden Court in the Four Seasons led to dinner, which led to a promise of a future get-together. Normally Bernie would have attempted the assumptive closing technique to get his date in the sack; somehow his better angels prevailed, and Shelly ended up enjoying herself and looking forward to seeing this well-to-do fellow again.

Shelly Thornton was born in Spanaway, Washington to working-class parents. Her dad worked on the assembly line at Boeing; her mom cleaned houses. When she was five, her father slipped off the nose of a

747 while working on the windshield and fell to his death. The good fortune of working for the second-largest producer of passenger jets in the world showed up in the form of an excellent life insurance policy. The death of her father was tragic, but five-year-olds eventually scar over and move forward. Her mom no longer needed to work, but she kept at it. Always a tomboy, seldom a great student, Shelly was well liked by all her classmates. Her mom was a survivor and taught her to be one as well. Never afraid to speak her mind plainly and never one to take a back seat to anyone, she eschewed further education and started her own cleaning company.

She loved the independence and enjoyed most of her clients. If she was treated poorly by one of them, they were dropped immediately. In a matter of months, word spread throughout the wealthy techies in the Seattle area that Shelly's Sunshine Cleaning was taking new clients. She hired a second crew and called it good. Managing people proved to be less fun than actually doing the cleaning and visiting with clients. Her hardscrabble upbringing encouraged confidence and independence, even if she still envied those who were very well off.

Perhaps this tiny weakness allowed good ol' Bernie Chesnick to worm his way into her life. No, he wasn't handsome, but, at least in the early stages, he really seemed to be trying, and he *was* pretty rich. As they dated and eventually got married, Shelly seemed to rely on those memories of when he was actually *trying* to get her through the day. Now she had money—lots of it. She believed her husband was a shallow, obnoxious assclown who probably fucked around. Right now, that was okay; they never had sex anymore anyway. And she had the new house to work on. She'd make certain to get it when it came time to get divorced. She looked forward to working with the O'Malleys. They seemed like fun.

CHAPTER 5

Bill Owens was not a happy man. This case was testing his detecting skills as no other had. He'd joined the Bellevue Police Department three years ago. Born in Swanton, Ohio, he had gone to Toledo Police Academy for his basic training and served on the city's force for only six years before becoming its lead detective on their most sensational cases. His clearance rate was among the highest in the state. Then his personal life hit the skids.

Because he was gone almost sixteen hours a day, his high school sweetheart turned wife became lonely. Working as a nurse on the day shift at ProMedica Toledo Hospital offered her a challenging yet exhausting career. When she returned to an empty house after a grueling shift, she longed for a quiet dinner with Bill, sharing interesting things that had happened during the day. She even fantasized about helping with some of his cases, maybe even the ones that made the headlines.

Alas, that was not to be. Bill was a driven man, driven to be the voice of the victims of the mindless violence that seemed to permeate most of the urban colonies of these United States. Toledo was a city of less than 300,000 souls but still managed to murder almost forty of its citizens every year. Bill was determined to make a difference, if not in reducing this crime rate, at least in bringing to justice the seriously dangerous assholes still on the street. Most murders were senseless acts committed by the most obvious culprits. The spouse, the lover, the drunk, the druggie, these were the usual offenders, and rarely was much deduction required to solve a case. Once in a while, though, things weren't so simple, and that was where Detective Owens's star shone brightest. Certainly, he was intelligent and clever, but so were many other cops. What pushed him across the finish line first so often was his dogged pursuit of any case that came his way. It was also why his home life sucked and why his wife was shagging the head of oncology at ProMedica.

The divorce blindsided him, racked him with guilt, and instead of focusing even more on his cases, he became despondent. At first his superiors were understanding and helpful, suggesting he do some counseling. Yes, he told them it was a good idea, made sense, and all that shit, but not for him. He spent less and less time with his caseload and more at home with James Beam.

Two months later, the chief of police knocked on his front door with an ultimatum. "Bill, you've got two choices. You can sit here at home getting shitfaced all day long if you'd like. I've covered for you long enough and you've had plenty of opportunities to get over this thing. You're done here in Toledo. I don't want you around anymore. The other choice, and I'm not sure you're even up to it, is to take a job somewhere else. If you clean up your act during the next few weeks, I'll write a glowing letter of recommendation for you and personally talk to the chief there."

Bill's puffy face and bloodshot eyes looked stunned. "Where's *there?*"

"*There* is in Bellevue, Washington. They have an opening for a lead detective. I know the top cop there. He's good people. It's a bedroom community for Seattle. Lots of wealthy tech folks live there; not much violent crime. It's an opportunity for a fresh start—*if* you get your shit together. Lots of people get divorced; you're not the only one. Get sober *now*, get your ass on a plane to Seattle, and when you get there, here's the name of a therapist. Call her and see her, and if you don't, I don't really give a shit what happens to you. Got it?"

Bill, even through his alcohol-induced fog, was aware that his second choice was his only one. He put the glass, half full of amber-colored liquid, in the sink and turned it upside down. "I guess I need to thank you, sir, and also apologize. I've let my teammates down. Give me a week to get in shape, I promise, and then I'll head up to that fucking place where it rains all the time." His sloppy smile and back-handed compliment were evidence he had taken the first step in the right direction.

He had grown to like the northwest. Yes, it did rain frequently, but when it paused for an hour, a day, or a month, there were few places he'd ever been that were as beautiful. Bellevue, indeed, was a wealthy community and its police force was outfitted with the best gear money could buy. The cop cars were supercharged Ford Explorers, Police Interceptors, equipped with 400 horses of rapid transit. They were so well funded that annual refresher courses in *everything* were mandated, even for the detectives. Bill didn't mind; he was back at the top of his game in a new city with a new chief—and now with this *fucking* golf club murder mystery that had flummoxed him.

He had looked into every known associate of Jerry Johnson. His clients, his sexual liaisons, his wife and her friends, and his golf companions and club members. The deceased was a colorful sort, sure, but the detective couldn't find even a sniff of wrongdoing. The murder weapon had been wiped clean of prints, although there was that peculiar detail of the sand wedge only showing up between the time O'Malley had found the body and when the police had arrived at the scene. That was an oddity for sure, but what it meant he hadn't any idea.

Bellevue was far from a violent city, so Bill had carte blanche to do whatever he saw fit to solve this thing. It had been over ten weeks since the murder and he was no closer to a resolution than the day of the crime. All he had done was to rule out hundreds of possible suspects. He would do what he had always done, though; he would persist. He knew it was rarely the smartest or the luckiest who solved the crime; it was almost always the dogged determination of the most persistent investigator on the force, and that was Bill Owens.

With several projects in the planning stages and four under construction and now the Chesnick home, O'Malley and Associates had their hands full. A retirement community, a small boutique hotel, a 10,000-square-foot family compound in Woodinville, plus a small remodel in Madison Park were sufficient to fill their days. Also competing for their attention was Emma. Several sessions at Maltby GSDs' obedience class had opened their eyes to the superior intelligence of this breed. At any given time, there were from ten to twenty-five German Shepherds in attendance with their owners. One of the exercises was to put every dog in the class into a "sit" position. When that had been accomplished, each dog and handler took a turn at weaving through the rest of the animals, each dog holding his or her position. The more they worked with her, the more they were convinced of their decision to make her part of their family.

She went to work with the designers every day and both Valerie and Ilene became fast friends with her. Occasionally an unannounced vendor or solicitor would walk through the office door, which was on street level. The protectiveness and intense alertness of GSDs made certain it was a one-time event. Few dogs bark more or louder than a German Shepherd, and when that intensity was focused on an individual, it got their attention. There was never any threat or intent to harm, closer to "Hey, what are you doing here? These are my peeps, and next time, make an appointment." The ladies in the office were thrilled to have her there.

In the four years since starting their firm, Jenne and Kevin had never consciously decided which of them should take the lead with a client or even a presentation. Their confidence in each other was such that if one felt stronger about taking the lead, it was simply fine with the other. This attitude carried through when it came to site visits as well as research and selection trips. Sometimes they would make a presentation together or inspect a site under construction, but this was the exception, not the norm.

Kevin was saddled with the Woodinville project, while it was left to Jenne to interact with Shelly Chesnick. After the meeting with Tom Kronin, in which Shelly asserted her confidence in O'Malley and Associates, everything looked in order. Kronin was well known for his contemporary residential work and his professionalism. He had met Jenne at several industry functions, was impressed with her credentials, and actually appeared relieved that the O'Malleys were now on the team. All expected smooth sailing for the remainder of the construction process.

"Jenne, would you mind coming in for a sec? I'd like you to take a look at some of the tile selections that the other firm came up with." Jenne had driven them both to the meeting at the Huber Group in Seattle, and they were now back at the Chesnicks' rental home.

"Sure thing, Shelly. Good idea." They sat at the dining room table, now completely covered in plans, schedules, and finish selections.

"Jenne, I'm really glad you agreed to work with me on this project. I like Tom, he's a good guy, but he's not that easy for me to relate to. At least with you I feel like you're hearing me, and you value my input."

Jenne appreciated Shelly's no-nonsense, direct approach. "Shelly, first of all, it's your place, your home, and we would not have taken the job if we had any reservations about working with you. Secondly, much of what you've selected is excellent. You're well read and have a good feel for what works and what doesn't. I see a few things here and there that if we adjust them it might make for a better result. Let's go over them."

It was five o'clock by the time the two women had finished reviewing the majority of the finishes. The kitchen cabinets, the counter materials, the bathroom flooring, the shower and vanity selections, the engineered wood selections in the main living areas, the New Zealand wool carpeting in the bedrooms, the sound systems and low voltage selections, all comprised a vastly incomplete list of items to address. With the sheer volume of finish materials and selections available, it could seem overwhelming to the first-time home builder.

"Say, Jenne, what would you say to a nice glass of cold sauvignon blanc?"

"I'd say, 'Get your ass over here and hop in my hand.'"

Shelly's big grin exposed her vulnerable side. "I knew I liked you the first time we met. Thanks for working with me."

"It's our pleasure, Shelly. We're going to enjoy this hopefully as much as you."

"You probably think it's weird for me to be doing this without Bernie, yes?"

Jenne wasn't sure how to answer except to tread lightly. "I don't know about weird, but most of the time if it's a married couple we're working for, we deal with both of them. Thing is that everyone's different, and whatever works for our client works for us."

"Bernie's an annoying, obnoxious jerk. That, and as soon as we get our house built, I'm dumping the prick. I know it sounds like I'm a gold digger, but he really is a sorry excuse for a human being. When I first met him, I thought he was this loud guy, but he treated me well and it was kinda cute the way he tried so hard to impress me. At first his business took so much of his time that I didn't notice what a complete shit he is. Now, when he's not home, I love it. I'm certain he's screwing around on me, but instead of being angry, I just feel sorry for whoever he's fucking."

Jenne was not embarrassed by straight talk from her clients, but this seemed to push the envelope some.

"And that's not all, Jenne. You know all those stores he's got? He's not the most ethical guy when it comes to his customers either; I'm pretty sure he's screwing them too."

"Huh? What? What do you mean?"

"Well one thing I *know* he does is he switches out diamonds."

"What do you mean?"

"When someone comes in to have their rings cleaned or fixed, he takes the stone out and swaps it for a shittier one. Nobody can tell the difference. Then he sells the one he swapped for tons more dough. That's how he makes so much money. He's a goddamn crook."

"And no one's caught on to him yet?"

"Once in a while somebody who's really sharp and knows what the stone looks like using a loupe will catch him. Then he just says it was a mistake, he's really sorry, and he switches the original one back. He usually gives them something like a big discount so they'll forget about it and go away.

"What most people don't know is that the really good stones usually have serial numbers engraved on them. The Gemological Institute of America grades loose stones and issues a certificate with the serial number from the diamond noted."

"How come the people don't verify the serial number when they get their ring back?"

"The numbers are teeny tiny and can only be seen under magnification."

"Geez, Shelly, that's terrible. How come you haven't told anyone—or have you?"

"I wondered where all the money was coming from, but I never really knew for sure until just recently. One of my housecleaning clients took her ring to be cleaned and appraised and when she got it back, she said it looked a little yellower. I looked at it through a loupe and it looked like frozen yellow spit. It was really a piece-of-shit stone, almost worthless. There was also no serial number. The real one she had cost twenty grand. This one was maybe worth five hundred."

"What did you do? What did she do?"

"She knows I'm married to the asshole, so she felt bad. I told her I'd get the original one back and then I'd come up with a way to make sure he gets caught."

"How?"

"Leslie, the manager at the Seattle store, is a close friend, and Bernie keeps the stolen diamonds in the safe there. She's been with him since his days in the Market, when he was legit, and she's started keeping track of all the customers he's screwed. As soon as I'm done with this house, I'll force him to give me a divorce, and as soon as that happens, I'm gonna turn over everything to the cops. I hope the cocksucker gets ten years in the slammer. Excuse my French!"

This was a first for Jenne, and it made her a bit uncomfortable. "That's quite a plan you've got there, Shelly." Her sauvignon blanc hadn't been touched for some time. "Do you think you'll be able to pull it off?"

"I sure do. After I get the stuff to the police, he'll either have to sell out or go bankrupt, which I doubt. With most of his stores, he owns the land too, so if he liquidated everything, he'd still have some cash. At least that'll be enough to make everyone whole and still have some left over for me. If I can keep the house, great; if not, I'll sell it and go back to housecleaning."

Jenne was doubtful all would go as Shelly had planned, but she was certain that if anyone could pull it off, it would be Bernie's wife.

CHAPTER 6

Debi Johnson hadn't played since the death of her husband. If JJ were alive, she supposed she would still be practicing, at least trying to improve. Now, though, she really didn't give a shit anymore. She had only done it to keep her deceased husband happy.

Five years ago, while hitting the night spots with her girlfriends, she ran into a short chubby guy at the piano bar at the top of one of the new office towers in town. Everyone seemed to know him, and all appeared to genuinely like him. He was generous with his tips and always happy to buy the first round.

"How about a drink, sweetie?" was his opening gambit.

Her newly highlighted hair and low-cut blouse had apparently caught the gentleman's eye. Her generous breasts could always be counted on to encourage conversation; besides, she had never been called "sweetie" before. It wasn't long before JJ—that turned out to be his name—and Debi were engaged in a more intimate setting. A few short weeks later and they were engaged, period.

Debi had been the proprietor of The Hairport for seven years. She had always dreamed of owning her own shop. The previous twenty years she had spent renting a chair at several other locations in the city; she had built up a solid client base and vowed that as soon as the opportunity presented itself, she'd pull the trigger on her own store. There were only four other stations in the 800-square-foot street-front place, yet they managed to constantly stay occupied.

JJ proved to be a lover of life—of food, drink, and gambling. Oh, he had his jewelry manufacturing business, but that existed only to provide enough funds for all the rest. Debi loved the guy, though, and even with his many faults it was difficult to stay angry with him. Sadly, toward the end of the last year she became aware of his dalliances with other women; it wasn't that he didn't still love her, he just prized the hunt for strange pussy even more.

She did her best to ignore his wandering beaver basher, but eventually she had to issue an ultimatum. "JJ, I still love you and forgive you, but if you don't stop fucking around, I'm gonna go all Lorena Bobbitt on you, and I'm not kidding." Debi could be plain spoken on occasion.

This confrontation had curbed Jerry's affront to monogamy for a time, but he eventually reverted to his natural tendencies. The last months of his life were among the more tumultuous in their three-year adventure.

Johnson Jewelers had been a thriving fabrication outfit five or six years ago. Five craftsmen, mostly from southeast Asian countries, were kept busy ten hours a day, seven days a week. It was during this period that JJ's company provided the expertise to manufacture rings, necklaces, earrings, and all forms of jewelry, from gold, silver, and platinum in concert with diamonds and precious stones, from around the world. Several retail chains were clients of Johnson's, including Cascade Creations. As Bernie Chesnick's collection of jewelry stores expanded, so did JJ's volume increase. Though his workmanship was second to none, it couldn't be hurried. Chesnick was a royal pain in the ass as a client; he wanted everything *now*, yet he never felt the need to pay extra for jumping to the head of the queue.

The money was excellent at the time; however, it sadly curtailed JJ's extracurricular activities. Soon Chesnick started spreading his fabrication needs around, especially since JJ was hardly motivated to show him deference. As his larger clients continued to bleed away, forcing him to increase prices for the smaller ones, cutting his staff and lowering overheads was the only option.

Debi had come to the sad realization that her only inheritance would be a pile of debt, including the balance owing on Johnson Jewelers for the remaining six months of his lease. JJ had been generous with gifts of jewelry during their first year of wedded bliss; unfortunately, as their relationship turned south, his largesse also declined. A collection of exquisite diamonds in various settings were the chum Jerry had bestowed upon her during their courtship. She figured she could easily cash those in to stave off the bill collectors and lawyers. The only good news was hearing that the young lady who had purchased The Hairport was having a hard time making a go of it. If Debi could take it off her hands and scare up most of her old clients, she was sure things would be fine.

Because of their relatively new member status at Kelsey Creek, Kevin felt that joining one of the committees would enable him to expand his circle of friends, or at least acquaintances. The greens committee met once a month on the last Thursday of the month. The objective of the meetings, it seemed, was for the golf course superintendent to inform the committee members, who in turn would inform their constituents throughout the club, of past and upcoming maintenance procedures, budget requirements and constraints, and general agronomic practices.

This was Kevin's second meeting. He and the other nine members of the group were listening to Jimmy Kenealy, the super, detailing the results of the recent course aeration procedure. Apparently, all had gone well, and the course would be back in shape within a week or so. The recent use of the solid tines, in place of the hollow ones that extracted a plug, would allow the turf to recover more quickly, ensuring a happier membership. *Good to know*, Kevin thought. *Really happy to know this stuff.*

He had to remind himself of his original motivation for joining this team. Actually, he had learned a thing or two about golf course operations and was mildly surprised that it took nearly two million dollars in labor, fertilizers, fungicides, and insecticides, on top of the cost of replacing equipment every season, to keep Kelsey Creek one of the top courses in the state.

During the last get-together of this group, Keneally had toured them through the maintenance facility. There were gobs of equipment, for much of which Kevin couldn't fathom a use. The highlight, though, was meeting the crew members. Now, when Kevin walked by a fairway mowing unit or a worker repairing a sprinkler head, he was able to acknowledge them by name and thank them for their work. It felt good knowing that they knew who he was and that he could bring a smile to brighten their day. Much of the crew had been with the club for years, while a few were newcomers. There were several Hispanic fellows who spoke English, but only haltingly so.

One of these workers, Santiago, was an especially engaging teenager who always displayed a grin full of perfect teeth whenever he saw Kevin. "Mr. Kevin, Mr. Kevin, how is the game today?"

Kevin would always respond in the same way: "Santiago, I'll let you know after the round is over. Nice job on the traps today."

And then the smile would get even wider. "Si, si, after the round is over. See you next time, Mr. Kevin." It was a brief and shallow exchange, but it always lifted Kevin's spirits regardless of the state of his play that day.

Kenealy, too, had become very friendly, and he would always share the issues of the day whenever they ran into each other at the club. Every so often he would be at breakfast on Saturdays and would share pin locations and green speeds with Kevin before he ran into Jeff or Mani. Naturally these trivial subtleties wouldn't be shared with the others.

Life at Kelsey Creek Country Club had returned to normal now that a few months had scarred over the tragedy of Jerry Johnson's murder. The perpetrator of the crime had yet to be revealed, but according to the local gossip, Bellevue's finest were hot on the trail. Well … maybe not if you asked Bill Owens; that particular cop was frustrated as hell.

Bernie Chesnick had mistakenly thought joining Kelsey Creek would expand both his social connections and his customer base. As with most private country clubs, the members tended to gravitate to smaller groups of like-minded individuals. It could be similar golfing or tennis abilities, political beliefs, professional affiliations, or even ethnic or cultural similarities. Bernie thought himself better than most of humanity. He had money and a very attractive wife but was erroneously convinced that he also possessed a heightened level of sophistication. Alas, the doofus had all the self-awareness of the forty-fifth president of the United States.

His attempts to mix with some of the higher handicappers met with abject failure. In most foursomes there's an unspoken requirement to contribute in some way to the social fabric of the group, if only for four hours on the course and maybe a drink at the bar following the game. Bernie's less than impressive physicality combined with a voice that encouraged all comers to quickly search for a muting device made him one of the most unpopular members to ever grace the Creek. He was shunned by any group that experienced the discomfort his personality delivered. He took up more space, physically and emotionally, than three normal golfers, and no amount of encouragement by the professional staff could convince other members to endure his obnoxiousness.

Barely a year into his tenure at the club, he was now only seen on the course with an invited guest, or perhaps a new member not yet wise to the misery four hours' worth of Bernie Chesnick could produce. It was thought that he was single-handedly responsible for the resignation of some of the less confident members. On the occasion of a club tournament, where the teams were selected via a blind draw, the entire field held their breath, uttering promises to the god of their choice in the hopes they'd be spared from having to play with His Douchebagness. There was genuine sympathy for the unfortunate sods destined to endure his presence and not a small amount of snickering and sheer joy at having been spared.

This afternoon Bernie was teeing it up with an employee, Alex Hartmann, the soon-to-be manager of Cascade Creations of Bellevue. Hartmann had been lured away from Bernie's closest competitor several months ago and had been learning the policies and procedures of his new employer by assisting Leslie Barnwell in the Seattle store.

Having been in the retail jewelry game for over a dozen years, the last four as manager of the Diamond Ranch in Portland, Alex was credited with ensuring that the Cascade Creations store there always came second in annual sales. Bernie needed a hard charger to ensure his success at the new location, and from reports so far, he'd made an excellent hire. Although Leslie's experience was more substantial and her loyalty unquestionable, Bernie felt he needed a more aggressive male approach to launch the store's opening campaign.

Alex had mentioned during his interviews that he enjoyed golf, even hinted at being *accomplished* at it. Saying he could play to an eight handicap, Alex agreed to a fifty-dollar Nassau bet, giving Bernie a stroke a hole. A Nassau is really three bets: fifty for the front nine, fifty for the back, and another fifty for the total. It's the most common betting game on the links the world over.

Turning the front side with an appalling fifty-eight, Bernie was stunned he was able to break even with his new hire. That he hadn't even been marginally conscious of his playing partner's obvious attempts at throwing the contest spoke to the sludge occupying the man's cerebral cortex. Alex had three-putted four times, hit three out of bounds, and even managed an intentional shank, possibly the most difficult shot in golf, in an effort to tie with his new boss. He was exhausted by the sheer effort of coming up with new and interesting ways to fuck up the score so he'd lose to the guy.

Through sheer ingenuity Alex had managed to lose a hundred bucks to his new boss. If he was lucky, he'd never have to play another round with the man.

CHAPTER 7

Alex Hartmann was originally from the great state of Michigan. Bad Axe, Michigan, to be more specific. When a Michigander is asked what city he or she is from, the standard response is to hold up their right hand, palm facing out. Next, they'll point with their left hand to a specific point on their right, which now represents the map of the state. An odd but effective communication technique that never fails to amuse. Bad Axe is in the center of the thumb, and interesting is not normally the word used to describe the place.

As the county seat of Huron County, located at the top of the thumb in the "Mitten" that is the great state of Michigan, Bad Axe might be one of the least interesting places in which to come of age. Famous for sugar beets and corn, this agricultural capital of the state is geographically devoid of interesting attractions save for the tunnels of corn bordering the pancake-flat two-lane roads and the random corn maze challenges. Alex came into this world as the only son of a third-generation dairy farmer just west of what the smartass locals called "Nasty Hatchet."

With a population hovering near 3,000, the cultural attractions were few for a teenager struggling just to make it through high school. Sports held no interest for Alex; he was never a team player. Fifteen years laboring on a family farm was enough teamwork to last a lifetime. He was not alone in his boredom with his random place of birth, and he inevitably gravitated to other young men with the same affliction.

It proved a low hurdle to convince one of the itinerant farmhands to pick up a six-pack or two in exchange for a couple of cans. Alex and his two pals, Jamie Duggan and Bobby Dawson, started drinking as sophomores at Bad Axe High School, home of the "Hatchets." One of the three would hang out near the entrance of the local IGA store until said farmhand would approach and then proffer the arrangement. Their beverage of choice was Colt 45 Malt Liquor, less because of its suggested sophisticated taste and more because of its high alcohol content.

After several episodes with the vile stuff left the boys circling the porcelain god, they learned to pace themselves accordingly in order to maintain a constant buzz. The funds to sustain this habit through their remaining years of high school weren't a big obstacle, since all three were adept at supplementing their incomes through skillful withdrawals from unattended wallets or purses at the family homes. As often happens with idle, stoned young men, trouble ensued. It started with just plain rowdiness and belligerence, though this was immediately silenced after the local police paid a visit to their parents. A significant "grounding" was sufficient to curtail their antisocial activities for a time, though this predictably gave way to more covert endeavors.

Rather than stay local and face reprisals on the home front, the boys began taking their show on the road. First it was Port Austin or Harbor Beach, but then these too offered little to attract the threesome other than a safer location. As graduation approached, Alex, Jamie, and Bobby became spurned by the rest of the student body. They were considered "bad boys" or outlaws by the rest of the class, harmless drunks by the faculty.

The weekend before their final days at the home of the "Hatchets," they took their stash of Colt 45 and an ample supply of weed on the road to Saginaw, a city famous for auto manufacturing, biker gangs, and a random mention in "America" by Simon and Garfunkel. The city had been through some rough times, and several of its watering holes were favored by large, bearded miscreants outfitted with all things denim, adorned with swastikas and American flags.

It was into one of these establishments that Alex and his pals wandered—frankly just out of curiosity. Their fake IDs were only of average quality, but their thinking was that this place was too seedy to make an issue of it. Dark, dingy, smelling of smoke, sweat, reefer, and seldom-washed bodies, Harley's barely registered half a star on Yelp.

It was five or ten minutes before their eyes had adjusted sufficiently to assess their surroundings. "Well, lookee here, boys, we got some fresh recruits payin' us a visit." It was tough to see where the sound was coming from, but Alex suspected it was the 300-pounder stretched out on two chairs over by the pool table.

Jamie and Bobby looked as though leaving was their preferred move, but Alex had just enough of a buzz going to make the mistake of engaging the large specimen in the dirty overalls. "Recruits for what? We're just gonna have a beer."

"Looks like Whitey here got a mouth on him." Alex was a tow-head, very slender, and exhibited the prominent features of his Germanic heritage. He'd actually heard similar name-calling once or twice back in Bad Axe.

"That's okay, really, we were just gonna have a quick one and then be on our way." Alex, too, was feeling a little uneasy. "In fact, maybe we'll just leave you guys alone and find another place."

"Nah, you're here now. Pull up a chair; let me buy you and your pals here a brewski." Alex detected a slight lessening of the hostility initially exhibited by the biker. Seeing no easy way to escape, he and his friends sat at the table next to the apparent leader of the assembled gang members.

"My name is Gump, sorta like Forrest Gump but I'm way smarter. Our little group here is called 'The Saviors.' We're all born and bred here in Michigan. Our mission is to keep America white. That's what KAW stands for on all our bikes. Why don't you boys drink up and we'll tell you some stories?"

Having grown up in rural America, the three young men had had little exposure to anything other than white, conservative politics. When the news was on, back at the farm, it was usually Sean Hannity and the Fox crew. Rarely did a more realistic viewpoint invade their consciousness. The few itinerant farmhands they encountered, including those who purchased beer for them, were dismissed as nothing more than furniture; not bad, not good, just something less than a real person. With their white-bread background as a foundation and their brains fogged by alcohol and THC, it was but a small step to absorbing basic indoctrination at the hands of The Saviors.

The afternoon turned into evening while Alex absorbed the stories and escapades of The Saviors. Both Jamie and Bobby had managed to duck out of the place with hardly a glance from Alex, so engaged was he with the Gumpster. Evidently the leader of this merry band of ne'er-do-wells was a shrewd evaluator of future talent and was executing the closing of this deal nicely. Since they had made the trip in Jamie's car, Alex's trip home was not to be. Gump and his troupe were staying at a rundown fifties-flavored affair on State Street, where they offered their new recruit a room for the night. After staying with his new friends that night and the next five, Alex no longer cared to return to "Nasty Hatchet." With his passive absorption of all things Fox setting the table, it was a tiny progression to actively participating in the fervent gospel espoused by The Saviors. KAW was now tattooed across his upper back.

When Gump and his crew saw the passion of their newest recruit, they made him a gift of a 1975 Harley Davidson Sportster. After only a few minor falls and scrapes, he became one of the gang, doing his part to keep the country safe from queers, Chinks, Blacks, and any other riffraff not acceptable to them.

After seven years and several hundred thousand miles of bad behavior, Alex became disenchanted with Gump and company. It wasn't that he didn't believe in their mission; he was just tired of living in shithole motels, eating crappy food, and smelling like the alley behind an Irish bar on St. Patrick's Day. After finishing up an afternoon rally against the Muslims, Jews, and homosexuals in Indianapolis, he wanted no part of bunking with his smelly band of brothers. He hated to forego the sanctity of the heterosexual marriage festival combined with the bikers-against-abortion cornhole tournament that was slated for the following weekend, but enough was enough.

Alex Hartmann mounted his Harley and headed back to Michigan, even though he no longer had any connection to his family or friends in Bad Axe. Although they had made several feeble attempts to touch base with their son when he hadn't returned from Saginaw, they had given up after Jamie and Bobby had brought them up to speed on what had transpired. Sure, there were snippets of news in the paper and on the internet regarding The Saviors, but nothing that shed any light on the adventures of their former friend.

Alex, perhaps because of his lack of research, decided he'd move to Flint. Along with his crappy Jimenez JA9 handgun, he still had a few bucks from the last liquor store they'd burgled. It was enough to pay the rent for a month for a studio apartment on Dort Avenue. Due to its depressed state as a result of GM's departure, the rents were low but the prospects of employment even lower. Hartmann wasn't of low intellect. His life choices, at least so far, were more a function of terrible programming—remarkably inaccurate data input flavored by genuinely stupid role models.

He was bright enough to realize he'd been lucky to escape the long arm of the law during his time with the bikers. He was under no illusions that he could expect his luck to continue if he chose to exercise his acquired law-breaking skills in search of steady income. Flint was no Seattle or Santa Clara. If any employment could be found for a high school dropout, it would be on the lowest rung of the ladder. Alex took a job at a Subway, building sandwiches for people of limited incomes, which included most of the population of Flint.

He spent his off hours searching for something more up his very limited alley. The Genesee Mall seemed to have more activity than most of the city, so he spent countless hours visiting the retailers, filling out applications. He had no idea if any of his biker skills could translate to the retail trade, but he was willing to give it a try. Little did he know that seven years of bullshitting every human he came across, outside of his fellow gang members, would prepare him for a career in sales.

His first break came when he witnessed a window washer slip from his ten-foot ladder while squeegeeing the showroom windows of a national jewelry store chain. The unfortunate fellow bounced off the lowest step, breaking his right wrist and left ankle in the process. Though it felt somewhat unnatural to him, Alex tried to make the man comfortable until help arrived.

As soon as the mall police relieved him, he sought out the manager of the store and asked to be allowed to finish the window job. Alex had no idea what he was doing but somehow managed to complete the floor-to-ceiling windows.

"You're not a window washer, are you?" The manager was nobody's fool.

"No, you're right. I just wanted to show some initiative. I'm trying to find some work." For the first time in years Alex tried the truth, and shockingly it paid dividends.

"Julio runs our mail order shipping in the back office. He was just helping out with the windows, but now he's going to be laid up for some time. Let's give you a shot doing that. If it works out, maybe something else will open up."

And so began the career of Alex Hartmann, purveyor of fine jewelry.

Alex showed great enthusiasm for his job as a shipping clerk. The challenges were few and his eagerness to please the store manager was infectious to the other employees. He would occasionally sit in for one of the saleswomen when they had to adjourn to the restroom or go for a quick smoke, while in his free time he cobbled together a library of some of the older classic self-help books. Bit by bit the ex-biker absorbed the lingo of the trade, and when combined with the old lessons of Dale Carnegie and Norman Vincent Peale, it became obvious that Hartmann was destined for greatness.

In six months, the store manager promoted Alex to head of sales. The Genesee Mall store became the highest-grossing store in the chain during his first twelve months, and this was in *Flint*. It wasn't long before word of his aggressive, yet empathetic sales technique was tossed about at the Jewelers of America trade show in Chicago, where he was in attendance.

During the banquet on the final evening of the show, the award for retail innovation was presented to Alex Hartmann of Flint, Michigan. His acceptance speech was humble, with generous tributes to those who supported him back at the store. His internship in sales— basically his seven years with The Saviors—was referred to only in passing. "I'd also like to thank a man named Gump, who taught me about the important things in life and the things that make America great." Generous applause followed, along with pats on the back and envious smiles. When he was seated back at his assigned banquet table, he was approached by several independent store owners with offers of employment, each with handsome increases over his current wages, one even offering a percentage of the gross sales.

The Diamond Ranch in La Jolla was the operation offering the best package to Alex; besides, he'd always wanted to live in California. This affluent suburb of San Diego was heaven to him. The weather was spectacular—none of that cold, snowy, rainy shit like in Michigan— and he got to play golf year-round. On top of that, the people were very rich, and most were very white; not too many of the brown folks and very few Muslims or Jews. The one drawback was the significant population of "queers." He detested the gay community, but he had to admit those fuckers spent some big bucks on gold and diamonds. He figured as long as he could sell them stuff, he'd be able to force a smile and hold his breath. He never could understand why someone would choose to be that way. *Maybe they think it's cool,* he thought.

After twenty-four months in La Jolla, Alex was offered a position as general manager of the Portland, Oregon store. It was producing only 70 percent of its sales goal and the manager had been fired. It was difficult to leave Southern California, but Alex was a driven man. His childhood in Bad Axe and his years with The Saviors were never far from his consciousness, reminding him of his previous impoverished life, impelling him forward to achieve even greater success.

CHAPTER 8

It was six thirty on a Wednesday evening. This late, the month of September could produce chilly evenings, even with the sun shining, but tonight was what made living in the northwest worth it. Jenne was relaxing on the deck overlooking a burbling Bear Creek, the sun still ten minutes from setting and Emma dutifully at her side. Kevin had just crunched up the gravel road and crossed the small bridge that led up the drive to their house. The Train had played early today, and rather than meeting each other at the club for dinner, Jenne planned on throwing some king salmon on the grill.

As usual, when Kevin came up the small rise to their home, Emma went ballistic. The dog might have been somewhat on the hyper side, but there was no disguising her joy at seeing the pack all together once again. He joined Jenne on the deck to relax for a few minutes before they began dinner. "So how was it today, Kev? Make any money?"

"Had those low-down motherfuckin' three-puttin' blues today, hon. Couldn't get the damn thing in the hole." Jenne knew that in spite of his proclivity for colorful language, Kevin had enjoyed the day and had no doubt that next time out with the boys most of his cash would return to the nest.

"Well, I won't ask how much you lost. Just make sure you kick their ass next time. I spent a few hours going over some fabric choices with Shelly this afternoon. She's actually got a good eye for color and she understands scale and balance. It makes her enjoyable to work with."

"I'm glad things are going smoothly. I'm pretty sure if her dickwad of a husband was involved, it would be much more difficult. I'm still amazed at all that stuff she told you—the diamond-swapping, the screwing around … what a sweetheart of a guy."

54

"According to her, they spend very little time together, especially since the grand opening of the new store is happening next week. She told me he and the new manager of the place were playing golf today."

"I did see them out there. Looked like the guy could hit the ball pretty well. They were only a twosome. No matter how hard the pros try, they can't get anyone to play with Chesnick. He's such an unpleasant man. I guess I feel bad for Shelly, although she seems to have everything planned out for the most part."

"She *is* a determined lady, I'll give her that. Any word on the Jerry Johnson murder? It's been quite a while now."

"No news at the club. I saw Vince before we teed off, and when he checked in with Bill Owens, he was told they were following up some leads, but I think that's what they say when there's no progress. Hey, incidentally, Santiago says hi. He's that kid on the crew that I told you about; a real sweet guy. Told me, 'Say hi to Miss Jenne.' How does he know who you are, by the way?"

"Before I played last week, I stopped by Top Pot Donuts and picked up a dozen for the crew. When I dropped them off, they were in there on break and several guys introduced themselves. Santiago I remember; not great with the English yet, but that smile will take him anywhere."

Their quiet conversation was interrupted by the annoying first stanza of the Irish Washerwoman, the little ditty that signaled an incoming call on Jenne's phone. "Shit, who's calling right at dinner time?" she wondered aloud. "Huh, it's Shelly. Wonder what she's calling for."

"Hi, Shelly. What's up?"

"Jenne, really sorry to bug you at home. Can we get together in the morning? Something's come up."

"I've got an appointment at the design center in the morning. Can it wait until afternoon?"

"Um, I really don't think so. I'm sorry, but this is pretty urgent, and I know we've only just met and all, but I consider you a friend and I don't have many of those. If there's anything you can do to make it, I'd really, really appreciate it."

"Can you tell me over the phone?"

"No, I don't think so. It's private."

"Well, okay, I'll switch some things around. Where do you want to meet? Your place?"

"No, that won't work. How about the Starbucks on Northeast Eighth at nine?"

"All right. See you there."

"Sheesh, wonder what the hell that was all about?"

"I only heard your side of it, Jenne. What seems so important that she has to see you first thing? It's not like any design decisions are urgent or critical."

"I think it's something else, something personal. I guess I'll have to wait until tomorrow, but I'm not certain I want to get in the middle of something."

"I'm with you on that. Guess we'll know tomorrow. Can we eat now?"

The parade of cars going south on Avondale Road was nothing unusual. For those unaccustomed to the daily slog it was the source of much frustration; nonetheless, every day commuters took it in stride. Jenne had to admit it was something she had worried about when they had relocated to Woodinville, but as long as there were no accidents, it only added ten minutes or so to the commute. While seemingly mesmerized by the bright red taillights ten feet in front of her, she considered her upcoming meeting.

Shelly did not appear to be the type who rattled easily. If it were something regarding the new house, she could easily have discussed it on the phone. She'd find out soon enough.

The Starbucks Shelly had chosen was directly across the street from the Nordstrom's in Bellevue Square Mall, and it was one of the highest-producing stores in the country. While most of the Starbucks stores in Bellevue—and there were almost thirty of them—were less than 600 square feet, this was one of the largest at over 2,500. And judging by the in and out traffic, it needed to be.

Not yet seeing her client, Jenne lined up to order her short nonfat half-caff double-shot latte. "Better make that two so my date doesn't have to get in line." Jenne thought it best to get things under way as soon as Shelly got there. Luckily, she scored a table for two in a darker corner of the noisy place.

It was nine on the button when Jenne arrived. Twenty minutes passed as she sat at the table sipping her latte. She was not given to overthinking things, but her level of concern was beginning to rise just as Shelly rushed through the door. She quickly spied her designer from across the room and hurried over.

"Sorry I'm late, Jenne. I had to wait until Bernie left the house. I don't want him thinking I know anything. Thanks for meeting me, too. Is that for me?"

"Yes, it is. Shelly, how about slowing down for a sec and taking a deep breath? Whatever this is, we'll get through it."

Taking a sip from her now-lukewarm latte seemed to calm her some. "Thank you. This helps. I'm not sure where to start on this, but here goes. Leslie Barnwell stopped by the house yesterday; she said it was important that we speak while Bernie and that new guy, Alex, were out playing golf.

"You know how I told you about Bernie switching out good diamonds for shitty ones? I knew about it, but apparently, it's been going on ever since he moved out of that basement in the Market, so he's been doing it for almost nine years. Leslie told me he's got a couple hundred stones in the safe at the downtown store."

"Yikes, that's some serious money you're talking about."

"Thing is, that's not all. She told me that most of his other stores, at least a dozen of them, are doing the same thing. No wonder he takes hiring his store managers so seriously. He's looking for assholes and crooks, just like him."

"If what you're saying is true, Shelly, why not go directly to the cops now? Don't worry about your damn house—this is serious shit."

"I would, Jenne, but wait, there's more." Jenne had to hand it to Shelly, even in the midst of exposing her husband's crime spree she could insert the time-worn clause from a thousand TV commercials.

Jenne couldn't help but smile. "Okay, good one. What's the more?"

With their lattes all but forgotten, Shelly picked up the saga. "Most of the switching of the stones is done right there in the store. At least, it is now. Leslie tells me that years ago, when Cascade Creations was using Johnson Jewelers, Bernie tried to get Jerry to do some of the switching for him, but he said he didn't do that kind of stuff. Everyone knows that Jerry liked to gamble and loved the ladies, but evidently, he was fairly ethical when it came to his business. Then about five or six years ago Bernie started spreading his business around to other shops, sorta to punish Jerry for not assisting him in the grift. So I was thinking, could Jerry have suggested to Bernie that the police might be interested in knowing about his corrupt business model? And maybe … would Bernie be pissed off enough at JJ to whack him? I don't know. I thought I knew my husband, but maybe not. Maybe he *could* be that much of an asshole. I just don't know. That's what I wanted to run by you, and sorry in advance for involving you."

Jenne's mouth hung open throughout Shelly's unfolding story of corruption. "Whew, this thing just keeps getting better and better. Let me see if I've got this straight. Your husband, the owner of Cascade Creations, owns almost twenty stores on the West Coast. He's not only encouraged but directed most of his store managers to illegally exchange quality diamonds for seriously flawed ones. And then he either sells the good ones or keeps them in inventory. Right so far?"

"Yeah, but I think mostly, at least from what Leslie tells me, he keeps the good ones and only sells a few. That way he can cook the books while socking away all the good stones."

"All right. So, if he's got a couple hundred stones from the store here, then, conservatively, he must have at least, what, fifteen hundred or so?"

"Sounds about right; that's what I came up with."

"And what did Leslie say the average retail on those would be?"

"They're very good quality, so maybe twenty-five to forty thousand each."

"So that's like forty or fifty million dollars. Holy shit, Shelly! How can he count on the crooked store managers to play ball and not keep some for themselves?"

"She said he gives them a monthly quota. If they make their number, he rewards them with a percentage of the take. He checks the inventory himself when he's on the road and pays them in cash while he's there. The neat thing about that is it increases his payroll expenses and reduces his net profits, effectively reducing his taxes. If the managers took any of the stones, they'd end up having to swap them for cash somewhere. This way there's no incentive to double-cross him."

"So what's your hubby gonna do with all these diamonds?"

"Don't know, but I still wonder about the possible involvement in the JJ thing."

"The police have been working on that for several months now and they don't seem to be getting anywhere. From what you've said, I suppose there could be some connection. I just figure they would have looked into that. Tell you what, let me run this by Kevin and see what he thinks. If nothing else, we'll get another opinion. You should tell Leslie to be careful and just go about her business, and you and I will keep working on your house. Nothing important will probably happen immediately anyway."

At least, that was what she thought.

CHAPTER 9

Friday was not usually a full group for the "A" Train. Wednesdays and Saturdays always attracted the full complement, but Fridays not so much. Today Kevin, Jeff, and Mani were in the group, and the threesome teed it up just after one. Because there were only three today, it was every man for himself. There was a skins game, individual bets, and the usual "snake" game.

Mani was the highest handicap in the group and the only double digiter at twelve. The good news was that he got plenty of strokes from the other two. However, he didn't get to be a twelve by shooting even par; he was just a terrible chipper. Mani was the shortest man in the club, measuring five feet *even in golf shoes*. Besides being somewhat weak at the short game, he was understandably distance challenged with his driving game.

What he lacked in distance his accuracy off the tee more than cancelled out, since he was *never* out of the center of the fairway. That his tee ball never traveled more than 180 yards was a major contributing factor. Born and educated in Tehran, he had moved to the States in the mid-seventies shortly before the removal of the Shah. His degree in civil engineering was welcomed by the first firm he applied to in Seattle.

Having the discipline and industry that was ingrained in him by his parents, he advanced rapidly in the firm. He eventually made partner and promptly bought out the other two owners. At sixty-five years of age, he had sold his firm, was in marvelous shape, and rarely missed a day at the Creek. He had started playing with the Train shortly before Kevin but had quickly become one of Kevin's favorites. Simply put, he had a charming personality.

While folks who played golf with him regularly never made serious fun of his lack of height, he occasionally endured it from those possessing very limited social skills. His friends knew it bothered him to a degree, but he always good-naturedly laughed it off. Mani was rarely seen without a smile on his face. He was always around for a game of "sinks" on the putting green and rarely missed a round with his fellow golfers on the Train. Mani also fancied himself quite the gin player and never failed to induce guffaws and belly laughs with his antics during a hotly contested game.

He had missed a game several weeks ago, and he was explaining why as the three competitors strode up the third fairway. "I had to go to LA to visit my wife's sister's family."

"Did you have a good time?" Jeff was more than happy to pry a little.

Mani's impish grin broke out with squinting eyes. "I'll tell you it was fucking awful." He still had a trace of the accent from his country of origin so that even when he used the word *fucking*, it still sounded elegant.

Both Kevin and Jeff were now looking expectant, knowing that whatever they were going to hear would be worth repeating at some future social event. Kevin took the bait first. "Okay, Mani, tell us why it was so awful."

"The husband of my wife's sister is a born-again Christian. Every evening when it was cocktail time, he would tell me how wonderful life was now that he had found his Lord and Savior, Jesus Christ. You know, we were there for a week and finally I got tired of the hard sell." Mani was among the more patient individuals on the planet, so for him to be fed up was a very high bar.

"So, tell us what you did." They were approaching the green, where Mani was faced with a delicate lob shot over a gaping bunker. "Please tell us, Mani, you know, before you skull this sucker over the green." Jeff was a relentless son of a bitch; relentless but funny.

"Okay, here's what happened." Anything to delay the formidable pitch he was faced with. "The last night we're there, he goes on and on again with 'Unless you accept Jesus Christ as your Lord and Savior, you're gonna burn in hell.' I said, 'Jonathan, who the fuck is this Jesus

Christ character you keep talking about and how can I accept him if I don't even know who the fuck he is? I'm a goddamn Muslim. We don't do Christ. I never heard of the guy until I moved here. Please leave me alone.'"

Both Jeff and Kevin cracked up, along with Mani, who had tears in his eyes, he was laughing so hard. "The only problem is that my wife is pissed at me for swearing in front of her sister. It'll take her a little time to get over it. Looks like I'll be here at the club most of every day, at least for a while."

The group finished their round by five and headed to the bar for the winner to pick up the drinks tab. Naturally Mani was the big winner, the lob wedge into the cup on three contributing in large measure to his success.

Since Jeff needed to pick up his kid from the gym, he managed a quick beer and took off. Mani was reluctant to get home too early, not wanting to experience the wrath of Yasmina, his wife, who was still harboring a grudge. With Jenne sharing a drink with the office gals, it was TGIF after all. Kevin consented to a shot of gin with his friend. Now that Emma was a steady employee, the Friday celebrations were held at the studio.

Mani was finishing up his third glass of merlot and snatched the fifty-dollar bill Kevin had placed on the table. He may have been in the doghouse at home, but he was ecstatic with the day's winnings.

"It's been a pleasure doing business with you, Kevin. We just have to do this again sometime." Kevin couldn't help but smile at the infectious glee on the diminutive Persian's face.

"Mani, it's been great fun. I sure hope you don't piss Yasmina off anymore. I don't think I can take these losses. I'm gonna head on out. See you tomorrow."

Mani went to the locker room to shower and hit the sauna, then headed home to face the music. By the time he walked up the stairs to the upper level parking it was close to eight thirty; the sun had disappeared almost two hours ago and there were only one or two cars remaining in the lot. He'd parked underneath one of the 200-year-old red cedars that had been spared during the recent expansion of the practice area.

Because Mani's new Lexus was equipped with auto locking and opening, he just needed to grasp the door handle to unlock and open the door. As he did so, he heard a rustle behind him, a scrunching of the cedar droppings. The third glass of wine may have contributed to the outcome of the confrontation, although that's still an open question.

When turning to investigate, Mani lost his footing slightly and half fell, half slid against the frame of the door. As he did so, an individual in a balaclava was already on the downward swing with what was discovered to be a fifty-six-degree Vokey sand wedge. Just prior to cleaving Mani's skull, it grazed the very top of the door frame and bounced off the side of his head. Shortly before losing consciousness, Mani had the presence of mind to curl into the fetal position, which may have saved his life. The assailant took several more ferocious swings at the fallen victim before a shout rang out across the lot.

Maryann was done for the day and had just reached her vehicle when she saw the altercation. "Hey, hey, what's going on over there?"

The attacker stopped in mid-swing, dropped his weapon, and bolted into the adjacent Kelsey Creek Park. After hustling over to Mani's vehicle, Maryann saw the poor man lying bloody face up and unconscious, sand wedge across his chest.

The EMTs arrived within ten minutes, a testament to their training, funding, and professionalism. This was Bellevue, after all; these services were important, and folks had no problem paying taxes to make certain their public employees were among the most qualified in the nation. Mani was knocked out, but he was alive.

The only employees left at the club were Maryann, Bret, and Vince; the GM had stayed late dealing with the new state laws concerning sales tax on golf rounds. Vince, ever the professional, whose number one priority was taking care of the members, followed the emergency vehicle to Overlake Hospital while making calls to Yasmina, Bill Owens, and Kevin O'Malley along the way, in that order.

All were stunned, especially Kevin, who had left Mani only an hour ago. Bill, who arrived at the scene shortly after the ambulance departed, watched intently as the crime scene techs processed the evidence. Two attacks at a private golf club in twenty years would have been unusual; two in three months was just bizarre.

Rather than complicate matters at the hospital, Kevin was able to reach Yasmina, who was awaiting a report from the doctors. "Yasmina, I'm so sorry. I just left him at the club only a short time ago. I can't imagine how this could have happened."

He'd only met Mani's wife once or twice at club functions, but from what he could gather, she was a tough woman who wouldn't wilt under difficult situations. "Kevin, thanks for calling. I know how much Mani enjoys your company. The doctors said they would be out in an hour or so. First reports are that he suffered a concussion and probably has some broken ribs. They don't know yet if his arm is fractured, but they have assured me that he will pull through, but it may take some time before he recovers consciousness."

"Geez, Yasmina, that's terrible. I'm really glad he's going to be okay, though. When he wakes up, please let him know I called. I'll get over to see him tomorrow morning."

"Will do, Kevin. Please say hi to your wife. Bye now."

Kevin, who had arrived home only fifteen minutes earlier, was now staring at his phone while Jenne looked on. "What the hell's going on, Kev?"

"You heard most of that, I think. Basically, someone attacked Mani with a club, just like JJ. What the fuck? At least he's going to be okay, they think. Might have some broken ribs and a concussion, but at least they're pretty sure he'll pull through."

"This thing's getting a little scary, don't you think? Nothing ever happens like this here. I'll bet that Owens guy is going to start feeling the heat, and I wonder if there's anything to that Chesnick connection that Shelly and I discussed."

"From what you said that guy had somewhat of a motive to go after Jerry. I can't imagine how that fits with poor Mani, though. I'm gonna call the other guys and tell them what's happened. I'm certain they'll want to know."

The techs had rigged up their portable LED floodlights and were now processing the second crime scene at Kelsey Creek Country Club within the last three months. Standing just to the left of the old cedar,

Bill Owens watched as the investigators collected, measured, and studied, hoping to find something that would reveal the attacker. "Looks like a similar club to the one that killed Johnson, am I right?"

Bill was glad to see Julie Thomas on the case tonight; she was a capable, seasoned veteran, but not one given to guessing until all the data had been gathered. "What I can tell you, Bill, is that the make of the club is the same. It's a Vokey and there are no prints on it. The guy must have worn gloves."

"Guy?"

"Well, if it was a woman, she's got one hell of a golf swing. You see the dent it made in the roof just before it hit Mr. Darzi in the head? If the guy hadn't been as short as he is, he wouldn't be at the hospital, he'd be at the morgue. It took someone with a great deal of power to do that. By the way, the wedge isn't exactly the same. This one's a fifty-six-degree model, with twelve degrees of bounce, whatever the hell that is."

"Same person, you think?"

"Awfully similar not to be. Guess it doesn't pay to be a golfer today. We'll be wrapping things up in an hour or so. Any luck with the dogs tracking through the park?"

"Not yet. They'll keep at it for a while, but I'm not holding my breath. Way too many smells in that place for the dogs to follow anyone, but I guess it was worth a try."

Kevin found himself at the Bellevue Police station the next day. In light of the events of the previous evening, Detective Bill Owens thought it prudent to once again revisit the Jerry Johnson homicide by interviewing any and all persons within JJ's circle of friends. That Kevin had been in close contact with both victims shortly before their attacks was a connection too close to ignore. Owens had been able to reach Kevin the previous evening and schedule the interview. An unexpected twist was the arrival of his wife, Jenne, along with a client, Shelly Chesnick.

The surprise on the detective's face at seeing three people in his interview room rather than one was evident. "What's this all about? I was just planning on interviewing Kevin regarding last night's attack on Mani Darzi. I don't think it's necessary for all of you to be here."

"Actually, Detective Owens, we think it might be." Kevin always got a little aroused when Jenne took control of a situation, even though he knew full well it wasn't the appropriate time or place. "This is Shelly Chesnick. We're not certain that what she has to say will have any bearing on your case, especially after last night, but the three of us thought you might want to have a listen on the off chance it does."

Owens's raised eyebrows indicated that his curiosity had won over his need to direct the conversation. "Okay, Shelly. Thanks for coming in. Please tell me what you think might have a bearing on our situation." The detective's professionalism had reestablished his status as the leader in this discussion.

Shelly proceeded to tell the story of her husband's years of theft and dishonesty. She left nothing out, including her plans to divorce him after she finished her house. She explained that after discovering the full scope of his corruption, she could no longer delay exposing him. When the connection with Johnson Jewelers was revealed, Owens placed his elbows on the table and leaned forward, perhaps to focus even more intently.

Upon finishing her narrative, Shelly took a deep breath and sat quietly, somehow looking small and very vulnerable. Jenne felt for her. Though they'd only known each other for a short period, she got the feeling that at a different time and place they might have become close friends.

The stillness in the room was broken when Owens scraped his chair back. "Ms. Chesnick, that was quite a story, and thank you for coming forward with it, despite you not being invited. It's because of folks like you that we're able to keep the good guys safe and take the bad ones off the street. Because I'm going to have to get a number of other agencies involved, I'm going to have to ask the three of you to keep things under wraps for a little while. Cascade Creations has stores in four states, so there's that. Much of what you're telling me crosses state lines, and there are federal crimes that have taken place. I'm thinking the FBI will want to set up a task force and not make any arrests until everything is in place. You should just go about your normal activities until we alert you that a raid is imminent. As far as the connection to the murder of Jerry Johnson, well, that's something *I'm* going to have to look into.

"Last night's attack, at least on the surface, doesn't have any jewelry connections that we know of." Owens directed this next at the two women. "Thank you very much for volunteering this information. You two can go now while Kevin and I discuss Mani's friends and associates from the club. There's immense pressure from the public on this and we really want to resolve the situation. Thanks again, and I won't keep your husband very long."

The women left the station while Kevin filled the investigating officer in on the folks that Mani was close to at the club. Word had filtered down from the hospital that he was now conscious and was already complaining about the food—definitely a good sign.

"So, Kevin, any idea why anyone would want to go after Mani? Everyone seems to like the guy, according to the club manager. The two attacks are too similar not to be connected, though for the life of me I can't conceive of a motive for this one. It sure looks like Chesnick *could* have had something to do with Johnson's murder, and we'll be all over that angle. Problem is, that won't fly for Darzi's assault. I'm gonna head over to the hospital to have a chat with him now that he's awake. Care to visit your buddy?"

They arrived at Mani's room just as Yasmina was leaving. "He's hurting a lot from the broken ribs, and apparently his vocabulary hasn't improved any. When I get him home, we'll have to work on that." She said this last with a smile, relieved that her husband would soon be released.

Kevin paid his respects with some gentle ribbing. Mani's head was wrapped like a Sikh's, dried blood seeping through the folds of bandage. "How's it feel, Mani?"

"Hurts like a mother. My head feels like it's gonna explode, and every time I take a breath it feels like someone's sticking a knife in my ribs; other than that, no problems. Good thing I'm vertically challenged. If I was a few inches taller, the doc says that fucker would have killed me."

It went on like that for a few minutes until Kevin said goodbye and left Owens to ask his questions. He'd been told that the guy had had his face covered, but maybe Mani could remember something that would help his investigation.

CHAPTER 10

In the days that followed, the O'Malleys went about their business. Shelly continued working with Jenne on her home, although some of her enthusiasm had dampened. Kevin was still tied up with the family compound client but still managed to get to Kelsey Creek on Wednesday.

It would be several more weeks before Mani would be able to join the Train for a game, but that didn't stop him from showing up for gin when his pals had finished their round. Chris, Danny, and Jeff were all very happy to see him, bandages and all. Everyone wanted to know who the culprit was, even though Kevin had filled them in on what little progress had been made.

As one of the other club members joined the fivesome to make it an even number, Mani thought it an opportune moment to share a joke. "Okay, listen up, you guys. There were four people on a plane: the pilot, an eighth grader, the orange president, and a preacher. They run out of fuel, but there's only three parachutes and they have to figure out who goes down with the plane. The preacher says he has to survive in order to save his flock, so he grabs a parachute and jumps out. The president says he's the smartest man alive and the leader of the free world. He grabs a chute and jumps out the door. The pilot looks at the eighth grader and says, 'Look, son, you've got many more years ahead of you than I do, so you take the remaining parachute. I'll go down with the aircraft.' Mani was grinning from ear to ear, the last vestiges of accent from his home country just a little thicker, lending some excellent timing to the story.

"The kid looks at the pilot and says, 'Don't worry, sir, the smartest man in the world just jumped out of the plane with my backpack.

There are still two parachutes left.' Loud guffaws rang around the card room. Mani was thrilled to be back among his peeps. Life was good even with sore ribs and a five-inch scar on the side of his head.

The grand opening of the Bellevue Cascade Creations store went off without a hitch. Bernie had scheduled it for a Saturday evening to take advantage of the weekend walking traffic through the Old Town area of the city. For folks arriving in cars, valet parking—free, of course; no tipping—was a must.

Both Bernie and Alex were decked out in tuxedos. Bernie's cummerbund had had to be let out and fastened in back with a safety pin. There were balloons for the kids and champagne for the adults. Bernie had closed the Seattle store and brought Leslie and her staff over to help with the crowds. The small two-lane section of Main Street that fronted the jewelry store was backed up for a thousand yards in both directions. Bernie had even hired off-duty cops to assist in traffic control. The objective, Bernie had instructed his employees, was to make the public aware of their location and comfortable with the ease of access, not necessarily to make sales.

Heavy crowds in a jewelry store are not necessarily conducive to sales. Rings and watches are small items, precious stones even smaller. Presenting the expensive trinkets on velvet pillows with customers standing elbow to elbow was just not possible. Better to display all his wares effectively with highly engineered accent lighting to encourage his visitors to schedule an appointment at a time when a much more personal experience could be arranged.

At Bernie's request, Shelly had also put in an appearance. The loud, obnoxious jeweler was blissfully unaware of the extent to which law enforcement was assembling to gather enough evidence to put him away.

Alex Hartmann was enjoying himself. He'd come a long way from Bad Axe, Michigan. Now in formal wear, he was a respected manager of the flagship store of the wealthiest independent jewelry store chain in the US. He'd give anything to see the faces of his biker buddies now.

When Alex had signed the deal with Bernie, he'd made sure to get a piece of the action. Since net figures were fairly arbitrary, he had negotiated a percentage of the gross. Bernie knew that Alex was killing him in Portland, so he considered bringing the talented sales manager on board a win-win for Cascade Creations. Alex was certain to make his new store profitable, and the Oregon location should be able to gain significant market share from the Diamond Ranch in his absence.

The new Bellevue store manager reflected upon his initial discussions with his boss regarding his business model. While the incentive of the gross sales was one thing, Bernie had offered an even greater spiff if he met his monthly "recovery" quota. Since Alex was not above committing fraud, deception, or even larceny, the opportunity to line his pockets with even more cash was appealing. Although he had heard of unscrupulous jewelry shops swapping out good stones for bad, even he was amazed by the efficiency of Bernie's enterprise. He was told by Bernie to keep his mouth shut during his month-long apprenticeship with Leslie Barnwell in the Seattle store; apparently her morals were on a much more solid footing than her employer's. That Leslie had confided the graft to Shelly was not within the realm of their suspicions.

Shelly left the festivities early, wanting to get away from the horse's ass for some peace and quiet. With all that she had gone through lately, the constant pressure of living with Bernie and knowing the shit he was involved with, she was especially thankful for the one bright spot in her life—her newfound friendship with Jenne. It had started as a business relationship, but now, with all that had transpired, she considered the designer to be a close friend—actually, her closest. She hoped that when all the dust had settled, she would remain so.

Bernie and Alex had closed the store by ten and were the last to leave. It was suggested that they have a nightcap somewhere to decompress. Bernie wanted to hit the local meat market watering holes, but Alex needed to make certain they were both on the same page and was able to steer him to a quiet table at the Westin Hotel bar. It *was* quiet—that is, until Bernie arrived.

"SO, WHAT DID YOU THINK? GREAT TURNOUT, EH?"

After a month in his employ, Alex still couldn't get over how irritating Bernie was. He'd been successful in the past by responding in almost a whispered voice, which seemed to suggest to Bernie that he was being a big fat loud annoying asshole, and it seemed to work now, as well. "Yes, Bernie. I thought it went exceptionally well. I was able to schedule a dozen appointments for folks to come in to look at specific pieces; in fact, I'm certain that we can top the sales numbers of any of the other locations.

"Let me see if I understand this 'recovery quota' thing. If my number is, let's say, fifty K in swapped diamonds and I hit the number, I get twenty percent of the take, correct?"

Now that they were discussing exactly how to screw their customers, Bernie had no difficulty in lowering his voice. "That's right. We base the value of the stones on their wholesale cost. For every five grand you're short of your quota, you lose five percent, so if your take is only thirty grand, you get nothing. Shit, you can make your quota with only two or three diamonds. Should be no problemo."

Alex could only hope this guy would just leave him alone and let him take care of business. He'd agreed to switch companies because he wanted to make some serious money, but having this asshole for a boss was already beginning to worry him. The more he made and the faster he made it, the sooner he would be able to move ahead with his other plans.

Arranging coordination between the states would have been a real pain in the ass if the FBI hadn't gotten involved. Bill Owens's first call was to Special Agent Matthew Steele of the Seattle field office. When he had first moved to Bellevue, Bill had been forced to attend a mandatory orientation class to familiarize himself with the additional law enforcement agencies based in the northwest corner of the US. After enduring the monotonous drone of the facilitator for several hours, they had met during a coffee break. Both were new to the area, Matt Steele from New England.

After Bill initiated the conversation by making fun of Matt's Boston accent, they became fast friends. Both spent over sixty hours a week dealing with caseloads that were normally handled by two officers. Even though Matt was frequently called away from the area, they still found time to get together a few times a month. While it would have been unprofessional for them to discuss ongoing cases, nothing stopped them from revisiting older ones that had been declassified.

When the scope of Chesnick's lawlessness had been outlined, his FBI buddy was all in. While Bill was focused on the murder of Jerry Johnson and the attack on Darzi, Matt was busy bringing the local offices in Oregon, California, and Arizona up to speed. He let Bill know that his people wanted to hit all the stores at once to avoid anyone slipping through the cracks. They would be ready to go within a week to ten days. There were still victim and former employee interviews to complete to lay the foundation for the prosecution that would be forthcoming.

That the two golf club attacks were connected was almost indisputable. Both were done with Vokey wedges and both with the same angle of attack. In each case the club was left behind, although strangely, it had not been there immediately after the Johnson homicide, so someone had placed it there when O'Malley had returned to the clubhouse. He could see that there might be a connection with the Chesnick situation, but how did that fit with Darzi? He'd just do what he always did, keep turning over stones until something made sense. Sadly, he had no fucking idea how he was going to solve this thing.

Ginny Paterno had managed the Scottsdale operation of Cascade Creations since its opening five years ago. Before that she had owned a small store in Mesa where she had managed a steady, if not impressive, income. Bernie had got wind of her operation after overhearing several of his competitors gossiping about her lack of scruples when it came to misrepresenting the quality of the precious stones. She had been his first choice to run the Phoenix area store, which had, up until now, been his most profitable. She constantly exceeded her quota of "recovered assets" and, because of this additional source of income, had salted away an impressive nest egg.

She waited on a young couple who were looking at loose diamonds from which to select a stone for an engagement ring. The attractive young bride-to-be, obviously of Hispanic descent, was as giggly as a young schoolgirl sharing her first boy crush. Unfortunately for Ginny, this particular woman was Special Agent Victoria Ruiz of the Phoenix Bureau of the FBI. She had been briefed on the fraudulent activities of the jewelry store chain and was here to gather as much information on the Scottsdale branch as she could.

Ruiz and her fake fiancé chose a flawless one-carat stone valued at $30,000. They would be back later in the afternoon to pick up the ring after it had been mounted in the setting they had selected. Ruiz, in spite of her youngish appearance, had been with the bureau for eight years and was well schooled in the chicanery that unscrupulous jewelers could foist on unsuspecting customers. Based upon the intel from Matt Steele in Seattle, there was a likely chance that the beautiful diamond she had selected would be replaced by one of equal size but of lesser quality in both color and clarity. If that were the case, she would document the episode and use it for justification to obtain a warrant to search the premises.

Similar stings were occurring at more than a dozen other Cascade Creations locations. Additionally, there were ongoing interviews of past and present customers, all designed to create a mountain of evidence with which to convict the unscrupulous ring of thieves.

When the phony couple returned to pick up their engagement ring, Ginny made certain to pay close attention to their reactions. She had a good eye for fakes, and with these two she had her suspicions. Rather than swap out the flawless diamond for something worth a third of the price, she *did* swap it out, but with a stone of equal clarity with only a few inclusions. If they complained, she would be surprised; the stones were very close.

"I know she switched it, Tom. The first one was flawless; this one has a few inclusions." Ruiz had managed to view the first diamond through the jeweler's loupe but did not have the opportunity to do so when they picked up the ring. She was now viewing it through her own handheld lens and was certain this was a different diamond from the original.

"Whoever Matt got his intelligence from was spot on. This outfit is a shit show. I'll bet they've swindled hundreds of customers without anyone suspecting a thing. Just think of all those young brides with stars in their eyes being conned. Goddamn, that pisses me off. I can't wait to bring the hammer down on these assholes." Having Victoria Ruiz pissed off was not advantageous for those who went afoul of the law, as dozens of felons now behind bars could attest.

As soon as the FBI agent left the showroom, Ginny got on the phone to Bernie. "We just sold an engagement ring to a couple that I'm concerned about."

"WHY? WHAT'S THE PROBLEM?"

"I'm not really sure. Just something about the woman sent up a red flag. I think she knew more than she let on. I wanted to let you know in case something comes up at one of your other stores. Probably nothing, but worth staying vigilant."

Evidently the threat of being discovered was enough to cause Chesnick to dial down the volume. "It's most likely just your overactive imagination, but I'll alert the other stores that are on the incentive program and tell them to keep their eyes open. Talk to you later."

Without so much as a thanks, he hung up. Ginny was very close to throwing in the towel. Bernie was an extraordinarily unlikable fellow.

Special agents for the FBI are very careful people. Unfortunately, those managers that were on the incentive program were also very careful, and because they were crooks and were screwing their customers, they were suspicious of everybody. Over the next four or five days, Bernie received calls from two other managers with similar reports to that of Ginny Paterno. Perhaps, he thought, her imagination wasn't so overactive.

Bernie was a pompous ass, but that didn't mean he was a *stupid* pompous ass. One alert from a store manager could be written off as alarmist or someone with an overactive imagination. Three within the span of a week was definitely cause for alarm, and while Bernie didn't have a formal contingency plan in place, he thought it prudent to circle the wagons.

He began by driving to the Portland store to retrieve the "recovered" stones from that location. That was followed up with a private charter to Phoenix and then to Orange County. Normally he would have flown commercial but having to explain a sack full of near-flawless diamonds to security was a risk to be avoided. The charter pilot couldn't have cared less. From John Wayne Airport to LAX and then up to San Francisco, Bernie collected all the stolen merchandise from the previous two years. The two-day trip netted more than twenty million in diamonds at wholesale cost.

The safe at the store in Seattle already held more than five years' worth of pilferage and was the only repository close enough to home for the crooked jeweler to trust. Besides, Leslie was the most dependable member of staff. She was an exemplary employee, and while he was certain she knew of, or at least suspected, his unlawful activities, he felt certain she would never expose his wrongdoings. Hell, he paid her too well.

The Worldwide Super Fortress safe, a six-by-three-foot impenetrable behemoth, now held almost fifty million dollars in diamonds. Even Bernie was impressed by this accumulation of chunks of carbon that were formulated three billion years ago. They would be secure in there for now, but he needed to come up with an alternative repository just in case the long arm of the law had other ideas. It was hard to believe that so much money could barely fill a Cracker Jack box, but that was the beauty of the stones. They were very light, portable, and passed for currency in every country in the world. Who wanted gold? That shit was way too heavy, and paper money took up much too much space. No, diamonds were Bernie's best friend.

CHAPTER 11

It was Saturday afternoon at Kelsey Creek Country Club. The overcast skies suggested rain might be in the offing, but in the northwest that was not an unusual occurrence. Bernie Chesnick had resigned himself to the fact that he would never have a regular game here at the club. That no one liked him was never in doubt, and a personality makeover was out of the question. The only people he could play with were guests. Vendors and employees were the only potential candidates, and he was rapidly burning through his list of vendors; even *they* had trouble putting up with him.

Today, Alex Hartmann was the unlucky half of the twosome. "PLAY THE SAME GAME AS LAST TIME?"

Alex was quickly developing a monumental dislike for Mr. Chesnick. He knew he'd have to put up with him for a while because he worked for him, but he'd be damned if he had to associate with him during his off hours. Besides, he really hated this repulsive club. Bunch of assholes. Alex figured he might be able to forego any future invitations if he just beat the man senseless and embarrassed the shit out of him. What could Bernie do? He wouldn't fire him; that would make him look foolish with the members of the Jewelers of America, and he couldn't stand the humiliation.

"Tell you what, boss, let's up the stakes. Hundred Nassau with automatic presses at two down work for you?"

Bernie looked surprised, especially since he'd taken a Benjamin from Alex last time. The thought of knocking some of the arrogance out of his new employee was too much to pass up, though. "SURE THING. IT'S YOUR FUNERAL."

An automatic press means that when a player loses two holes in a row, a new bet begins for the same stakes as the original bet. Although theoretically possible, it's unheard of to lose every single hole, but Bernie Chesnick managed such a feat on the front nine. At the turn, he was five hundred down but still certain he could manage a comeback. He was somewhat surprised, however, at the improvement in Alex's game since their last outing.

"TELL YOU WHAT, ALEX. YOU GOT ME PRETTY GOOD THERE ON THE FRONT. HOW ABOUT WE DOUBLE THE BACK, GIVE ME A CHANCE TO DO SOME DAMAGE?"

This stupid motherfucker just will not learn, Alex thought. *Fuck him, I'll just take his money. Maybe that's the only way.* "Okay, Bernie. If that's the way you want it, let's tee it up."

Bernie's game improved slightly on the back nine, while Alex's putting deserted him on several holes. As a result, the carnage was limited to only four bets at 200 each, for a total haul of 1,400 bucks.

Bernie's bombast had diminished quietly over the final four or five holes. Not having the douchebag screaming in his ear was an unexpected bonus for Alex. Maybe now he'd never ask him to play again.

"Your game was excellent today, Alex. I think I'm gonna need more strokes next time we play." Bernie's smile appeared forced as he complimented his store manager.

If I have to play with you again, I'm going to have a stroke, thought Alex.

"Alex, I got so wrapped up in our match that I forgot what I wanted to tell you. Several of the store managers have reported suspicious customers in their stores recently. They think maybe it could be the cops checking us out. I told them to be cautious with any 'recovery' activities, at least for a while. I'll suspend the quotas for now until things cool off a little."

"That sounds a little ominous. Do me a favor and keep me in the loop. We'll just stay busy with our appointments and not bother with any recovery operations. We should have plenty of business anyway, especially after that turnout at the opening. Oh, and thanks for the cash." Alex hoped sticking the needle in would dissuade Bernie from any future invitations to this disgusting place.

"I don't expect any problems, but yes, good idea to keep a low profile for a while."

Leslie Barnwell had put up with a lot of shit from Bernie Chesnick over her ten years with Cascade Creations. Her excellent management skills and client-based sales approach were the chief reasons the Seattle store had moved from its hovel in the Pike Place Market and was currently the most successful store in the city. Sure, the advertising helped a great deal and that ridiculous jingle was ubiquitous, but she was confident her skills were responsible for Bernie's success.

Before Bernie had opened his second store in Portland, Leslie had known he was pulling the old switcheroo with diamond rings that were in for repair or cleaning. She never said anything because, well, he was the boss and she needed the income. At the time she was a single mom raising a twelve-year-old son on her own, and every nickel counted. She was put on commission after her first six months and things improved dramatically from there. Now, at forty-eight, she lived in a comfortable house in the Queen Anne neighborhood and had been seeing Mike Lyons, an electrical engineer with Boeing, for the last fifteen months. Leslie, an avid hiker, loved nothing more than to hit any of the many trails winding through the foothills of the Cascades. Within forty minutes from her home she could find herself lost among the giant cedars and firs with Mike, initially a reluctant but now enthusiastic convert to her woodsy lifestyle.

With her red hair and crooked smile, she still managed to get a second look from the many single techies inhabiting the high-rise condos that had sprung up over the last dozen years or so in Seattle. With her son now out of college and a healthy start on her retirement nest egg, she was happier than she had ever been. Except for one niggling little thing: her boss was a fucking crook.

She had chosen to ignore it at first and pretend it didn't happen. When Bernie saw he could get away with it, he became indiscriminate in his choice of targets. Leslie made it a point to leave the showroom during the more flagrant thefts, afraid that she would be considered an accomplice. The scale of thievery had now escalated to the point where she was very uncomfortable in her position and actually thought she might be at risk as an accomplice. It was with this in mind that she had contacted Shelly and revealed the extent of her husband's unlawful activities.

Leslie was just finishing putting the loose diamonds in the safe for the evening when she noticed the additional velvet sack of stones on Bernie's shelf. The huge strongbox had seven different shelves and compartments, with the top one dedicated to Bernie's works in progress and his personal items. With him at the golf course for the afternoon, she didn't expect his return.

The store was locked, but she still felt nervous and stole a look over her shoulder to make certain she was alone. She picked up the sack, turned it upside down on a velvet countertop, and was stunned by the hundreds of glittering diamonds. She quickly picked up her loupe, examined a few of the jewels, and gasped at their perfection. There were some with minor inclusions, but they were few and far between, and the color and clarity of these purloined pieces was spectacular. She couldn't even hazard a guess at the sum of money she was seeing. She quickly scooped them up and returned them to the safe, now understanding where Bernie had gone when he had left town for a few days. Apparently, he had thought it necessary to consolidate the stolen diamonds. She needed to talk to Shelly again.

"Shelly, I think your husband is planning something." As soon as Leslie got to her car, she rang Shelly.

"What do you mean? Did he say something?" Shelly had kept her word to the detective and hadn't mentioned the ongoing FBI investigation to Leslie.

"No, but when I went to put the loose stones in the safe, I noticed a cloth sack on Bernie's shelf. It was full of diamonds—really expensive ones. He must have collected them from the other stores when he was traveling the last couple of days."

"Leslie, do you think you can stop by the house Monday morning? There's someone I'd like you to talk to." Shelly figured she'd get Owens to come by and talk to Leslie; that way she might be of some help to the police.

"What about Bernie? Will he be there?"

"No. He signed up to play in one of those Monday pro-ams. It's the only way he gets to play with the other members, since they all think he's a dork. At least he'll be out of the house early."

Leslie was somewhat concerned about who she would be talking to, but Shelly was trustworthy, so she wasn't that worried. "Okay, I'll get one of the other employees to open the place up. See you around nineish?

"Works perfectly. See you then."

Bernie and Shelly didn't talk much these days. She detested him, and he knew it. *That's fine with me,* he thought. *Never should have married that goddamn housecleaner anyway.* He was worried. He had chosen his managers well, especially those in the twelve stores that were participating in the program. That he could have amassed that many quality diamonds in such a short time period was impressive, but things seemed to be unraveling.

The downtown store was closed on Sunday, unlike the suburban showrooms that were open seven days a week. He let himself into the store around eleven o'clock and walked directly to the bullet- and fireproof safe that took up most of the closet in the back workroom. With a spin of the dials and a snick of the deadbolts as they retracted, he swung the heavy door open. His heart quickened as he anticipated the heft of the deep blue sack full of exquisite stones. It felt almost like one of the beanbags he had used when he had last played cornhole. He imagined himself trying to throw a fifty-million-dollar bag through a plywood target. God, it was great to be filthy rich.

He pocketed the diamonds, locked the safe, and closed up the store. He trusted Leslie to run his business, but he didn't trust anyone with fifty million dollars. He'd have to find another place to keep them, at least for a while until this shit blew over.

Shortly after noon he returned to his Clyde Hill rental home. Shelly was out with that designer looking at tile and stone selections for the bathrooms and the kitchen of their new home. *Check that,* he thought. *I'll never set foot in the goddamn place. She can have it.* Bernie was a boorish jerk, but he was a realist. He knew his marriage to

Shelly was on borrowed time. He figured she could keep the house and he could keep his fifty million. She'd never know, anyway.

One of his clients, a hotelier on his third wife, had been kind enough to give him one of those room safes that guests put their valuables in while visiting his hotel. He had converted two of the guestrooms into a conference room and no longer had any use for the thing.

Bernie had almost thrown it away, but Shelly had insisted they keep it. "You never know, we might need it someday."

Their rental home was one story in the front and two in the back where the hillside sloped away. In the northwest, folks referred to this style of house as a "daylight rambler," where the lower level was unfinished and contained the furnace, water heater, and laundry room. Being mechanically challenged, Bernie seldom ventured below the first level of the house, although he found himself there now.

He spotted the old hotel safe squeezed in between several boxes of outdated tax returns and other crap that his wife would never part with, stored on unfinished plywood shelving. *If anyone wanted, they could just take the damn thing*, he thought, but it would be fine for a few days until he could figure out something else. The combination had to be set every time the small door was closed, so he entered his birth year after stuffing the diamonds away.

CHAPTER 12

Although he was thrilled to have waxed Bernie at Kelsey Creek, Alex still felt uneasy at the prospect of Cascade Creations being investigated. He had spent the last few months as basically a gopher for that Barnwell bitch who managed the Seattle store. When Bernie had coaxed him away from the Diamond Ranch in midsummer, it was with the promise of running his largest retail operation that had sealed the deal.

Construction hiccups and problems with inspections—Bellevue was notoriously strict when it came to honoring building code requirements—had delayed the opening of the store. Because of that, he had been forced to endure weeks of "this is how *we* do things here at Cascade Creations" from the original hire of Bernie's who had managed his earliest store. Now that he had his own store to run, he was apprehensive, contemplating that one of his major sources of income might disappear.

He hadn't planned on making a career of the jewelry business. If his days with The Saviors had taught him anything, it was that he had the freedom to associate only with those of his choosing. Sure, those guys were two-bit smelly hoods who lived hand to mouth, but they had each other to stumble through life with, and their disdain for those unlike them was genuine. Until the election of the current occupant of the White House, both Alex and his former mates had been certain this country was going down the shitter.

Now that "The Donald" was running the show, things were looking up. With his new wall, the brown people from Mexico would be kept at bay. He'd already clamped down on those coming from "shithole" countries, and it appeared he was trying to find ways to keep the Africans from voting. Yes, things were definitely improving, but until even greater strides were made, Alex was going to find a way to make enough dough to settle with those of his choosing.

He had researched such groups in Eastern Oregon, Eastern Washington, and Northern Idaho. Most were made up of thugs pretending to be activists. They mostly wanted to just fuck off all day without having to work. Occasionally they'd commit some petty crime or roust some homeless Black person, but they were mostly ignorant folks with nowhere near enough gray matter to enlighten them any further.

Alex believed in the tenets observed by his former biker chums. The KAW ink across his shoulders was a constant reminder of the vigilance required to keep the Blacks, Chinks, Muslims, queers, and Jews from ruining the good old US of A. The challenge was one of finding a group with similar principles yet folks with enough BBs to keep him from getting bored.

An outfit called the White List had established a collection of like-minded believers on a small island located just off Lopez Island in the San Juan Island Archipelago. This collection of 172 islands was a boater's dream, with the added benefit of being in the "rain shadow" of the Olympic Mountains. Its annual rainfall was a third of that of Seattle's, and the surrounding waters kept the temperatures incredibly mild for a location this far north.

For the last month, Alex had corresponded with the founder of the group and the owner of the island, Robert Klein. What set these folks apart from the bottom feeders that comprised the majority of the secessionists was the requirement that any candidate for enlisting was required to donate $500,000 to the organization. The funds were required to continue to improve the infrastructure on the island and to fund future development of their web presence.

Unlike other separatist groups that disrupted small rallies and protests, the White List focused their efforts on sedition by peppering mainstream messaging websites with innuendo and fabricated stories elevating the white race.

According to Klein, who documented his settlement with photos and plans, there was an 8,000-square-foot main house with its own power, water, and high-speed internet. At present there were seven members of the group, all of whom were computer geeks. Klein had mentioned to Alex that they were looking for a marketing person to find new and ingenious ways to promote their message of hate. When asked about the steep buy-in, Klein had said only that it was essential to eliminate the wannabes and to fund the movement. Oddly enough, the place was called Trump Island but had nothing to do with the forty-fifth president or his family. The name had existed prior to any Trump relatives emigrating to the United States.

The more Alex traded emails and phone calls with the founder, the more it seemed like the ideal setup. Folks with that much dough couldn't all be stupid, and their obvious presence on the internet convinced him that they were philosophically aligned. Alex had never been interested in any kind of relationship with a member of the opposite sex, but Klein assured him that, if he were so interested, women could be provided. It wasn't that he was attracted to men—the thought made him shudder—he just wasn't interested. When he hung with The Saviors, there was the infrequent hooker or biker groupie, but those were just to show the guys he wasn't queer.

A weekend trip to the island had convinced Alex that this was going to be his future home. Klein was the owner of a Grand Banks 60, one of the world's finest cruising trawlers, which he berthed at Shilshole Marina when it was necessary to travel to Seattle. When Alex took him up on an invitation to Trump Island, they traveled in style aboard the beautifully designed yacht. The thirty-acre paradise was on the small side, but the isolation was complete. The only access was by private boat or seaplane or helicopter. Any need for supplies, medical attention, or companionship was just a short boat trip away.

Alex had taken this gig with Chesnick because he sensed an opportunity to earn a pile of money quickly, and if not *earn*, then he could find a way to steal it—it was the jewelry business, after all.

"Jenne, can you come by the house in the morning? Leslie's stopping by to talk to Bill Owens and that FBI guy. I know I shouldn't ask, but you've been in this from the start and, honestly, your support means a lot to me." Shelly blurted it all out as soon as she climbed into Jenne's Macan. "Leslie called me last night and told me that Bernie had collected all the stolen diamonds from the other stores and now they're in the safe in Seattle. I'm pretty sure he thinks something's going on."

"It sure sounds like he's making plans to do something. Did you arrange it with Owens?"

"Yes. When I told him what Leslie had said, he immediately got hold of that Steele fellow and they said tomorrow would be fine. Can you make it?"

"I'm not sure what I can do, but yes, I'll be there. Do you still want to go to the tile and stone showroom?"

"Ya know, Jenne, my heart just isn't in it right now. This is gonna sound silly, but you know what I'd really like to do?"

"I give up. What?"

"I'd really like to go to the club and just bash the living shit out of some balls on the range. Would you care to join me?" Shelly's impish smile was so infectious that Jenne found it difficult to imagine anyone refusing her anything.

"You're too much, Shelly. Okay, let's do it."

"Um, Jenne, one more thing."

"What now?"

"What the fuck is all this hair and slobber all over your car? Last time you took me somewhere, this thing was spotless."

"Emma. She's a fabulous companion and I wouldn't trade her for anything, but this is what you get. If you don't like hair all over your car, don't get a German Shedder."

Sunday afternoon was normally referred to as "hit and giggle" golf. The rather sexist idiom referred to couples' golf, which was primarily a social event with no serious gambling. Since Jenne was spending the afternoon with Shelly, Kevin ended up getting a game with Danny and Jeff. Mani was still stiff from his broken ribs but had managed to spend an hour or two on the putting green, honing his skills. Mani joined the other three on the first tee, proposing a bet that involved putting only, which the rest of the group was more than happy to accommodate.

"Hey, Kev, isn't that Jenne's car?" Mani had been the last to leave the first tee and managed to see the gray Macan as it pulled into the parking lot.

"I think it is, Mani. You three go on ahead and I'll catch up. I'd like a word with my wife.

"Hey, kiddo, what are you two doing here? I thought you were spending the afternoon looking at tile and stone selections."

"We were, hon, but Shelly's upset with the direction things are headed with Bernie. She thinks he's wise to the FBI's investigation, and we're meeting with Leslie, Owens, and the FBI guy tomorrow. She thought she'd have more fun hammering balls on the range than looking at porcelain tile."

"Geez, that doesn't sound good. Anything I can do?"

"I don't think so, at least not right now. We can talk tonight when you get home. I'm just gonna hit some balls with Shelly."

"Okay, see you then. I'm gonna see if I can hitch a ride up to the green with Kyle here." The assistant pro had just pulled up in a golf cart and offered Kevin a lift.

"Hey, Kevin, I was just told I could play in that pro-am event here tomorrow and I need to put a team together. Can you play?"

"Well, I did have a meeting tomorrow morning with the team, but it looks like Jenne's going to be tied up. What's your tee time?"

"We're off early, eight fifteen. That work?"

"Should be fine. Who else have you got?"

"Still working on it. I'll text you tonight. C'mon, hop on. I'll drop you off with your group."

The four "A" Train members had a wonderful day. Kevin, Jeff, and Danny had a spirited game of "skins," while Mani challenged the three of them to a putting contest on every hole. As they came up to the clubhouse from the eighteenth green, they ran into Jack Lewis, the head golf professional.

"Kevin, I just got some news I don't think you're going to like."

"That doesn't sound good, Jack."

"Here's the deal. You told Kyle you'd play with him tomorrow, right?"

"That's correct."

"Well, he had trouble filling out his group at the last minute, so he asked Bernie Chesnick. I know how you hate playing with the guy. Hell, everybody does, but Kyle's only been here for a couple of months, so maybe you could cut him a little slack."

"Ugh, shit. This looks like it's gonna be a real fun day. Who's the fourth?"

"He couldn't find another member, so he asked Bernie to bring a guest."

"This just keeps getting better and better. Maybe the guest will be okay. He couldn't be any worse. At least I can ride with Kyle."

Kevin was dreading the four and a half hours he needed to spend on the course with Chesnick. He showed up just thirty minutes before tee time, hit a handful of range balls, struck three practice putts and threw his bag onto the cart with the assistant pro. "Kev, Jack told me about your issues with Chesnick. Sorry, I didn't know."

"No worries, Kyle. You're new here, and what the hell, I can put up with almost anything for a short time. Hell, maybe we'll win something. Who's Bernie's guest?"

"Guy's name is Alex. He works for Chesnick, and I have to say, he doesn't look all that happy to be here either. Must be doing the boss a favor. He's playing to a seven, though, so maybe he'll help us."

They all showed up at the first tee and Chesnick did the introductions. "THIS HERE'S ALEX, THE MANAGER OF MY NEW BELLEVUE STORE."

Kyle was correct; Alex looked miserable. He just *had* to be doing this to pacify the boss. "Alex, nice to meet you. Let's kick some ass out here today." Kevin was at least going to try to be hospitable. He wondered, though, if this guy had anything to do with Chesnick's ring of crooks. *Ah, well*, he thought, *only four more hours to go.*

While Kevin was enduring quality time with Bernie Chesnick, Shelly was having coffee in her Clyde Hill home with Jenne, Leslie Barnwell, Bill Owens, and Matt Steele.

Owens took the lead. "So, Shelly, what's so important that we needed to get together?"

"As I told you, Leslie called me yesterday with some information that I think you need to hear directly from her."

Leslie told the two guys her suspicions regarding her boss. "It looks as though he's collected all the stolen diamonds from the rest of his stores. He was gone for a couple of days using a small chartered plane, and when I locked up the store Saturday evening, I noticed a sack of stones on his shelf. I looked closely at them and many were flawless stones worth tens of thousands. If he's consolidated all these diamonds right now, it might be because he suspects something, so I thought you should know."

Steele and Owens both faced each other with raised eyebrows. It was the FBI agent's show at this point, and he took over. "Thank you, Leslie, for coming to us with this. We have done some preliminary investigatory work and I suppose it's possible someone picked up on it. We were prepared to move on every store at the same time later on this week, but if all the stones are here, we'll need to rethink that. Your testimony will help us quite a bit, but we'll need some sort of confirmation with a few of the other managers to really nail this conspiracy. Normally, the first one to confess gets the best deal, so we'll definitely work that angle. Maybe some of the customers will be able to help, but I'll bet most of them aren't even aware that they were screwed.

"I'm going to huddle with the rest of the agents involved to see the best way to do this. In the meantime, just do what you'd normally do and, of course, please don't mention any of this."

"Of course. He's gone today, but he should be in the office in Seattle tomorrow. I'll just do my best to avoid him."

"Thanks, Leslie." Steele turned to look at Shelly and Jenne. "You two have been very helpful and the agency certainly appreciates it. Do your best to stay out of this now. Things could get a little dicey."

The meeting broke up, with Steele heading to his office to come up with a way to accelerate the takedown of Bernie Chesnick. Owens returned to the Bellevue station to bang his head against the wall. He'd made almost no progress on the Johnson homicide and the Darzi attack.

Shelly and Jenne spent a little time reviewing finish selections for the house, but only halfheartedly. Shelly had no qualms about making sure her husband paid for his crimes, but the excitement of creating a new home was overshadowed by her close involvement with the FBI in their pursuit of Bernie. They finally gave up, Jenne heading to the office and Shelly cleaning things up at home.

Leslie got to the store shortly before eleven and proceeded to remove the loose stones from the safe for presentation to prospective couples. There were only two people with access: her and Chesnick. The employee opening the store would be responsible for watches and baubles, but loose diamonds were too fungible to allow access by anyone but the most trustworthy employees.

While she generally paid little attention to the items on her boss's shelf, she couldn't help but take a peek just to reassure herself that she had really seen what she had. It was gone. The blue velvet sack containing the stolen diamonds from the past ten years was no longer in the safe.

She immediately got Shelly on the phone. "They're gone, Shelly. All those stones are missing. Only Bernie and I can get into that safe, and I'm certain nobody has messed with it. Your husband must have stopped by the store yesterday, when we were closed, and taken them. I guess he's getting a little paranoid about things."

"I know he was here yesterday while Jenne and I were at the club hitting range balls. The lazy shit left crumbs and soda can rings all over the furniture. I remember because I had to clean it up."

"Could they be in the house somewhere? If he took them yesterday, then they're not in a safe deposit box or anything; the banks would have been closed. He's playing golf today and I can't imagine he left them in the car or something."

"Leslie, I'm calling Jenne to see what she thinks, and then I'm gonna talk to that FBI agent. It could be it's time for him to do something."

CHAPTER 13

Like most pro-am events, this one was taking forever. A normal foursome should complete their round of golf in four hours or less. Most club tournaments take a little longer, maybe four and a half or so. This death march was going to go over the five-and-a-half-hour mark. And Kevin O'Malley got to spend every minute with the most annoying schmuck in the club. A smile came to his face as he recalled Jeff's comment to him describing Chesnick. "That Bernie, he may not be the biggest asshole in the world, but when the guy who is dies, then Chesnick's next in line."

The only blessing was Kyle. Kevin had only known him superficially, nodding hello as he passed him in the pro shop or the dining room. He turned out to be engaging and very funny too, especially when making fun of Chesnick after several topped shots and shanks. Alex was quiet, with seemingly a bit of a chip on his shoulder. Kevin brushed it off as the discomfort of having to play with his irritating buffoon of a boss.

As they approached the twelfth green, Kevin saw a couple of the greens crew working on one of the sprinklers; apparently, they had had a leak the previous night. One of the workers was Santiago Hernandez, who was busy, his head stuck down into the hole they had dug. "Hey, Santiago, hola. Que estas haciendo?" Jenne had taught him how to say "What are you doing?" in Spanish last week.

"Mr. Kevin, hola." His big toothsome grin appeared immediately, and just as quickly, it disappeared.

"Santiago, everything okay? I see you're working late today." The greens crew was usually gone by late morning, especially when there was a tournament. Since most of their maintenance needed to be accomplished by first light, their day started at four a.m.

"Si, si, things are good. We just need to hurry and repair this." Santiago may have said all was well, but his furtive glances at Kevin and his playing partners said otherwise. "Have a good game, Mr. Kevin." His dismissal of the group was also somewhat out of character.

Kevin thought the interaction was a bit odd and told himself to remember to ask the superintendent if all was good with the young man.

Since Bernie and Alex were riding in the same golf cart, they had plenty of time to discuss business. Bernie let Alex know that he was going to tell all the managers who were working the diamond con to play it straight for the time being. Bernie, being the pretentious jerk that he was, bragged to the new manager that he had consolidated all the confiscated diamonds and as soon as he could he'd stash them in a safe deposit box.

Having no friends and a wife who despised him, Bernie tended to glom on to whoever was handy. Without an empathetic bone in his body, he had no comprehension of how others saw him and cared even less. Alex was handy, ergo it was his burden to shoulder for the day. That Alex might not have been the most benign individual with whom to share his cleverness never entered Bernie's mind. The most important lesson Alex had learned during his stint with The Saviors, aside from to take a shower at every opportunity, was to never, ever pass up the chance to make a quick score.

"So, Bernie, what are you going to do with all those diamonds? Sell them individually? Cash them in?"

Now that they were discussing illegal activities, Bernie appeared to have the presence of mind to lower his normally verbose discourse. "I'm thinking of leaving the country."

"*What?* You just opened your biggest store. You just hired me. What the fuck?"

"Please don't raise your voice." This was priceless coming from Bernie Chesnick, thought Alex. "I've only just started plans. My wife hates me, which is fine because I can't stand her either. I couldn't care less about the new house, and my chain of jewelry stores that I built from scratch, well, I no longer give a shit. Forty or fifty million dollars should be enough to provide a nice life for me on one of those Cayman

Islands, where I won't need to worry about taxes or the law. It's not like I'll miss my friends; I don't have any. This club sucks too. No one will play with me. Fuck 'em all. I'm outta here."

Alex was stunned at this revelation. It was also the first time he'd seen any passion in the man. Almost as if the years of being ostracized had finally driven him to a tipping point. "So, what about me?"

"What about you? You'll figure something out. Maybe my wife will take over things and you can work for her. You can even *have* her if you'd like." This was definitely a different side of Bernie, one that convinced Alex he was serious about skipping town.

The remainder of the round was completed with very little being said between the two jewelers. Kevin and Kyle, on the other hand, enjoyed each other's company as well as the surprising silence coming from their playing companions' golf cart.

Shelly had Jenne on the phone as soon as she disconnected from Leslie. "Apparently Bernie took the diamonds out of the safe yesterday. Leslie thinks he might have stashed them somewhere here in the house until he can find a better place."

"Shelly, you need to get in touch with that FBI agent. It sure looks like the shit's gonna hit the fan pretty soon, and he'll know what to do. I'll come over now and give you a hand looking around." Jenne didn't want to be in the middle of this thing, but she was, and she wasn't going to ditch her new friend just because it was inconvenient.

Her next call was to the Seattle field office of the FBI. She was fortunate to catch Steele in the office, and he was more than willing to speak to her. "If you're telling me that he's moved the jewels from the safe at the store, then he must be getting ready to do something. We had planned to round up all the crooked managers simultaneously tomorrow, but I think we'll move that up to closing time today. They won't expect anything, and they won't be able to contact your husband either. What time do you think your husband will be done at the golf course?"

"They teed off early, but those events take a long time, and then they have to have a few beers after, so I'm thinking he'll be done by around two."

"Okay, Shelly. I hate to tell you this, but we're going to have to arrest him before he leaves the club. I don't want to give him any opportunity to leave town, and it appears that he's planning to. Do you have any idea where he might have stashed the diamonds?"

"Agent Steele, you can do whatever you like with that asshole. I have absolutely no feelings for the man, and the sooner he's put away, the better off everyone is. Leslie thought maybe he brought them home with him, but I haven't seen anything here. I suppose I can look around."

If Steele was surprised, he hid it well. "I'll touch base with you later in the day after we take care of business. After we pick him up, I'll be able to send a couple of agents over to help look for the stones."

Shortly before noon, Jenne arrived at the Chesnick household. "Did you say anything to that FBI agent about where the diamonds could be?"

"I told him what Leslie said, and he promised to send some guys over *after they've arrested Bernie.*"

"Oh shit, Shelly. I'm sorry you're going through all of this. It's got to be awful for you."

"It's not a lot of fun, but I'd be lying if I said I wasn't a little bit happy that my stupid husband is going to get what's coming to him. The bright spot is that I'll be able to get on with my life regardless of how this mess ends up, and, hey, don't forget I wouldn't have met you and Kevin if this house thing hadn't happened."

Jenne never ceased to be amazed at the resilience of this woman. Somewhere, someone, some day would be very lucky to tie the knot with the soon-to-be-former Mrs. Chesnick.

"So, you have any idea where that shithead of a husband of yours might have hidden millions of dollars' worth of stolen diamonds?"

"No, not really. Remember this house is just a rental. We've only lived here for a year. Let's just start going room by room and see if we get lucky."

The house was only a two-bedroom affair, so by late morning they had covered the two bedrooms, kitchen, and family room that comprised the main floor with no success.

"What about downstairs, Shelly? Think it's worth a look?"

"We may as well, although most of it's just mechanical stuff, the furnace and water heater, and the washer and dryer, of course. Bernie is a moron when it comes to fixing things and he's never done the laundry in his life, so I can't imagine why he'd even go down there."

They poked around the laundry area for a few minutes before going into the furnace room, which was partitioned off. The last time Shelly had been in there was six months ago when she had boxed up the previous two years of her tax returns. She still kept her small house cleaning business separate from their joint returns. It had been incorporated before their marriage and she had insisted on preserving that separation.

"What's that safe doing up there with those boxes, Shelly?"

"It's one of those hotel room things. Bernie wanted to throw it out, but I told him just to hang on to it; you never know."

"Help me get it down." It wasn't very heavy, since it was made to be bolted into the hotel room closet from inside. When they pulled it out from the tight space in between the banker boxes, it slipped and clattered upside down onto the floor.

"Ah shit, lost my grip." Shelly wasn't bothered by the mishap; after all, the safe was steel and relatively indestructible. "Let's get it up on this shelf and see if we can get it open."

When they lifted it up and turned it over, they heard what sounded like a rainstick being flipped. They stared at one another, knowing without a doubt that it was the sound of the stolen diamonds bouncing around the metal interior.

"They've gotta be in here. Shelly, do you know what the combination is?"

"Not for sure, but I've got a good idea. He always uses his birth year, so let's give it a try."

She promptly turned the four dials to 1961 and twisted the small knob. Because the velvet sack holding the stones had been turned upside down during the mishap, there were over a hundred loose diamonds of various sizes scattered inside the small safe. A number of them spilled onto the concrete basement floor and bounced like the shards from a broken crystal goblet.

Just as the two women began collecting the runaway stones, the first stanza of the Irish Washerwoman caused them to jump. "Whew, that scared me. It's Kevin. Let me get this."

"Hey, Kev, what's up? Are you guys done?"

"Kyle and I are grabbing a beer and a sandwich here at the club. Numbnuts said he had to get home."

"But it's only one o'clock."

"I know. Usually the guys stay for a bit, but Bernie said he had to leave. I can't say it bothers me."

"Shit, Kevin, the FBI was going to arrest him at the club when he got ready to leave. We thought it would be closer to two or two thirty."

"Yikes, that doesn't sound good."

"We've got to call them right away. Lots of stuff going on. I'll fill you in at home. Goodbye."

Kevin was left to ponder the cryptic response he had received from his wife while Shelly immediately called Steele.

"Agent Steele, Bernie's on his way here. He left the club early. Also, we found the diamonds."

"We're on our way. We'll get there as soon as we can. Can you hide them from him?"

"I'll figure something out. Please hurry." She disconnected.

"Bernie will probably be here in fifteen minutes, Jenne. I'm certain he'll want to pick up the stones."

"Let me take them home with me. If they're not here, he can't take them. You should be able to stall him long enough until the FBI guy gets here. I'll leave now and I'll stay on the phone with you until Bernie gets here. If nothing else, it should at least distract him."

Shelly's blank look suggested this confluence of events might have nudged her into a cul-de-sac of inaction, but she quickly snapped out of it. "Okay, get going. I'll call you when His Highness pulls into the driveway."

Jenne gathered up the diamonds, jumped into her car, and took off. As she rounded the turn onto Northeast Eighth Street, she saw Bernie's navy-blue Tesla zipping by with nary a glance in her direction.

As soon as she hit the 520 heading east, she called Shelly. "Is he there?"

"He just pulled into the garage. Let's pretend we're talking about the house."

"You do that on your end; I'll try to figure out what's going on. Did Steele say how long he'd be?"

"He said they were on the way … Yes, Jenne, I really like that glass subway tile you found for the splash in the kitchen. What type of grout should we use?"

"Okay, I guess he's right there. Maybe just ignore him."

"And that slab you selected for the laundry room I think is wonderful. Maybe we should … he's headed downstairs. Shit."

"Did you put the safe back on the shelf where we found it?"

"Yes, I'm pretty sure I …"

"Shelllly."

"Uh oh, guess what just happened."

Just then, tires screeched in the driveway as two unmarked sedans arrived.

"Gotta go, Jenne. Matt's here, shit's hitting the fan, call you in a bit."

Bernie was arrested with little fanfare save for the constant drone of "I'M INNOCENT, I'M INNOCENT, YOU COCKSUCKERS ARE GONNA REGRET THIS."

After Steele and the other three agents had removed Bernie from his home, Shelly nearly collapsed from exhaustion. The last vestiges of adrenaline draining from her body left her empty and feeling very alone. She'd told Matt that she'd given the diamonds to Jenne to make sure Bernie didn't get them in case his arrival was delayed. Now that everyone was gone, she just sat there and experienced her solitary sanctuary. Then she smiled and thought, *I never have to hear that son of a bitch's voice again. Wonderful!* She picked up her phone to fill Jenne in on what had happened.

Kevin had just spoken to his wife as he walked up the hill from the club to his parked pickup. She was on her way home with a bag of stolen diamonds and Bernie had been arrested. With all that was going on, it was a wonder O'Malley and Associates was still in business. *Thank god for good employees*, he thought.

As he was about to climb into his Honda Ridgeline, he noticed Jimmy Keneally driving by on his Toro Workman maintenance vehicle. "Jimmy, hold up for a sec." Kevin flagged him down.

"Hi, Kev. What's up?"

"I bumped into Santiago today while he was fixing a sprinkler. He didn't seem his usual jovial self, and I just wondered if things were okay with him. I don't know what his visa situation is, and I know our fearless leader in the White House has the ICE agents all riled up, so I was just wondering, you know?"

"I know what you mean. He *has* been a little more subdued lately. I know he's got a green card, because we check for that, but I'm not certain of his family situation. I think he falls into that Dreamer category so, I don't know, maybe that's got him concerned."

"Well, when you see him, tell him I was asking about him."

Kevin got behind the wheel and drove up the hill, heading back to Woodinville. Just as he pulled on to 140th Street, he noticed Santiago sitting at the bus stop, looking somewhat dejected. Kevin pulled over.

"Santiago, need a ride home?" Kevin wasn't certain where he lived, but it couldn't be too far out of his way.

The young greenskeeper still had an uncertainty about him but managed to nod as he climbed into the passenger seat.

"Hi, Mr. Kevin. I live over near Crossroads if that is on your way."

"I'm headed right by there—no problem. Say, you look like something's bothering you. Can you tell me what's got you worried?"

"I don't know. I think I may be in trouble. I'm afraid for mi padre. He is one of the Dreamers."

"I'm pretty sure he's safe for now, Santiago. They only seem to be rousting immigrants who have criminal ties."

If anything, the look on the youngster's face darkened considerably. "Mr. Kevin, I think I have done something wrong. I'm worried for my family."

It was possible that whatever Santiago thought he had done wasn't wrong, and perhaps Kevin could relieve his concern. "Why don't you tell me what happened? I promise I won't tell anyone unless you agree." It was a promise that he really hoped he could keep.

"The man you were with today, I saw him hit Mr. Johnson."

Kevin wasn't sure he had heard correctly. He quickly pulled into the Kroger parking lot and stopped in a deserted area. "Santiago, what did you say?"

"I saw the man hit Mr. Johnson with the club on the Glow Ball night."

"Which man? Why were you there? Are you sure?" Kevin realized his hurried, anxious words weren't helping ease Santiago's discomfort. "I'm sorry. Let's slow this down a little. Which man did you see?"

"The one you were playing with today."

"The big loud one?"

"No, the skinny one with the blond hair."

"Alex? Are you sure?" Kevin was shocked and had no idea where this was going.

"Si, I am sure. I saw him take the club and keep hitting Mr. Johnson. I was working that night because when we have the Glow Ball, many things get broken and we have to fix. I was taking the sand trap rakes back to the shop when I heard the skinny one yell things at Mr. Johnson while he was hitting him. He ran across the creek to the fence on seven, where he went through someone's yard and left. When I saw him throw the club into the creek, I pulled it out and put it back with Mr. Johnson. I am afraid I did something wrong."

"Did you wear work gloves that night?"

"Si, always. Jimmy makes us wear them."

Well, that explains the lack of prints on the wedge and how the club happened to appear in between the time I found the body and when the police arrived, Kevin thought. "Santiago, did you see them together before Mr. Johnson was attacked?"

"No, only when I heard the skinny one yelling."

Kevin recalled his promise to Santiago, but he just had to let Detective Owens know what happened. The kid was likely to be an accessory or something because of messing with the crime scene, but if there was any justice at all in the world, he was sure that could be overlooked. "Why did you put the club back with Mr. Johnson?"

"I did not want to get involved with the police. I thought if I put the club there, the police would see the fingerprints and catch the man."

Santiago had done the best he could under the circumstances, but now Kevin had to get him to tell his story to the police. "I told you I wouldn't tell anyone unless you agree. I know the policeman in charge. I will tell him what you told me only if he promises that you will not be in trouble. Will that be okay?"

Santiago's eyes wandered over the parking lot while he considered this. Mr. Kevin had never been mean to him or lied to him, so he trusted him. "Si. It is okay."

Kevin immediately got Owens on his cell and related Santiago's story. As expected, the detective vowed there would be no retribution against his, at the moment, only witness to the crime. "Can you bring him down to the station?"

"It might be better if you could meet us here to get his statement. I don't think he feels all that comfortable surrounded by cops." Owens was more than accommodating and said he would be there in fifteen minutes. While they waited, Kevin attempted to get his wife on the phone to bring her up to speed.

CHAPTER 14

By the time Matt Steele arrived at their offices in the Jackson Federal Building in the heart of downtown Seattle, it was early afternoon. Although he very rarely got upset, the discomfort of having to escort Bernie Chesnick through forty-five minutes of bumper-to-bumper traffic while he screamed obscenities at decibel levels approaching a Seahawks playoff game had pushed him over the edge.

FBI agents are notoriously polite, and Special Agent Matt Steele was a poster boy for this well-deserved reputation. "Mr. Chesnick, this is your final warning. If you don't SHUT THE FUCK UP, we will pull over to the side of the road, where I will let you out of the car. Then we will escort you to the back of the car, where we will open the trunk and I will personally shove your large fat ass inside and shove a gag in your mouth. Does that meet with your approval?"

Something in Steele's demeanor must have wheedled its way through Bernie's bluster, because the thief finally got the message. "When can I make a phone call?" This question arrived at normal conversational levels.

"When we get to the office, we will allow you to make a call."

"In private?"

"Yes, of course. You'll probably want to talk to your attorney, and you will have privacy to do that."

Bernie had no intention of calling his attorney. There would be plenty of time for that later. What he really wanted was to find a way to get the diamonds back. While his narcissistic tendencies prevented him from dealing with the very real prospect of spending years in the Big House, he was somehow convinced that if he could keep the diamonds, his future prospects of girls and booze on Grand Cayman Island would be assured.

Bernie had no friends, only employees. Because Alex Hartmann was committed to the "incentive program," and also because Bernie had done a background search on his new manager before he had hired him, he was aware of his ties to The Saviors. He had supposedly cleaned up his act after finding employment in the jewelry industry, but Bernie figured once a crook, always a crook, which made him prime material for his little band of thieves. Now he was hoping Alex could be motivated to recover the hard-earned fruits of *his* labor.

It took another hour before Bernie was allowed his call. "Alex, I'm calling from the FBI headquarters. I've been arrested."

Alex was surprised but not shocked. After all, the guy *was* a fucking crook and he'd been at it for almost ten years. That he'd gotten away with it for this long was more of a surprise. "Why are you calling me and not your lawyer?"

"My wife, that bitch, she gave the diamonds to that decorator so I wouldn't get them. Then she called the FBI on me and they picked me up. She'll probably turn those over tomorrow, so I need you to get those stones before the cops do."

Alex *really* couldn't believe this. Millions of dollars in diamonds and this clown wanted him to go fetch them. Jesus, what a fucking rube. Just for shits and giggles he thought he'd string him along. "And why would I want to do this for you?"

"If you do, I'll share them with you. You can have twenty percent."

This was priceless. Here was this clown, in custody with no hope of freedom, telling Alex he could have 20 percent of something that, if he could manage to confiscate, he'd have *all* of. No wonder the only profit this clod ever saw from his stores was the stuff he stole. "Gosh, Bernie, that sounds like a great idea. Where are they now?"

"They gotta be at O'Malley's house somewhere in Woodinville. Look it up, and when you get them, put them away so nobody can get them."

"Sounds like a plan, Bernie. I'll find a way to get back to you." *Sure, I will, when pigs fly. Some days just turn out unexpectedly,* thought Alex. A few hours ago, he was playing golf and was told he might no longer have a job. Now his moron of a boss had just offered him fifty million dollars in diamonds. Go figure.

Armed with Santiago's eyewitness account of Jerry Johnson's murder, Detective Bill Owens put out an APB for the arrest of Alex Hartmann. There were still plenty of unknowns—the motive, how Hartmann had managed to get Johnson alone—but these could be dealt with after his apprehension.

Alex, on the other hand, was traveling north on Avondale Road with the O'Malley residence as his destination, his JA9 jammed into his belt. The handgun was among the crappiest ever manufactured. No wonder Gump had given it to him. He had found the home on Google Maps and was surprised at its remoteness only a short distance from town. Bear Creek Road angled off Avondale and then a right on Mink. At five p.m. in late September, even this far north, there was plenty of daylight left.

The turnoff to the gravel road that led to the O'Malley residence was easy to miss. The drive, barely wide enough for a single vehicle, featured thorn-laden blackberry vines, their sole purpose seemingly to scrape the sides of his ten-year-old Honda Civic, severely limiting his speed. He had to stop twice to make certain he was still headed in the right direction; it was a very long driveway. About a half mile into the thick northwest forest, a small wooden bridge crossed over Bear Creek. That was when Alex began to hear the sound that German Shepherds make when they sense something or someone's presence exclusive of *their* pack.

Jenne was getting the details of Santiago's statement to the Belle-vue police from Kevin. "So, this is the guy you played with today?"

"Yup, I can't believe it either. Anyway, I'm on my way home and I can fill you—what the hell's that racket?"

"It's Emma. She hears someone coming. Maybe UPS. I gotta handle this. See you in a bit."

Jenne looked out of the window to see a shabby gray Civic crossing the wooden bridge. Emma was going apeshit. "Emma, Emma, quiet." As expected, the dog had no ears when a trespasser was near. It was rare for a vehicle, other than theirs or a delivery truck, to venture this far off the beaten track, and this particular auto looked a little suspicious.

Alex drove up the small rise to the A-frame structure that was surrounded by decking that extended to the edge of Bear Creek.

Not knowing who the driver was, Jenne held Emma by the collar as she walked out to the small front landing. At no time did Emma stop alerting, and Jenne did nothing to discourage her. Alex opened the door and stood by the car some twenty feet away.

In between the ferocious barking, Jenne managed to get a few words out. "Can I help you?"

Alex had planned a simple stickup; show the gun, take the diamonds, and leave town. This dog, though … this dog complicated things. "Your name is Jenne O'Malley, right?"

"Yes. What do you want?" Emma was straining at her collar and her barking became even higher pitched.

"Chesnick's wife gave you some diamonds. I'm here for them." As he spoke, he pulled the JA9 from his waist and pointed it at her. "If I were you, I would tie up that fucking dog before I shoot it."

"Who are you? What do you want them for?"

"My name is Alex and I work, or rather worked, for Bernie Chesnick. Now, get me the diamonds."

The tumblers suddenly clicked into place for Jenne. *This* was the guy who killed JJ. Since she had just spoken with Kevin, she assumed that Alex didn't know he was a hunted man. Maybe if she told him the cops were onto him, he'd take off. "The cops know that you killed JJ. They're looking for you."

Alex froze. He had thought he'd covered his tracks well enough, but evidently, he had not. Still, he could get the stones and head up to the San Juans before they knew where he was. "You've got two choices, lady: either tie up that fucking dog right now or he's dead."

"Um, it's a she."

"Tie it up or it's an it."

Jenne fought to contain the barking, snarling animal while she tied the leash around one of the vertical support beams. Emma had her soft collar on, not the choker, but hopefully it would hold.

Alex gingerly walked around the dog and followed Jenne into the house. The diamonds were sitting on the quartz counter, the deep blue velvet bag still cinched tight.

Alex grabbed them, checked to see they were indeed the stones, and turned to leave.

"Why did you kill JJ?"

"Why do you care?"

"He was a good friend, that's why."

"You wanna know? I'll tell you why. He was a fucking Jew, a kike. Those fuckers are taking over the world. We're better off without them."

"JJ wasn't Jewish! He was raised Catholic. What's wrong with you?" Jenne's anger always got her in trouble, but right now she was yelling at a guy with a gun.

"Then what was he doing at a Jewish club? Tell me that."

"You killed him because you *thought* he was Jewish, because you *thought* all the members were Jewish? You attacked Darzi too, didn't you? Did you think *he* was Jewish too?"

"Nope, I went after him cuz he's one of those Muslims. I know the difference."

Jenne was scared, but she was scared and very pissed off. "Get the fuck out of my house. The cops will get you soon enough."

"Lady, you seem to have forgotten who has the gun here. Now hand me your phone."

Jenne handed him the phone. As Alex turned to leave, he noticed Emma had quieted down. What he failed to notice was the *reason* she had quieted down. German Shepherds are incredibly intelligent animals whose intelligence is only surpassed by their sense of loyalty and duty. Emma had quietly chewed through the thick leather leash that had tethered her to the post.

Alex was out of the door with the diamonds, one foot off the landing, when he heard a faint rush of air. It was the sound of Emma's fur being ruffled by her thirty-mile-an-hour leap as she buried her one-inch incisors with 240 pounds of pressure into Alex's bony little ass.

He was thrown face first onto the gravel drive while Emma literally tore him a new asshole. Jenne had known how loud Emma's barking could be; she hadn't known that Alex's screaming would be even worse. Somehow, he managed to get onto all fours and crawl to his car with the eighty-pound animal still attached to his ass. Forgotten was his shitty little pistol and Jenne's phone, but he still gripped the little velvet bag.

Alex was able to climb into his Civic and managed to bash the door into the dog's head to get her to let go. Emma yelped and fell stunned into the drive. As he drove down the hill, Jenne could see small chunks of gravel embedded in the side of his face, and she could still hear his screams.

Jenne located her phone and immediately called her husband while she reached over to console her dog. "Kev, that guy you told me about, he was just here."

"What? Are you okay?

"I'm a little shaken up. He pulled a gun on me; he wanted the diamonds. Emma ripped him up pretty good, but he got away." Everything came out in a rush, her pulse still hammering in her ears.

"Jesus, Jenne, I'm really sorry I wasn't there. I'm ten minutes out right now; I'll be there shortly. I'll call Owens on the way."

"Actually, Kevin, Emma took really good care of me. I don't know what I'd do without that dog. Come home."

As Jenne disconnected, Emma slowly got up and leaned into her. "There, there, Emma, good girl. Thanks for watching out for me, sweetie. Let's go get some water." Together they walked slowly over to the dog's water bowl.

The traffic had thinned somewhat, and Kevin found himself doing seventy in a forty-five zone before he realized it. His wife and dog had been robbed at gunpoint by a murderer and he hadn't been there. When he finally reached Owens on the phone, he lost it.

"That goddamn killer just threatened my wife with a gun. She's lucky she wasn't killed. Thank god for that dog."

"Kevin, slow down. Talk to me. What's happened?"

Taking a deep breath, Kevin told the detective what he knew.

"It sounds like he might be injured, so we'll check all the ERs and the walk-in clinics. I'll let the Woodinville police know what's happened. Maybe they can track him down. I'm coming by your place now to interview your wife. I'm sure she's shaken up, but she might have some information that could help us. I'll be there in fifteen."

Kevin sped across the wooden bridge much faster than he should have, spewing gravel before he slammed on the brakes in the courtyard.

Emma bolted out of the door, tail wagging, barking with joy. Her dad was home.

Jenne walked slowly to him and they embraced. "Honey, you scared the shit out of me."

"Well, you should have been here. It *was* scary. Emma saved the day. I really think that guy might have some bathroom issues for a while."

When she started making wisecracks, Kevin knew she was starting to calm down. "Owens is coming by to talk to you. He thinks you might be able to help them find Hartmann."

"I don't know if I can help, but fine, I'm happy to talk to him. Let's dial it back a bit, Kevin, how about a glass of unoaked chardonnay to smooth out the rough day?"

"Wonderful idea, baby. Let's sit on the deck and watch the creek until Owens gets here."

Ten minutes of silence were pierced by Emma's shrill barking. "I guess the detective is here, Kevin." Sure enough, the Bellevue officer had just turned onto the wooden bridge.

After the day Emma had experienced, there was no way any other stranger was getting inside their house. Kevin met Owens out on the front landing while Jenne attempted to calm her lifesaver down.

The detective seemed uncertain whether he should get out of his car. "Is that the animal who did the job on Hartmann?"

"It is. Do me a favor, just stand up next to your car and don't move. Don't look at Emma and don't reach out for her. Just stand still."

Bill Owens did as instructed but was definitely not comfortable. As soon as Jenne opened the door, Emma bolted straight at Owens, barking ferociously. The nervous tic in his right eye was a definite indication of a normally controlling individual being forced to totally cede that position to another.

Within fifteen seconds Emma calmed, the barking stopped, and she was licking Owens's hand. He exhaled the gulp of air he'd been holding the entire time. "Okay to move now?"

"Yup. You're a friend now, but I wouldn't make any sudden moves toward me or Kevin. She gets annoyed about stuff like that."

"Jenne, believe me, that isn't going to be a problem." Emma sauntered over to her dog bed, curled up in it, and relaxed. Her eyes never left Owens, though; she was a protector, after all.

Jenne was debriefed, and other than some details about the murderer's car and his injuries, she could offer no additional information.

"So, this guy murdered Johnson because he thought he was Jewish?"

"That's what he said. Apparently, he has no use for anyone other than *his* kind."

"Did he say how he got Johnson back out on the course that night after he dropped his wife off?"

"No. I wondered about that. Maybe JJ knew about the shenanigans Chesnick was up to and he tried to blackmail him. Hartmann could have promised him money if he met him on the course. It still seems a bit complicated, but I think this guy is a kook anyway. Maybe we'll never know. It pisses me off, though, that he got away with the diamonds."

"We'll catch him. When there's a murderer on the loose and we know his identity, we'll get every jurisdiction involved. Don't worry, we'll get him."

But they did not get him. Alex was indeed in pain as he tore down the long gravel drive. Tiny bits of the rock that comprised the O'Malleys' driveway were embedded in the left side of his face, but that was the least of his concerns at the moment. Only by tilting his left shoulder into the side window to relieve any pressure on his right buttock could he manage to drive. The goddamn dog had really done a number on him. He should have shot the thing.

He was no doctor, but it felt as if his glute had been ripped from his tailbone. His ass was bleeding profusely, and even the slightest pressure on that side rendered him lightheaded. Driving with his left foot was his only option. Now that the cops had found him out, he needed to disappear, and he thought he knew how to make that happen.

Robert Klein had told him that he was welcome to join his little community whenever his finances made it possible. He figured fifty million dollars in diamonds made a lot of things possible. He was able to reach Klein on his cell, although driving left-footed with the phone scrunched against the window almost proved to be his undoing. The phone slipped, and when he swerved left to try to catch it, his right buttock planted itself firmly in the blood-soaked seat.

Just as Klein answered, he screamed in agony. "Alex, Alex, what's going on? What happened?"

"Ahhh ... I had an accident, a run-in with a German Shepherd. My ass is seriously injured. I have money and I need transportation to your island. Where are you now?"

"I'm on the island. If you can make it over to Shilshole, I can be there in three hours. You may have to wait a little, but I'll be there—slip J-42."

"Okay. Hurry." Alex generally knew how to get to the marina, but now he'd have to use surface streets. They'd probably figure he'd head north or south on I-5 or east on I-90. There was still some risk he'd be seen going through Kenmore and Ballard, but at least the sun was dropping, and the odds were marginally in his favor.

The driving was difficult and painful. When he arrived at Shilshole, he found a parking slot in between two full-sized pickups where the possibility of being seen was minimal. After his shitty little Civic was turned off, he leaned against the wheel and actually cried. *Goddamn, this fucking hurts. If I ever get the chance again, I will kill that fucking dog.*

Alex must have dozed, even through the pain. The exertion of the escape and the loss of adrenaline had left him exhausted. It was time to meet Klein and his fancy boat, but first he had to get to the slip. He reached into the glove box and pulled out a screwdriver. First things first. Since he'd never see this piece-of-shit car again, he thought it prudent to remove the plates and maybe buy a little time. They'd eventually find it, but it was a big world out there and he could have gone anywhere.

Walking the 200 yards to Klein's slip was unbearably excruciating, but after leaving a trail of blood, he managed to limp up to the *Purity*. It was the leader's clever name for his yacht.

Owens, on his way back to the station, had put a call in to Special Agent Matt Steele to inform him of the situation. The diamonds were gone, and a murderer was on the loose. Steele said that because the killing could be considered a hate crime, the FBI would now be involved in the manhunt. "Any help you can give us will certainly be appreciated, Matt. Logically it seems he'd take one of the main roads out of the area, although according to Mrs. O'Malley, he could have a serious injury. I've got folks checking on the clinics, but so far, nothing."

"Let me get on this, Bill. We'll get the son of a bitch. Those diamonds are important to our case against Chesnick. Even though we've picked up all the managers that were part of his crew, having that evidence is crucial. I'm certain one or two of the gang will roll over for a reduced sentence, but we still need those diamonds."

Hours turned into days and days into weeks. Hartmann's car was finally discovered at the marina, covered in seagull shit after not being moved for a week. It was surmised that he had left on a boat ... to somewhere.

Since Seattle was within a five-hour range of hundreds of islands and two countries, the challenge of finding Hartmann was daunting. Even though a liveaboard had seen a skinny guy limping down one of the docks at dusk on the night in question, the lead went nowhere. The witness hadn't seen the guy get on a boat, nor had he seen him return.

Shilshole was a massive marina with over 1,400 slips. The *Purity* *was* a large expensive yacht, but this was Seattle, the home of a significant number of people with more money than God; there were many large expensive yachts.

A month went by with no sightings of the racist. The FBI was still involved, although they had pared down the number of agents involved; their plate was full of miscreants.

The Bellevue police detective was hellbent on finding Hartmann and was beside himself with the lack of progress. Both law enforcement agencies had interviewed Chesnick so many times that they could no longer stand the sight of the man, yet he could offer no help as to where his former manager had gone. It now looked like Chesnick might get off at the low end of the one- to twelve-year sentencing guidelines.

The managers who were arrested all pled guilty to theft, easily rolled over on Chesnick, and, depending on their track records, were given probation or minimum sentences. They were, however, ordered to make restitution, which was made even more difficult by the absence of the little blue velvet bag.

The agents traced Hartmann back to his days in The Saviors, even interviewing his old mentor, Gump. The origins of the killer's white separatist inclinations were obvious now. Border agents and the RCMPs were alerted in British Columbia as well as Alberta, yet there was no word from them of any Hartmann sightings.

Kevin and Jenne fell back into their work routine, mopping up their existing work and preparing to continue the design of a multi-million-dollar log cabin on the cliffs above Deer Harbor on the west side of Orcas Island. They had partnered with a nationally renowned architect, known for his work with log construction, who lived on Lopez Island. Ground was scheduled to break in October, with construction taking the better part of two years. It was a beautifully designed home, one they were excited to be a part of.

Shelly was busy trying to put her life back together. She had skillfully wrested control of Cascade Creations from her convict husband and proceeded to liquidate the business. Since the corporation was a private one and she was listed as the CEO with 50 percent of the stock, she just assumed control.

Her first move was to cancel all advertising contracts and get that goddamn jingle off the air; if she never heard it again, it would be too soon. The few leases the stores had were bought out. The remainder of the stores were owned outright and these she shuttered, then listed the real estate at fire-sale pricing. Because of their locations, they were quickly snapped up, ensuring that the now-former Mrs. Chesnick would not be destitute. Her divorce proceedings had begun the day after Bernie was arrested.

Jenne and Shelly had become best friends and golfing buddies while work continued on *her* house. Now that she had dissolved Cascade Creations and sold off most of the property, she found herself with more than enough money to complete the project—and maybe even live in it.

Bill Owens had interviewed Shelly about her husband perhaps a little more than necessary. She confided to Jenne that she thought the detective had other things on his mind than just information about Bernie. She admitted that she too found Bill attractive and had already had a lunch date with him.

CHAPTER 15

As for Alex, he was ferried to Trump Island by Robert Klein. As soon as he was on board and making twenty-five knots past Golden Gardens Park in the luxury of the *Purity*, he began to relax.

One of Klein's followers, Tommy, took the wheel while Klein took a look at Alex's wounds. "Goddamn, that looks like it hurts. We really should get a doctor to fix you up."

"Obviously, that won't work. Let's just do the best we can, and I'll live with the results."

"It looks like you've got some tendon or ligament thing hanging out of the bottom of your right buttock. Dog must've had one hell of a bite. I can pour some peroxide over it to clean things up, but I'm not a doctor. I can't do any stitches."

"Can you tape it up? Maybe it'll heal up on its own."

"I can try, but no guarantees. This thing looks nasty."

So, Klein did his best. The peroxide fizzed and bubbled while Alex howled like a woman giving birth. The best Klein could come up with was a roll of duct tape from the engine room, which he used generously to pull the muscle back into what he presumed was the proper position. Twenty-year-old McCallum's served as an anesthetic, but no amount of it could dull the pain.

Alex drank enough of the single malt Scotch to help him pass out that first night, but if he thought that was going to be the worst of the pain, he was mistaken. He awoke the next morning with a massive headache, an upset stomach, and an urgent need to void his bowels. It was *then* that the pain hit the high notes.

He could not sit on the toilet seat, only brace himself against the tank and a nearby sink. Even the smallest push to void his waste sent lightning bolts of agony through his body. Both Tommy and Klein had spent the night on the boat with their patient and now looked at each other with what might have been empathy while they endured the killer's screams.

As the weeks passed, Alex's wounds *did* heal, and his infection passed. Klein's handiwork as a physician, however, left something to be desired. Alex's ass was no longer an attraction for prisoners everywhere. His right buttock was misshapen and sported a fist-sized knob on the anus side of the thing, further complicating his bathroom habits. To top it off, he now walked with a noticeable limp, as if his right leg weighed thirty pounds more than his left. Emma's handiwork had ensured there would be no tight jeans in Alex's future.

On the brighter side, Alex's philosophy of life dovetailed admirably with that of the other seven disciples on the island. The White List was fast becoming known as the wind beneath the wings of the white separatist movement in the western US.

Rumor, innuendo, and fabricated stories of misdeeds by Black, gay, and brown people, along with nasty tales of Jews running the world and the country taken over by Sharia law, were placed on the Facebook pages of those harboring even a hint of bias. The five men and two women were hackers whose sole mission in life was to purge the country of the impure. The marketing skills Alex had acquired helped them to phrase their stories properly and then direct them at the appropriate demographic group.

Klein's self-appointed job was to keep things running smoothly and secretly and to continue funding the endeavor. His fifteen years as an investment banker had rewarded him with a significant war chest. The half-million buy-in from his *team members* was basically to ensure their loyalty to the program. His boat was paid for, as was his island, and his diversified portfolio was worth north of a hundred million.

The fifty million in diamonds that Alex had stolen was interesting, but frankly it was of no concern to him. He gladly took what Alex had told him was $500,000 worth of the stones and that was that.

Robert Klein was born and raised in Willard. This small rural town in northern Ohio lies less than thirty miles directly south of Sandusky. Primarily agriculturally based, the town boasts only 6,000 souls and has a declining population. When Robert was born during the early sixties, the town was 95 percent white. There were few African Americans, few Hispanic folks, and very few Jews.

His father was a deputy sheriff, his mom a homemaker as dictated by the senior Klein. It was difficult to say where his father learned his intolerant ways; however, he was determined to pass them on to his son. It wasn't uncommon for him to come home for dinner bragging about some Black guy he'd arrested for speeding even though the guy was only two miles over the limit.

Robert Sr. was a two six-pack a night drinker. The more he drank, the louder he got. If Fox News had been available at the time, it would have been a constant in the Klein household. While he wasn't particularly physically abusive to his wife or son, he made up for it verbally. When he was of high school age, Robert made a point of hanging out with his like-minded buddies whenever his father was off duty. He felt bad for his mother having to endure him, but not nearly bad enough to be there to dull the pain.

Robert was an intelligent kid and a bright and accomplished student. Graduating high school as its salutatorian earned him an acceptance as well as a scholarship to Cornell University.

The Ivy League school was known for developing leaders of industry, giants in politics and law, and was basically a ticket to a wealthy future upon graduation. Ithaca, the home of Cornell, is located in the Finger Lakes region of New York State and is the home of the Ithaca Gun Company, makers of fine shotguns.

The liberal idealism of Cornell was not as comfortable for Robert as for most of the students. Over time he became more of a loner on campus and spent more and more time in some of the local bars.

On one occasion, while watching a Bills game at the Palms, Robert was slapped on the back with more force than just a friendly tap. "Tommy! How ya doin?"

Robert turned to face a tall red-bearded man with bulging biceps and a weightlifter's physique. "I'm not Tommy." He needed to shout above the noise; the Bills had just scored.

"Shit, dude, sorry about that. You look just like Tommy Burns from the back. Let me get you a beer. Didn't mean to whack you like that."

"No worries. Just nursing this one, watching the game."

"Name's Kenney, Kenney Boyce. Me and a few of my buddies hang out here." He slid onto the adjacent stool while offering his hand.

"I'm Robert Klein. I've only been in here a few times. Seems like a good place to watch the game."

"You at Cornell?"

"Yup. I'm at the business college there."

"So how come you're not hanging with the frat boys or your pals?"

"Sometimes I like to go off by myself. Every so often the politics there wear me out."

"I know what you mean. I dropped out of the ag college after a year. Started working at the Ithaca factory and met a couple of really good guys there. We hang out, go shooting, hit the titty bars. Tommy's one of them; the other is Pete Simmons. They'll be here soon; I'll introduce you."

Robert wasn't a big shooter, but the titty bars sounded interesting.

Kenney's buddies arrived shortly, and true to his word, Tommy Burns could have been Robert's doppelganger.

The four young men had a few beers and swapped lies, as young college-age men everywhere are wont to do. Tom and Pete were both from western Massachusetts and had attended Cornell for only six months before losing interest. It wasn't the difficulty of the curriculum that fomented their disillusionment with college life—after all, these were very intelligent men; it was no easy feat getting into an Ivy League school. The majority of the student body were liberal idealists. Very few of them had been raised by bigoted parents whose view of legitimate human rights was a society of only white folks.

Robert was happy to meet even a few people whose upbringing merged so well with his. Although these three had dropped out of college and were satisfied assembling shotguns and pistols at the Ithaca Gun Factory, Robert's goals were a little loftier. While he wasn't naïve enough to think his dream of an entirely white country would come to pass, that didn't stop him from dedicating every fiber of his being to the movement.

Even though his social activities were entirely off campus with his intolerant pals, he studied diligently. Rather than thinking less of him for his conscientious attention to his curriculum, his friends actually admired his dedication. When he graduated seventh in his class and accepted a position at a prestigious Wall Street investment banking firm, they were sad to see him off. When they heard of his success and his dedication to the cause through snippets on the internet, they bragged of their exploits with him.

Robert never forgot his college buddies. After making a ridiculous pile of cash through legal yet dubious investments, he once again reached out to them. He informed them of his intent to purchase Trump Island and to use it as a headquarters for spearheading a covert operation to accelerate the white separatist movement throughout the country. He let them know in no uncertain terms that if they wanted to be a part of his strategy, they needed to dedicate themselves to a comprehensive computer science program and master it. "You three are smart enough to have been accepted to Cornell. Get off your collective asses, learn the science, and join me in this crusade."

The Ithaca men saw the light and joined their former college friend. Robert and his three teammates became the foundation of the new White List, headquartered on Trump Island. Ever the pragmatist, it was Kenney who suggested to Robert that future conscripts should have to pony up half a mil if they wanted to be a member. "I like your thinking, Kenney. Let's make history."

As fall turned to winter in the Seattle area, the golfing frequency diminished. The "A" Train now played only once or twice a week at the most, and frequently it was while enduring the persistent drizzle that established the stereotype of the weather in the northwest.

Mani was back to full health and seldom missed an outing. The day was a rare clear one for mid-December, the hard frost finally dissolved by the low-angled sun. The group was Kevin, Mani, Jeff, and Chris today, with Jeff and Kevin taking on the other two. Mani, because of his higher handicap, was the only one getting strokes. The prospect of seeing the sun shining in the winter months in this corner of the country almost always ensured the locals would be in good humor, and this Wednesday was no exception.

"So, Mani, the ribs are all better? They don't bother you anymore?" Jeff's question could have been taken as concern for his friend, but the others knew it was probably just a setup for a zinger.

"Yes. No more pain, and the doc says I'm cleared for any type of physical activity."

"Geez, Mani, you'd think since there's no more pain you could maybe swing a little harder, get that swing speed up to maybe fifty or sixty miles per hour." Laughs all around, even from Mani, whose legendary lack of distance never stopped him from kicking a little ass now and then with his prodigious short game. The average swing speed for professionals was in the one twenties; most amateurs were high eighties to low nineties. Mani's was probably low eighties, but that never stopped the ribbing.

"Kev, did they give up on finding the guy who clubbed me in the parking lot?"

"No, definitely not. I saw Bill Owens the other day and he had no clues, but he's determined to get his man. The problem is that the guy just disappeared. Nothing at the borders, nobody saw him leave the marina, and the state cops from the entire West Coast have been on the lookout with no luck. Owens seems like the type who doesn't give up easily, though."

"I still can't get over his motive for going after me. I was raised Muslim, but it's not like I'm practicing."

"From what I hear about these white separatists, they see the white race as superior to all the others. They want a world that separates the races, controlled by whites. Most of these groups are not Mensa candidates, and they usually do something stupid and are disbanded. Lately, though, there's been a movement, heavily focused on an internet presence, that seems very well funded, and they're giving the Feds a run for their money. Owens told me that Matt Steele is heading up a task force to look into any local connections. The FBI thinks, because of the internet angle, whoever is leading the movement could be using the tech talent here in the northwest to help their cause."

The other three had stopped to listen to Kevin's take on the separatist movement.

"Kinda hard to believe some people still think that way." Chris offered his two cents.

"I guess there's no discounting how you are brought up. Most of these guys are from fucked-up homes, or were bullied, or just have low IQs and get taken in by the rhetoric. The thing that has the FBI concerned recently is how focused and methodically much of this internet assault has been developing. They don't think it's the usual bottom feeders. They say a lot of the gofers are still knuckleheads but that whoever is driving the bus is a real threat."

"Do you think that all this drivel you're spouting is gonna make us forget your three-putt back there? It's a 'snake,' Kevin; don't forget to mark it down. That'll cost you fifteen." Kevin had to hand it to Jeff, the guy had his priorities straight.

"The other thing that's got the FBI pissed off is the missing diamonds. That's allowed Chesnick and his crooked associates to skip some serious jail time. He'll still be off the street for a while, but geez, what an asshole." While the local news had constantly kept the public informed about the developments in the Cascade Creations case, Kevin was privy to the inside scoop because of Jenne and Shelly's relationship.

"I'm just thrilled that turd isn't a member anymore. I'm glad the board kicked his ass out as soon as he was found guilty." Mani had only played with him once, but the unpleasantness apparently lasted a lifetime.

CHAPTER 16

The Christmas holidays came and went with little further development in the search for Alex Hartmann. Bill Owens was now frequently seen with the former Mrs. Chesnick, and they became one of the regular couples, along with the "A" Train members, at events and dinners at the Creek. So much so that eventually people stopped inquiring about his quest to locate the only real enemy Kelsey Creek had ever known. Owens was a genuinely likable fellow, and now that Shelly's asshat former husband was in jail, her circle of friends widened considerably. That the detective was still troubled by his hunt for Jerry Johnson's murderer was no secret, although he brightened considerably whenever he was around his new lady friend.

Shelly's residence was going through the finishing touches by the time spring rolled around. Carpets, cabinets, slab and tile work, lighting trim out, plumbing fixtures, painting, and landscaping all came together at the same time. It was no wonder folks building a custom home for the first time either ended up divorcing or so exhausted that it was no longer any fun.

In Shelly's case it was nothing *but* fun. She got to spend time with her BFF, she didn't have to get approval from anyone, and she had plenty of money to hire the best subcontractors available. Her new home, understated and fitting seamlessly into the site, was met with approval from the entire neighborhood. The news about the homeowner's husband being a convicted felon should have met with disdain, but Shelly knew how to take care of people.

After the last workers' vehicles were gone, she made it a point to visit each of her neighbors, apologize for the inconvenience of all the traffic, and present each with a $200 gift certificate to Bis on Main, the excellent local eatery for the well-to-do.

O'Malley and Associates had as much work as their small firm could manage. A steady influx of new clients along with their existing portfolio left little time for recreation. Golf on Wednesday for Kevin and on Thursday morning for Jenne was all they could manage, save for the weekends.

The Orcas residence was taking more and more of their time. Frequent plane trips to the island for meetings, along with the constant requests for information from consultants and contractors, filled most of their days.

As for the little colony on Trump Island, they had made considerable inroads with their campaign of racism and homophobia. January was a milestone for the White List.

Through their constant barrage of separatist encouragement on every platform available—Facebook, YouTube, Twitter, Reddit, Snapchat, Instagram, to name just a few—they managed to foment enough hate to fuel the largest protest in the history of the movement.

On Martin Luther King's birthday on the Capitol Campus in Olympia, Washington, almost 1,000 disillusioned, disenfranchised, racist, homophobic souls showed up to affirm the superiority of the white race.

Not since Charlottesville had there been an outpouring of such hate and ignorance. The time and place had been promoted on social media by the White List since Thanksgiving. Ancillary signage and headwear, along with bottled water and energy bars, had been provided.

Klein had seen to it that the tools for treachery were in place the morning of that third Monday in January. He and Hartmann had taken the *Purity* to Oro Bay on Andersen Island, which is just north of Olympia in the southern end of Puget Sound. There they transferred the items to one of the separatist's boats, which ferried the supplies the final leg to Olympia.

Although Hartmann had put on some weight, shaved his head, and now sported a stubby beard, he still kept out of sight. These physical changes, along with his grotesque limp, would make recognizing him all but impossible, but he still wasn't taking any chances. Klein, on the other hand, preferred anonymity, hence the subterfuge with the support materials.

The MLK protest, as it came to be known, quickly grew out of control. There were no counter-protestors, but that made little difference. When 1,000 people, regardless of their political beliefs, are stoned, stupid, and mostly roided out, bad things happen.

It started with a neo-Nazi Neanderthal turning to a New York separatist with a Brooklyn accent and called him a fudge-packing faggot Jew boy. Apparently, the accent was determinative of his sexual and ethnic proclivities. Of course, such a slight couldn't go unanswered, and so the melee began.

When the state police couldn't handle it, the National Guard was called in. By the time the Guard arrived, a dozen cars were on fire, fifty or sixty were injured seriously enough to require hospitalization, and eight people were dead.

Klein and Hartmann listened with glee to the news reports all the way back to Trump Island. The White List was not just reporting on things now; it was *making* them happen. News reports of comments by the orange president were encouraging as well. "Some terrible things happened in Olympia today, but people, a lot of people are saying that most of the trouble was caused by liberal mothers with baby strollers giving the finger to these fine Americans. Let us support those poor men who gave their lives for this country."

There were times, Klein thought, when God was on his side. Certainly, the opportunity for the growth of the movement looked promising.

It was mid-April when the foundation was prepared, and construction had commenced on the Deer Harbor log home. Traditional construction requires framed two-by-six exterior walls that are filled with insulation, finished with sheathing, then siding, and then drywall and paint on the interior. Log construction consists solely of logs stacked horizontally on each other, which are then chinked to fill in the imperfect joints of the logs. The exterior siding, the insulation, and the interior drywall are not needed.

The O'Malleys had taken a Kenmore Air floatplane from Lake Union in downtown Seattle directly to Deer Harbor on Orcas Island. From the flight dock, the general contractor and architect picked them up for the half-mile ride to the construction site, where a huge crane was lifting the logs into position. It was the first such project for the interior design firm and they were fascinated by the process. The logs had been harvested from British Columbia, then assembled at the lumber yard before being numbered sequentially, disassembled, and shipped to Orcas Island.

After several hours at the site, which were spent reviewing interior walls, spaces, and details, Kevin and Jenne decided to call it a day. The return flight to Seattle would depart from Rosario Resort, located off East Sound near the center of the island. The drive to Rosario was a narrow two-lane road through hills dotted with farmland and through the town of Eastsound, eventually arriving at the resort, which sits at the base of Mount Constitution in Moran State Park.

The resort featured the original mansion built by Robert Moran in the early 1900s and offered a small marina and landing area for seaplanes delivering tourists to Cascade Bay.

The O'Malleys arrived early and spent their waiting time over lattes and croissants at the resort restaurant. They chose a quiet corner and watched the sporadic comings and goings of the trawlers and cruisers visiting the island. This early in the season meant very few visitors to Orcas, mostly sport fishermen and neighboring island residents out for the afternoon.

"Check out the size of that one! Gotta be over fifty feet, ya think?" Kevin had noticed a large trawler that had just entered the mouth of the bay.

"Wow, that thing sure is a beauty. Wonder where they're from."

The luxury trawler came to a stop several hundred yards from the marina, which was not built to accommodate a ship that size.

"Looks like they're dropping anchor out there. No way they could get any closer." Kevin stated the obvious while the young woman waiting on them asked if they'd like anything else.

"We're good, thanks. Any idea who owns that boat?"

"Gosh, no. I've seen it once or twice and heard it belongs to some rich banker guy who lives here in the islands, but no one knows for sure."

"Does he just stop here to eat or visit? What for?" Being nosy wasn't a problem for Jenne.

"Actually, it's the first time he's been here to the resort. The other time I saw it was over on Lopez, near Fisherman's Bay. They were probably at the Village Market getting groceries, so maybe he lives on one of those smaller islands over there."

As they contemplated this minor mystery, the Kenmore Air Otter droned in for a landing. "Looks like our ride's here, Jenne. Let's go."

The pilot pulled up to the dock and one passenger deplaned. As the O'Malleys walked past, they noticed the man seemed somewhat unsure of his footing on the floating dock, still rocking from the wake of the plane. He looked of Hispanic descent, small, wiry, with a trim beard and wearing a Padres baseball cap.

Jenne and Kevin boarded the plane just as the dinghy from the trawler pulled up to the dock. They watched as the previous traveler cautiously stepped down into the inflatable boat, which returned immediately to the trawler.

As the seaplane began to taxi into takeoff position, they noticed the expensive yacht had pulled up anchor and turned back into the sound. Even though it was a fair distance away, they could still make out the name *Purity* on its polished teak stern.

The team on Trump Island was ecstatic over the results of the MLK Birthday massacre. Their behind-the-scenes orchestration and assistance to key members of the movement had yielded dramatic results, the only question being how best to follow it up.

Gang fights and a few dead bodies were good for publicity, but there was little sympathy for Nazis, racists, and homophobes no longer among the living. Robert Klein wanted the next target for the White List to be noticed, to be historical, and to impact the one-percenters, especially the liberal one-percenters.

Alex wasn't as blessed cerebrally as were Klein's Cornell pals. What he lacked in smarts, though, he made up for in creativity and vengeance. A former single-digit handicapper, he could no longer swing a club. He could barely walk down to the dock, never mind eighteen holes on the golf course. He had millions of dollars' worth of diamonds, but nothing on which to spend it. Alex was dedicated to keeping America white, yet what fueled his fire even more was the hope that someday, some way, somehow, he'd find a way to kill that fucking dog who'd ruined his life.

Just recalling how that asshole Bernie had forced him to play with Jews and Muslims at a club that fucking *allowed* them to be members set him off. At the very least, private clubs could keep people out; they were *private*. The other country clubs in the Seattle area seemed to be able to limit their membership to only a token few of the unwanted. It just seemed to make sense that any organization that allowed anyone other than white Christians in should be made an example of.

Eventually, through his persistence, Alex was able to convince Klein of their next target. When February rolled around, they were on the same page and strategies were beginning to materialize. Researching specific elements of the plan took time and even some subterfuge. The biggest hurdle, though, was in locating exactly the right talent to execute it.

Boyce, Simmons, and Burns had dedicated themselves to computer science to further their separatist ambitions, and their above-average intellects had provided fertile ground for their development. Their singlemindedness enabled them to locate and recruit a golf course maintenance worker who had been fired from his job at El Paso Country Club.

It seemed a long way to go for a simple groundskeeper, but he needed to meet some specific requirements. Jesus Martinez was just the man they were searching for. His experience had made him the next logical choice for assistant superintendent at the exclusive club, and it would have if not for his conviction for distributing fentanyl among the crew members and their acquaintances. His source, which he would not divulge, somehow managed to get the stuff into El Paso from Ciudad Juarez, that infamous city just across the Rio Grande.

Jesus had been on the crew for half a dozen years before he stumbled onto questionable ways to supplement his income. The greens crew at the club were seasoned veterans and were dedicated to their profession. The occasional injury, however, forced them to miss a few days, and the resulting loss in hourly wages was devastating to their families.

At first Jesus did one of the men a favor by supplying him with opiates to relieve his pain and shorten his downtime. As frequently happens, word spread among the crew that their crew leader could help them out if necessary. One thing led to another, and eventually Jesus became the go-to guy for prescription painkillers.

His supplier suggested fentanyl patches might be another option for his crew members if nothing else was working, and he had a source for these. It was a small step from helping out those on the crew to supplying illegal opiates to others who had heard about their availability.

Eventually the police got wind of his activities and Jesus was arrested and charged. Nevertheless, his greenkeeper friends at the country club would not testify against him, and the case was dismissed. He was fired from the maintenance crew and was unable to find other work. His reputation was now that of a drug dealer, so he became one.

For six months Jesus developed suppliers and distributors. There was no avoiding the more ruthless side of the business, yet he found he was up to it. He had started out trying to help out his friends on the crew, and the club had fucked him over for it. That he had broken the law had no place in his reasoning that he had been wronged, and the chip on his shoulder grew bigger, not smaller.

He thought his first killing would have bothered him more, but no, it did not. The guy was stealing from him and had to be made an example of. Soon word on the street was "Don't fuck with Jesus; he'll make you pay."

"Jesus Martinez?" His burner phone had buzzed; maybe the new supply of patches was in.

"Yes, who's this?" Only a select few had this number and this caller was not one of them. Jesus suspected something was up.

"My name is Robert Klein. My organization has a proposition for you, one that could make you a very rich man."

"How did you get this number?"

"Mr. Martinez, our organization is far reaching. We are able to search and locate phones, track work and financial histories, and more. We know you were fired from El Paso Country Club for just trying to help your crew. We also know about your drug dealing and your small organization. We would like an opportunity to visit with you, show you what we have in mind, and you can see if you are interested. No pressure, just a meeting."

Jesus was nonplussed. Whoever this was, they knew a lot about him. It couldn't be the law, though; not if they just wanted a meeting. "How do I know I can trust you?"

"Our organization is called the White List. Google it. That will tell you all you need to know. Once you've checked us out, call me back. We'll arrange to have you visit us securely. We'll show you our plans, and I think you will be impressed. Call me after you look us up." The connection ended.

Jesus wasn't used to being told what to do, but the guy seemed *really* confident in his proposal.

The information on the internet regarding the White List was intriguing. Most of the info was second or third hand and some was just rumor. The White List was a small, well-funded group that supported any and all white separatist movements. It was said they were located somewhere in the northwest and the group had been behind the MLK massacre.

Jesus was Mexican. He had been born in Juarez and emigrated to the US with his mother when he was five. What the hell did a white separatist group want with a Mexican? Either he was going to be some sacrificial lamb, or they wanted something else.

"Is this Klein?" Jesus called early the next morning.

"Yes. Mr. Martinez?"

"You people are white separatists. I'm a fucking Mexican; what do you want from me?"

"Yes, we know you are Mexican. There are times when our organization allows us to associate with non-whites for the overall good, to further the cause. Your particular talents and skills are exactly what we need for our next target. You will not be accepted by most of our group, but you will be paid handsomely. You will be set for the rest of your life."

Jesus already didn't like these guys, but if there was that much money involved, he could hold his nose until they paid him. "Okay. I will listen to what you have to say."

"Will next week be acceptable for you to visit?"

"Of course. I'm the boss; no need to get anyone's permission."

"I will send a private jet for you on Tuesday morning. You'll fly to Seattle and be driven to Lake Union, where you'll catch a floatplane to Orcas Island, where we will pick you up."

Jesus was thinking, *These guys may be white assholes, but they sure as shit must have some money.* "Okay. I will see you then."

CHAPTER 17

Klein and Boyce had picked up Jesus at the Rosario Marina. Klein had greeted him cordially, if not warmly, while Boyce kept his distance: this *was* a Mexican, after all. If Jesus was disturbed at all, he didn't show it.

After arriving at Trump Island, he was shown to the guest quarters by a bearded fellow with a shaved head. The unfortunate fellow had what appeared to be a painful limp that prevented him from moving with any speed. "Robert says to make yourself comfortable. Dinner's at six thirty, when he'll talk to you about our plans."

They must really need me for something, thought Jesus. He was looking forward to finding out exactly *what* they needed him for.

A small table had been set in one of the conference rooms off to the side of the huge great room. One of the two female members of the small group doubled as the chef for certain occasions. Normally each member would fend for him- or herself when it came to meals. A weekly visit by a domestic services company from Lopez Island was sufficient for house cleaning, laundry, and weekly meal preparation for the rest of the crew.

Dinner was grilled Alaskan salmon, asparagus spears, and garlic mashed potatoes, accompanied by a robust Santa Barbara pinot noir. Robert Klein, Alex Hartmann, and Jesus Martinez, in spite of their differences, thoroughly enjoyed the meal, but the fun part was over. It was time to talk business.

They moved into the well-appointed great room and sat by the fireplace. The cool and damp late April in the San Juans still warranted an evening fire by which to enjoy a fine port and Dominican cigars. Jesus was getting antsy for these two to explain what he was doing here, but he decided the best approach was to let them have all the rope they wanted.

"We're making plans for an attack this July, Mr. Martinez, and we'd like to hire you to help us execute it."

"Please call me Jesus. I prefer it, and I'd like to address you as Robert, just in case I decide to take you up on your offer. What is so special about me that you have to send a private jet to fly me here and a yacht to deliver me to your lovely island?"

Klein took the lead. Hartmann was here because it was his idea and because he had inside knowledge of the target. "Your background and your current occupation are essential to what we have planned, Jesus. We're certain, with your expertise, we can pull this off with no risk or danger to you. You'll be compensated handsomely, enough so that you can retire to wherever you'd like and live in luxury for the rest of your life."

Jesus was interested, but he hadn't got this far in life by being a sucker. If it seemed too good to be true, it usually was. "Please tell me your plans and my part in them."

"There is a private golf club in Bellevue, just outside of Seattle—Kelsey Creek Country Club. We are planning a surprise for them in July, while they have their biggest event of the year. They always expand their greens crew for the summer, and with your experience, you should easily be able to get hired. We need you to make that happen. We understand you were fired from your previous golf course job, but that should be no problem. We will be able to come up with good referrals and a clean record for you."

"I don't see that being much of a hurdle. May I ask why this place is your target?"

"Of course. I'm sure you know that, in spite of us needing you, our ultimate goal is separation of the races. Most private clubs, regardless of stated policy, usually find a way to stay exclusively white and Christian. Sure, they'll have the occasional token Jew or Black; for the most part, though, they manage to keep the undesirables out.

"This place doesn't care who they let join. It's practically a fruit salad in there. They have a number of Jews, some Blacks, a few Muslims and Asians. They even allow homosexuals to become members. We plan to make an example of them and show people what happens if you let the races mix."

"And exactly how are you planning on teaching them a lesson? What does my working there do for you?"

"We still have to iron out a few things, but we're very close. Why don't we proceed like this? You go down there and get hired onto the crew. I'll arrange a place for you to stay and pay you a quarter of a million dollars up front just to get started.

"We will firm up things on our end and fill you in just as soon as we have everything in order. You will be paid an additional five hundred thousand the day prior to our operation and five million after its completion."

Jesus had been doing very well as a drug dealer, but this was in another league altogether. "Okay. I'll go and see if I can find a job. I'll need to buy a car, though. I don't have any transportation."

Hartmann spoke up for the first time. "How about you use some of that money we're giving you to buy some piece of shit? They'll expect you to be driving a junker anyway; you're Mexican."

Klein looked disapprovingly at Hartmann. Jesus noticed the glance and nodded at his benefactor. In the future, Jesus knew where to go if things went off the rails. While Klein was indeed a racist, he knew how to look at the big picture. Hartmann was just a hater and had difficulty grasping the probability of future events.

At the May meeting of the greens committee, Jimmy Kenealy was bringing the members up to date on the state of the golf course. "We've hired two new crew members to get things ready for the upcoming tournament season. One of them has plenty of experience and knows his way around equipment, fertilizers, and chemicals. We were lucky finding a guy who knows as much as Jesus does. Any questions?"

Kevin, who was only half paying attention, had some questions regarding the KCCC Invitational, the foremost member guest tournament in the northwest. "Jimmy, what kind of shape will the greens be in by mid-July? I know we had to re-sod a few areas due to some winter kill; will they be healed by then?"

Jimmy smiled, knowing his answer would satisfy. "No problem, Kevin. We'll have those things rolling at twelve and a half on the Stimp."

"Beautiful. We'll have those guests pulling their hair out." Green speeds at average golf courses usually hovered between eight and ten. Private clubs were typically a little higher, with professional tournaments normally played on greens rolling north of twelve. "Thanks for the update, Jimmy. Great job on things."

The meeting broke up, with Kevin and Jeff, also a member of the committee, heading to the bar to chat over a beer.

"So, who are you gonna saddle with your sorry game for the big event?" Kevin couldn't resist giving the needle, knowing full well that Jeff's game could definitely stack up well with anyone in the club.

"Funny man, Kev, funny man. I thought I'd try to get Bernie Chesnick. Maybe they'll let him out of the slammer for the tournament."

"Good one, Jeff. C'mon, who's your partner gonna be?"

"My brother's visiting, so I guess I'll be playing with him,"

"Geez, don't sound so excited. He's a pretty good stick, isn't he?"

"He's playing to a ten now, so yes, he's plenty good enough. Problem is, now that he's divorced, he tends to hit the bottle a little heavy. I guess it'll be up to me to watch him."

Kevin had played with Bert, Jeff's brother, a few times when he was in town. "He's from Bellingham, right? As I recall, he was always a lot of fun. Maybe every once in a while, he got a little tipsy, but that was about it."

"I think it's just the divorce thing that's got him. Maybe by July he'll be in better spirits and things will have leveled off some. Who's your guest?"

"I'm going to play with Bill Owens. He's a fifteen, but he's a competitor, and since he's been going with Shelly, both Jenne and I have gotten to know him better. He's a really good guy. He still hasn't given up on finding that Hartmann guy, but I think he's running out of stones to turn over. Anyway, it'll be fun to hang with the two of them during the social activities. Jenne and Shelly have become really close friends."

With two months to go before the big event, it looked as though the field would be full. It looked to be an event that would be remembered long after the final putt was sunk.

CHAPTER 18

"Robert, we found a source for that product you were looking for." Kenney had taken to hacking like a Pitbull with a pork chop. He was a natural at it. He loved a challenge, too. Robert had tasked him with finding a source for one of the key ingredients necessary for their July plans at Kelsey Creek.

"Where did you locate it?"

"There's several places that manufacture the stuff, but only in small quantities. There's an outfit in Shanghai that formulates it in quantity for vets and zoos. Apparently, it's used to tranquilize elephants and large animals. I guess it's pretty potent."

"You can say that again, Kenney. Fentanyl is about a hundred times as potent as morphine. This stuff is a hundred times more potent than fentanyl and it's very difficult to find in any quantity. Great job."

"So how much of this carfentanyl do we need to get?"

"Since it can be lethal in quantities as small as a grain of salt, we'll only need a pound of the stuff, but get two just to be on the safe side. You're going to have to find a way to get it here, though. We can't just air freight it."

"What about your buddy Jesus? You think he might be able to get it out of Mexico if I can get it smuggled into that country?"

"Good idea. Based upon his previous activities, I think there's a good chance he can help us."

After getting in touch with Martinez, the White List devised a plan to get the carfentanyl from Shanghai to Trump Island. It would travel by freighter from China to Columbia, where it would be transferred to a private jet. The aircraft would take it to Ensenada, Mexico, where a former associate of Martinez's would ensure it was loaded aboard a

Gulfstar 50 supposedly practicing for the Newport to Ensenada yacht race. After being smuggled into Dana Point, it would begin the last leg by private charter to Paine Field in Everett, where Robert Klein would be waiting to meet it.

The Gulfstar was owned by Donald and Ronald Aronofsky of West Hollywood. The brothers had attempted the production of several mainstream films, but their reliance on poorly written scripts had doomed the projects. The production of graphic porn videos proved to be more up their alley.

It wasn't that the films were so well made, it was more the marketing. Donald's business degree from UCLA had finally paid dividends. Their social media campaign was omnipresent. Even the most benign sites were inundated with pop-up ads leading the viewer to a number of sites offering access to the brothers' offerings.

Over a five-year period, their success was unmatched in the history of the film industry. Oscar nominations may have eluded them, but fame and fortune did not. While the brothers were renowned for their flashy cars, homes, and yachts, they were equally known for their affinity for illicit drugs and, to a lesser degree, the distribution of them.

What started as a way to ingratiate themselves with the actors in their productions soon became a steady flow of opiates to most of the others in their film company. Ronald became the conduit from suppliers to users and was always available if a member of their talent pool needed a fix.

The LA County Sheriff's Office, in conjunction with the FBI, had had the brothers on their radar for over a year; the time never seemed right, though, for an arrest. The sheriff's office wanted them off the street and in jail; the FBI wanted their *suppliers* off the street and in jail. So, they surveilled and waited.

The Newport to Ensenada yacht race was notoriously famous for partying and had been since 1948. The brothers, eschewed by the snottier members of the SoCal yacht clubs, were determined to take the trophy in their class the following year. The race had been run in April, when, unfortunately, their vessel had finished DFL, fueling the disdain showered upon them by the more serious sailors participating in the race.

They had vowed less partying and more training for next year's event. When one of their suppliers from Juarez offered them a hundred grand's worth of heroin and fentanyl to deliver a package to a courier at the Dana Point Marina during the return trip, they jumped at the opportunity.

The FBI had seen the brothers depart from the Balboa Marina in Newport Beach. With their array of sophisticated tracking equipment, it was child's play to follow them down the coast until they docked at the Hotel Coral Marina in Ensenada.

The LA office of the FBI was staffed by a number of Hispanic agents; as a result, observing the brothers while they were in Ensenada was no challenge. They were seen in the hotel bar chatting with a known trafficker shortly after their arrival. When Donald was handed two packages the size of a Girl Scout Cookie box, wrapped in plain brown paper, they were photographed by the agents.

They were told not to approach either the supplier or the Aronofskys under any circumstances but to make sure the transfer was verified. The objective, they were told, was to follow the packages, document all the players in the chain, and strike when the drugs reached their ultimate destination.

Inside each package were sixteen one-ounce glassine envelopes, each containing one ounce of carfentanyl. The single ounce was sufficient to tranquilize 2,000 elephants. After returning to their yacht, Ronald, the slower witted of the two, carefully opened one of the packages, chose one of the envelopes to keep as a souvenir of their journey and perhaps experiment with later, then carefully rewrapped the tidy bundle. His brother would have been pissed if he had been aware.

During the brothers' return trip to Newport Beach, they made a brief stop and tied up at the outermost slip on J dock at the Dana Point Marina. At that precise moment, the two packages were transferred, shutters clicked, and photos were forwarded to the home office. The courier subsequently made the trip to John Wayne Airport in Orange County, driving a ratty fifteen-year-old Corolla but scrupulously adhering to the speed limit.

If the agents on the case knew that the packages contained carfentanyl, they would have understood the necessity for the number of cutouts being used during the delivery of the drugs.

They followed the courier to one of the many private hangars at the small airport until they lost sight of him as he went inside. Judging by his empty hands upon his reemergence ten minutes later, the agents assumed the goods were now on the private charter plane within.

The tail number of the Cessna Citation XLS was dutifully recorded and phoned in to headquarters. The mandatory flight plan showed a landing at Paine Field in Everett, Washington.

As soon as the charter was airborne, the Southern California agents alerted Matt Steele, the SAIC of the Seattle Field Office. Steele immediately dispatched two agents to be at the airport when the drug-carrying charter landed. The agents were cautioned that the mission was to find out the ultimate destination of the drugs, not to apprehend the courier.

Since the drugs were no longer in California, the Sheriff's Department convinced the FBI to let them visit the Aronofskys when they docked at the Balboa Marina. The consensus was that if they could find drugs on the Gulfstar, they would arrest the brothers. If not, they would present them with evidence of their trafficking and attempt to leverage them into ratting on their Mexican supplier.

Three deputies boarded the sailboat as soon as it pulled alongside the dock, with Clyde the drug-sniffing Malinois accompanying them. The brothers were mildly surprised to see the lawmen, but only mildly. They were well-known porn producers, drug users, and providers, after all; occasional altercations with the police were expected.

Ronald and Donald were seated in the center cockpit as the deputies boarded, confident that they were safe, at least from possession. Clyde skipped aboard as well; his days in the DEA had prepared him for almost any situation.

"Welcome aboard, deputies. What can we do—?"

Before Donald's first sentence was finished, Clyde went apeshit. His ferocious barking and alerting at Ronald's left pocket startled even the deputies. Clyde was used to heroin, fentanyl, and several other opiates, but this was a new one. It was new, but still an opiate. Clyde's amazing nose, 50,000 times stronger than a human's, had immediately found a target.

With Donald looking worried and Ronald getting red-faced, the handler tried to quiet the dog with treats while his partners frisked the obvious culprit. The sealed envelope was confiscated, and the brothers enjoyed a trip to the sheriff's office for further questioning.

The FBI was notified immediately, and the envelope sent to the lab for analysis. Within an hour the granular substance was determined to be carfentanyl, perhaps the most concentrated opiate on the planet. A follow-up call to Matt Steele was made.

Steele had heard of the drug and the stories of heroin being laced with it to provide the ultimate high. Because the midwestern states had experienced a rash of overdoses as a result of this combination, he was determined to keep it from doing the same in Seattle.

The two agents heading to Paine Field were notified of the incredibly dangerous drugs that were headed their way and told to be very, very careful. It was more important than ever that they track the shipment.

Stationed at the side of the hangar where the private charter was expected to arrive, the agents observed a well-built man of approximately six feet, possibly in his mid-fifties, heading their way. Dressed in jeans, a leather bomber jacket, and deck shoes, the man constantly checked his watch.

Fifteen minutes passed before the beautiful private jet approached, then pulled into the hangar. The powerful telephoto lens on the agents' camera was able to photograph the actual handoff of the drugs from the pilot to the man. They were immediately emailed to Steele in Seattle.

They followed the man to a waiting van and driver and tailed the vehicle as it headed north on the Mukilteo Speedway. They discussed possible destinations for their quarry, but none stood out as likely. When it became obvious that the van was headed for the Whidbey Island Ferry Terminal, they again contacted Steele.

"Looks like they're headed for the ferry. The next departure is in five minutes."

"Okay, do what you need to. Just don't let him see you. We don't want to scare him off. We've sent the pictures you forwarded to Washington. Hopefully they'll have an ID on the guy soon."

As often happens in the off season, vehicles pay the fee at the booth, then drive right onto the boat without having to wait in line. Because the ferry load was so light, there was concern that the agents could be spotted if they boarded directly behind the van.

Out of an abundance of concern, they held back. Unfortunately, the blaring of the ferry's horn signaled its departure as the boarding ramp was retracted. Since the Whidbey ferry departed every half hour, they contacted Matt and explained the situation.

"Well, shit. Not much you could do, I guess. I'll contact the Island County Sheriff's Office and have them tail the van. Meantime, you get on the next boat and catch up to them. It's an island—he can't get off it without being seen."

The sheriff's deputies trailed the van as soon as it left the ferry terminal, while the two agents boarded the next boat to the island.

Its relentless pressure to place the white separatist movement front and center on social media in concert with claiming responsibility for the MLK massacre had positioned the White List on the FBI's most wanted list.

Klein was not paranoid, but he had a healthy respect for his intuition. While he was leaving the hangar, he had the feeling of being watched, and it had stayed with him during his Uber ride to the Whidbey Ferry Terminal. He paid the driver another fifty to continue his travels up the island until he reached Coupeville; then he could return.

Just before the ferry docked, Klein slipped into a restroom located on the lower car deck, where he remained until the boat returned to Mukilteo. He arranged for another Uber ride to take him to the marina at the Port of Everett, where he boarded the *Purity* and headed for Trump Island.

The carfentanyl was not selected because it was inexpensive. Because its efficacy for what Klein had in mind was second to none, the two and a half million dollars in product and fees for the delivery would be worth every penny.

When Hartmann had first suggested the private club as a target, Klein had been skeptical. The more he thought about it, however, the more he realized how spectacular the publicity would be and the more enthused he became about the mission.

The Kelsey Creek Men's Invitational was always held the second week in July. While it was mostly rainy and overcast from November through April in the northwest, the summer months were dependably sunny, with very infrequent rainy days. The second week in July rarely produced unpleasant weather.

It was a member guest competition, highlighted by lavish dinners on Friday and Saturday evenings, followed by dancing. The event was flighted by handicaps, with the lowest net team overall crowned the winner. The golf was spirited and competitive, but all in attendance recognized that first and foremost it was a social event.

Preparations for the affair were begun weeks ahead of time, the greens crew working feverishly to have the course in the finest shape of the year. Since half the field was made up of guests, it was a marketing opportunity as well.

During the tournament, the course was closed to all other play. Many of the tee boxes would be set up with kiosks for snacks, beer, and booze. Others would offer the opportunity to donate to some cause or other, while still others displayed spanking new automobiles to be awarded to the first hole-in-one. The entry fee included everything from breakfast to lunch to dinner, all of it accompanied by excellent wine and beer selections.

The event took the efforts of the entire staff, including additional temporary workers, to pull off. Many of the members' wives volunteered to assist at the various stands, scoring tables, and wagering stations. Vince Walker, the GM, spent most of the event weekend at the club, so demanding was the work schedule.

Klein had picked up the two one-pound packages from one of the private hangars at the airport. Martinez would meet him on the *Purity* in the evening to review the final plans for their undertaking. For the last six weeks they had strategically placed tidbits on much of social media, suggesting that an upcoming happening would spur the movement forward, enticing more of the true believers to join the cause.

Because Hartmann had pestered the shit out of Klein to be able to view firsthand the fruits of their efforts, Klein had made a generous donation to the Stripes of Honor program the first week in June. The foundation, which provided scholarships for the children of fallen or disabled veterans, received much of its funding from charity golf tournaments throughout the country.

Not only had Klein contributed significantly, he had also volunteered to assist by manning the donation kiosk on the fourth tee during the KCCC Invitational. The local chapter was thrilled to have found such an upstanding benefactor in their community.

Klein was secretly elated at the prospect of witnessing the outcome of their efforts. That Hartmann was along was of no concern to him; it *had* been his idea, after all. With the extra fifteen pounds Hartmann had gained, along with the beard and shaved head, Klein was confident he would be unrecognizable.

Martinez had shown up punctually at seven p.m. to finalize things. As Klein handed over the packages, he again cautioned, "Jesus, this stuff is very, very fucking toxic. I mean it. Do not touch it without gloves, a respirator, and a sealed suit. Make sure you wear whatever they use when they're spraying pesticides on the golf course."

"I understand. Very bad stuff. I will execute the plan just as we discussed. I've already got most of the other materials I'll be needing on hand, but I'll need to have you or Hartmann get the rest of the coconut oil. Do you have the second installment of my compensation that we agreed upon?"

"I do. I was supposed to give it to you the day before you complete your task, but I think it best we don't see each other until it's all over. Would you prefer payment in cash or in diamonds?"

"Diamonds?"

"Yes. One of our group provided his buy-in in the form of diamonds. They're a hell of a lot easier to carry around than stacks of Benjamins, but I'll leave it up to you."

Klein figured Martinez had more cash lying around than he cared to admit; the drug business didn't use American Express or Visa. He supposed this guy might think he'd try to screw him over; however, killing lots of golfers was one thing, pissing off a drug dealer who had no qualms about killing was altogether another.

"You make a good point. I'll take the diamonds."

Klein hadn't cared one way or the other, but he was happy to fence the stones Hartmann had given him.

CHAPTER 19

Friday morning arrived with blue skies and bright sunshine. Temperatures would rise from the current fifty-five degrees to a comfortable seventy-eight. Whenever Kevin stopped to appreciate where he lived—the air quality, the mild climate, the comforting politics—he was reminded of the song from the ancient TV show *Here Come the Brides*. Composed by Hugo Montenegro and performed by Perry Como, the first line of "Seattle" talks about *the bluest skies you've ever seen and the greenest greens you've ever seen* being in Seattle. They were right, he thought, especially on a day this flawless.

The putting green was filled with participants searching for some elusive final adjustment in their putting strokes. Breakfast had been served; there was coffee, juice, and pastries available on tableclothed stands in the courtyard for those latecomers. There was joking, wagering, and backslapping as former guest partners met old acquaintances and new ones were introduced.

Vince Walker was glad-handing the contestants, both members and their guests, and beaming like he'd just won *American Idol*. This premier event was not only a terrific time, it was the best marketing tool in the manager's arsenal.

The head pro was also making the rounds, answering questions about rules, and explaining the tournament format. The folks staffing the kiosks on the tees were finishing their setups and the volunteers were heading out to their holes.

With this many golfers in the field, it would be a shotgun start, meaning the entire field would start at the same time on different holes. At exactly nine a.m. the groups would head out to their assigned tees, and at nine fifteen the shotgun—in this case an exploding firecracker—

would be fired. With a tournament field this size, a five-hour round would be expected.

Shelly and Jenne had set up chairs behind the sixth green on the remote chance that a hole-in-one should occur. Since the prize was a new Lexus, the insurance company required that two witnesses be present. The ladies enjoyed sitting under the sun umbrella, chatting away the morning while visiting with every group that went through.

Kevin and Bill had been fortunate to be paired with Jeff and his brother, and they were looking forward to a thoroughly enjoyable round. They were assigned the fifth tee on which to start. Kevin noticed that Bert had lost a little weight but otherwise looked happy to be playing with his brother. Jeff, too, looked glad that Bert was there. Perhaps things had settled down with his personal life.

It was Bill Owens's first time playing in a big event and he looked nervous as hell. He was the high handicap in the group and that was always a recipe for anxiety. Kevin pulled him aside just before it was his turn to tee off. "Bill, relax. Just think about what you're going to do to that Hartmann asshole when you catch him. Now get up there and pretend that's his head you're swinging at."

Whether it was the distraction or not, Bill pounded the new Titleist two-eighty down the middle. Even he looked surprised as he picked up his tee.

"Yikes, Bill, take it easy on that poor ball, will ya? I don't know what your partner said to you, but whatever it was, stick with it." Jeff was a kidder, always quick with the jabs and occasional insults, but at heart he was all about keeping everyone happy, and he always found a way to put people at ease.

Jesus was responsible for holes twelve through fifteen. At four thirty he began by mowing each green, cutting new holes in each one at the precise location dictated by Kenealy, making certain all the traps were raked, and moving the tee markers to the proper distance. The mowers were equipped with lights so that all the chores could be accomplished by the tournament starting time.

Jesus could have done the work with his eyes closed. He didn't need the lights. Rather than focusing on what he was doing, he was going down his checklist of items he would need for the evening. He had the carfentanyl, of course, and the stearic acid, and he had been assured he would get the rest of the oil by the evening.

Klein had been correct about the diamonds; they were a hell of a lot easier to move than trunks full of cash. He'd eventually need a way to fence them, but that was a problem for another day. If things went according to schedule, he would be a rich man by Saturday afternoon. He was marginally troubled that he was aiding white separatists in their cause, but the five-million-dollar payday would go a long way to easing his conscience.

Santiago's responsibilities included holes one through four. He was no longer worried about his family. The detective had assured him that because of his help in discovering the killer, he would make sure none of the ICE people would bother him. He had been told that even the FBI knew of his situation and they would keep their eyes on the ICE people.

He very much enjoyed the work here at Kelsey Creek. The members were always friendly and frequently brought the crew donuts and coffee or sometimes pizza and even some beer at the end of the day. This special tournament was exciting. He would do his very best to make certain not a blade of grass or a grain of sand was out of place.

That they had not caught the killer yet still bothered him, but the man was probably long gone, maybe even in another country.

The card table on the fourth tee that Klein and Hartmann had just finished setting up now displayed pictures and stories of the young recipients of the scholarships that the Stripes of Honor had provided. Convenient donation vouchers were available for those guests wanting to donate to this outstanding organization. The members only had to give the attendants their club number and the amount they wanted to donate. It would be added to their club bill at the end of the month.

Even though Klein had donated several thousand dollars to the cause, he had still had to attend an indoctrination session before the organization would allow him to represent them. The fact that his altruism was just an excuse to witness murder and mayhem wasn't lost on him. Just because his mission in life was to elevate the white race above all others, there was no excuse not to help the offspring of patriots who served this country.

"Alex, don't forget to get those two gallons of coconut oil over to Martinez before we're done here today."

Klein surmised that the look of disgust on Hartmann's face was less about the chore and more about his having to associate with a Mexican. "I'll be glad when we're done having to deal with that guy. I don't like him."

"This golf thing should be wrapped up by mid-afternoon. We can take all this stuff back to the rental car then, and you can use the golf cart to meet with him. We'll still have to come back and set up in the morning, but I expect there will be enough of a commotion by then that no one will see us taking off."

The format of the first round of the invitational was two-man best ball. The lowest net score between the two partners on each hole was counted. Jeff had been up a little late the previous evening, sharing some quality time and a bottle of Leonetti Cabernet with his brother. If he'd stopped at the wine, things could have been different; unfortunately, the port and cigar afterwards had an adverse influence on his usually flawless putting stroke. Bert, who had apparently backed off his heavy drinking, played brilliantly, carrying his brother's sorry ass. Their net score of sixty-five put them squarely in contention.

Kevin played well on the first nine but terribly on the second. Fortunately, Bill got over his nervousness and carded a respectable eighty-two, scoring only two over par on the final nine holes. Their team was one stroke higher than their playing partners and would probably end up being teamed with them the following day.

Rather than make the trip home to clean up and get dressed for the evening's festivities, both Bill and Kevin showered and changed at the club. There would be plenty of time for a sheet of gin rummy before they had to meet the women.

Shelly and Jenne had returned to their respective homes after their shift watching for aces on the sixth hole. Jenne would swing by to pick up Shelly after they had freshened up for the evening. Emma would be spending the night at her pal Rosie's home.

Rosie was another Maltby GSD that Emma had become fast friends with during the Saturday obedience classes. They often had playdates at each other's homes, their owners knowing full well that an exhausted German Shepherd makes for a happy owner.

It was decided that Jenne would drop Shelly off at the club and then take Emma to Rosie's, which was literally around the corner from the golf course. Shelly would rustle up the guys and meet back up with Jenne for the evening.

CHAPTER 20

The maintenance facility was deserted save for Jesus Martinez, who was supposedly fueling up the mowers and other equipment to be ready for the next morning. Santiago had left over an hour ago, and no other workers were expected until four in the morning. It was a slight risk to use the building to assemble his recipe, but the equipment and space was essential.

Santiago *had* left some time ago, but he had also left his cell phone in his locker at work. While his parents would be upset if he lost his phone, he would be even more so. His entire life was in that phone. Losing his wallet or his keys was far preferable to being without his phone.

He realized it just as he got off the bus. He crossed the street and waited for the next bus back to Kelsey Creek.

As he walked down the maintenance road to the facility, he noticed the gate was open and one of the club golf carts was outside the door. It was very unusual for someone to be there this late in the day, especially during a big tournament. He knew Jesus was filling up the tanks for the morning, but he should have been finished long ago.

Rather than barge in, Santiago cautiously stood on the uphill side of the gate where there were enough blackberry bushes to conceal him. It made sense to see who was there first.

Soon the large overhead door opened, and two men walked out. One, he was certain, was the new fellow, Jesus. The other looked vaguely recognizable, but only just. Santiago thought the man might be a soldier who had been injured, so serious was his deformity, or maybe he had been born that way.

Still, there was something about him that was familiar. The man with the limp was talking to Jesus, almost as if he was telling him what to do. Santiago was an intuitive fellow. His decision to leave his phone in his locker might have saved his life.

The dress code for dinner on the evening of the first day's competition was "country club casual." This meant that participants and their spouses could be dressed in anything from shorts to slacks to elegant evening attire.

The display of food, in sumptuous proportions, included everything from shrimp to mussels to crab to salmon to roast beef and filet mignon. The buffet on the first evening of the Kelsey Creek Invitational was reputed to be the benchmark against which all other private clubs in the northwest were measured.

Jenne pulled onto the entry drive for the club and drove down to the porte cochere to let Shelly out. As they pulled into the circle, she noticed one of the kiosk attendants returning a golf cart to the pro shop. Something in the turn of his head tickled a fleeting memory in Jenne, but she couldn't retrieve it. Immediately, Emma's ears swiveled in the same direction, her nose twitched, and her eyes flashed to the cart.

As Shelly cracked the door open to exit the vehicle, Emma jumped over the passenger seat, shoving her aside and vaulting past. "What the—? Emma! Emma! Jenne, what's she doing?"

Jenne had only seen Emma react this way one other time. Right now, she wasn't sure what was happening. The dog had never left the car while she was in it. "Emma, get back here! Emma!" Her shouts were useless.

Emma had gone from zero to thirty miles per hour in three seconds. As Hartmann turned to see what the shouts were, a numbing fear crawled up his spine. *That fucking dog again.*

He turned the cart in the opposite direction and floored it. Heading back out to the golf course seemed like the safest bet, but Emma had other plans. The electric cart, with a full battery charge, could easily achieve twenty miles per hour. This one was low on juice but still approached the top speed. Emma, though, could go a little faster.

As the cart zoomed by the elevated first tee, Emma chose the high road. Just before Hartmann cleared the front end of the tee box, Emma made her leap. This time her attack took on the meat of Hartmann's right shoulder. The scream was heard even above the cacophony inside the clubhouse.

With the Shepherd still fiercely holding on, he tumbled off the vehicle at the side of the path. There was no need for Emma to regrip; she had jaws that would never tire.

"HELP! HELP! PLEASE, PLEASE GET HER OFF ME …"

Many of the members who heard the loud screams were probably reminded of Bernie Chesnick, but he was still in jail.

Jenne, with Shelly still in tow, had turned the car around and followed the chase. By the time they arrived, Bill Owens and Kevin had also shown up.

"GET HER OFF ME! GET HER OFF ME, PULEEZE."

Jenne spoke first. "Emma, aus, aus." Emma immediately disengaged, walked over to Jenne, and sat, her eyes never leaving Hartmann and his never leaving hers.

"Holy shit, Kevin, guess who we have here. Bill, say hello to Alex Hartmann. I barely recognized him, but apparently Emma never forgets."

"You're serious? Hartmann? Really?"

"Really. I'll bet if you take a look at his ass, you'll see a row of Emma's teeth marks there."

By now half the members and their guests surrounded the killer and were hanging on every spoken word. The evening's entertainment would have some stiff competition.

"Okay, folks, time to go back in and enjoy the party. We'll take it from here."

Owens called for the paramedics as he left for the station with his prisoner. Hartmann's injuries weren't life-threatening, but Owens wanted him administered to quickly so he could interrogate him. It looked like neither couple would now be enjoying the dinner at the club. Jenne still needed to give a statement confirming that it was Hartmann, although Emma's bitemarks had erased all doubt.

The killer's presence at Kelsey Creek Country Club was what really concerned Owens. This guy had killed a man because he *could* have been Jewish. He'd attacked another because he was Muslim, and now he was manning a kiosk for the Stripes of Honor.

All of the support people for the tournament had had to register with their contact information for insurance purposes. Owens found that, although their names were fictitious, the registrations confirmed that there were two of them.

"Okay, Alex, tell me where you've been and what you've been doing."

"No. I want a lawyer."

Now that he had been mirandized, Owens became a little more aggressive with him. "Tell us who your partner is, and we'll take it from there."

"I want a lawyer."

Shelly, Kevin, and Jenne were sitting in another area of the station that was more suited to public use. Emma sat with them.

"Tell you what, Alex, we'll get you a lawyer. In the meantime, we're going to take you to a holding cell in Seattle. We'll be riding over there with Jenne O'Malley and her dog. She needs to give us a statement."

At the mention of riding in the same vehicle with Emma, Hartmann seemed to loosen up a bit. "If I tell you my partner's name, do I have to go near that dog again?"

"Tell us your partner's name and we'll keep you here for the night." Regulations would never have allowed a prisoner, especially a murderer, to ride with a civilian and her dog, but Hartmann didn't need to know that.

"His name is Robert Klein. He owns an island up in the San Juans."

"Who is he? What does he do? Is that where you've been hiding?"

"You'll have to ask him, and yes."

"Where can we reach him?" The fact that two people from a private island were manning a charity booth at a golf course that one of them, a murderer, hated because he thought it was Jewish was too pregnant with possibilities to ignore.

"He's staying on his boat. It's anchored off of Meydenbauer Bay in Bellevue. It's called the *Purity*, you can't miss it."

Owens left the interrogation room and immediately got Matt Steele on the phone. "Matt, we caught Hartmann. Actually, the dog got him again. It was beautiful."

"Great news, Bill. Congrats. We'll want to talk to him as well, since it *was* a hate crime."

"Of course. No problem. That's not all. He was here with an accomplice. His name is Robert Klein and he's on his boat over in Meydenbauer Bay. Can you pick him up?"

Steele was quiet for a moment.

"Matt, you still there?"

"Did you say Klein?"

"Yes. Is he someone?"

"If it's the Robert Klein that I'm thinking of, he's *really* someone. That fucker has been on our hate crimes list for six months now. He was reportedly behind that MLK massacre, and he's been inciting violence with the white separatist movement. He is supposedly the head of this 'White List' group that's ravaging the internet with all sorts of bad shit. We almost had him a couple of months ago, but he gave us the slip. We're certain he's managed to get his hands on a couple of pounds of carfentanyl."

"What did you say?"

"You heard me. I don't know what he has planned, but that shit is dangerous. We've got to get it off the street."

"Matt, a favor. When you get him, bring him here. If they've got something planned and it involves that drug, we'll need to get to the bottom of it fast."

"On it, dude. We'll call when we've got him."

CHAPTER 21

The maintenance complex was located on the opposite side of the golf course from the clubhouse. As such, Jesus heard nothing of the commotion and the apprehension of Alex Hartmann.

He had donned a respirator and face mask. He figured the additional clothing required for spraying chemicals on the course should be sufficient for his needs. There wasn't much to do to create what he needed to do the job, but the lethality of the carfentanyl called for extreme caution.

First, he heated the stearic acid until it dissolved to a milky liquid. Next came the coconut oil. It was a much thinner liquid, but the stearic acid would help thicken it into a slippery, pasty consistency. Adding just the right amount of the liquid, finally he achieved the consistency he was looking for.

Next came the really difficult step. Jesus had heard of this opiate before but had never seen any. That it took only a few grains on the skin to cause death was difficult to fathom. He cinched up his rubber gloves, making absolutely certain there was no skin exposed, and very carefully added the compound to the buttery liquid in the five-gallon bucket in front of him.

There were sixteen small envelopes in the first package and fifteen in the other. It seemed strange to Jesus that they were unequal, but he had plenty, so he wasn't concerned. He pocketed the odd envelope to make the total thirty, not thirty-one. His days in the drug business had taught him never to pass up an opportunity.

After both packages had been mixed, he covered the bucket with the sealable lid and walked outside to the dumpster. He removed the gloves, rubber jacket and pants, and finally the respirator and cap and threw them in the bin.

Now that the carfentanyl was mixed with the pasty coconut oil it would be less of a problem to handle. The next operation would only require rubber gloves, a paint brush, and long sleeves.

Robert was sipping a martini, chatting with Kenney in the spacious teak salon of *Purity*. The Grand Banks 60 was one of the finest cruising trawlers in the world. In this customized interior there were two master staterooms with en suite bathrooms, one forward and one aft. An additional smaller berth was tucked in behind the galley, which was outfitted with quartz counters and stainless-steel appliances. The center of the lower interior was dedicated to a lavish lounge with a sixty-inch TV, usually tuned to Fox News.

Three days prior, Kenney, Alex, and Robert had made the journey from Trump Island past Shilshole and through the Ballard Locks to Lake Union in the center of the city of Seattle. From there it was a short hop through the Montlake Cut, past the University of Washington's famed football stadium into Lake Washington. Since the yacht was much too big for any of the slips in Meydenbauer Bay, the only option was to anchor in the center of the tiny inlet.

The bay was surrounded by multi-million-dollar homes occupied by titans of the tech industry. Robert relished the easy access to his quarry yet enjoyed the quietness that being isolated from the other watercraft offered. It was necessary to take the inflatable dinghy into the Bellevue Park public dock in the morning, but that was a small price to pay for the solitude his yacht provided.

Matt Steele had hurriedly assembled a team of agents to pick up Klein. The enigmatic head of the White List had dodged them once, and there had been no recent reports of sightings. The occasional mention of him on Facebook or YouTube proved to be disinformation planted by the group.

Steele's branch had gathered overwhelming evidence that Klein and company were not only responsible for the deaths and mayhem at the MLK event but had lately suggested that something big was about to happen. The last thing the Seattle outpost needed was an uprising of uneducated, ill-informed, well-armed white separatist assholes. There was enough to do with jewelry theft rings and terrorist activities.

They didn't expect much resistance from Klein to their surprise approach, but there was no need to take any risks either. Steele and two others had borrowed a skiff equipped with a quiet electric outboard from the King County Sheriff's Department, whose responsibilities included patrol of the lake.

They launched from the public dock and quietly covered the two hundred yards to the sixty-foot trawler. As they approached the aft lower step, they killed the quiet motor and glided up to it.

"That must be Alex, Kenney. Hopefully he's picked up something for dinner. I don't think it's prudent for us to go out to eat anywhere. I thought he'd call for us to pick him up, but I guess he found a ride from the marina."

The weight of the three agents climbing on board suggested to Boyce that perhaps it could be someone other than their partner. He dove for the stateroom as the three agents burst through the doorway.

"Hold it right there!" Steele had pulled his Glock 23 and stopped Boyce in his tracks. Klein, astonished that someone was pointing a gun at him, had yet to put down his martini.

"Sir, we're with the FBI, and you are both under arrest. Please put your drink down. You're coming with us."

One of the other agents had radioed the Sheriff's Department, who now approached loudly on board a Willard Marine Sea Force 700 powered by a 230-horse inboard engine.

The two prisoners and three agents boarded the patrol craft and were whisked to shore, where police transport awaited. Normally Steele would have taken them downtown to his Seattle office, but he'd promised Owens first crack at these guys. Although his fellow agents weren't as certain, they deferred to their superior.

It was midnight by the time Steele had his two prisoners sitting in front of Bill Owens. A little tired, yet with energy reserves still untouched, the detective fleetingly thought about golf in the morning—mostly that there wouldn't be any. "Matt, how about you having a conversation with Mr. Boyce here, and I'll chat with Mr. Klein?"

Steele and Boyce left the room while Owens sat down across from Klein. "You're probably wondering how we found you, no?"

Klein apparently knew when to keep his mouth shut.

"We managed to catch up to your boy Alex. In fact, he's just down the hall there, a little injured but alive enough to tell us where you were."

Klein's raised eyebrows were a giveaway. Owens saw the doubt there. He couldn't know what Hartmann had confessed to or not.

"Alex tells us you've got big plans for tomorrow." Steele had shared his intel with his friend.

"Maybe. We'll see."

"He told us what's going down."

"Good, then you don't need me."

Klein was no dummy, Owens thought, but he had to find some way to ferret out the following day's plans.

"Enjoy your stay here. I'll be back." With that, Owens made the short trip down the hall to the interrogation room that held Hartmann.

"Alex, you'll be happy to know that we've picked up your buddy, Robert Klein. He's filled us in on your plans for tomorrow."

"Good to know. I need a doctor; my fucking shoulder is killing me. You need to put that dog away. It's dangerous."

"That dog belongs to a good friend, and it looks like the only person she's dangerous to is you. How about we let her visit with you?"

Hartmann's face showed real fear for an instant, but he recovered quickly. "I'm not falling for that shit again. If Klein's told you what's going down, then great, you won't get anything else from me. All I can tell you is some bad shit's gonna happen."

Hartmann's dedication to the cause was admirable. Stupid, Owens thought, but admirable. The guy was going away for life for murder, and a hate crime at that. There was little leverage he could use at the moment.

Owens met with Steele after leaving Hartmann.

"Any luck with that poor bastard? He looks like the dog did a number on him."

Owens cracked his first smile of the night. "That dog is something else. I'm glad she gnawed on the fucker; in fact, I wish we could lock her in there with him."

Steele grinned as well. "Yeah, if only. What do you think we should do from here?" Almost always the Federal Agents ran the show, but tonight Steele had no difficulty ceding that authority to his friend.

"Well, for sure something's going down, and I'd bet my life that it's going down at Kelsey Creek. Why else would they be there?"

"Okay, go on."

"It appears that neither one of these clowns is gonna say anything. Tee time tomorrow for the tournament is ten o'clock. How about we get nine guys from each of us, put one on each hole to monitor things, and see what happens? Everyone can get there a few hours early and scour the place to see if we can find anything. If the carfentanyl is involved, I can't see how they're going to use it. We'll bring the dogs to see if they can sniff out anything. The other option is to call the thing off, but then what? Close the place down forever? I'm stuck, Matt. What do *you* think?"

"I think your first thought is a good one. If we have that many agents and cops on site, at least we'll be ready if the shit hits the fan. We've got some sniffers too; we'll bring a couple of our Shepherds. We'll head back now, alert the troops, and maybe get an hour of sleep. I'll be back here at five thirty or six. We'll start looking then. Night, buddy. See you in the morning."

The O'Malleys, along with Emma, left for home around eleven. "Hell of a night, huh, Jenne? You and your girl here sure know how to show a guy a good time."

"I'm just glad they finally got that prick. And I'm *really* glad Emma gave him another ass-kicking."

"Are you upset we missed the big party?"

"Nah. Bill wasn't there, and Shelly just hung out and grabbed a bite, then left. I think Bill's staying over at Shelly's these days anyway."

"Are you telling me my golf partner is living in sin?"

"Hey, I'm happy for both of them. Shelly's been through a world of shit and I know Bill had a rough divorce back in Toledo. They're really good together."

"Agreed. I've gotten to know Bill pretty well. He's turned into a good friend, and from what I hear, he's a great detective. Pretty sure he's thrilled that Hartmann's no longer on the loose."

"What's the deal with that guy Klein they brought in?" Jenne's curiosity never took a holiday.

"Apparently he's the kingpin of some white separatist group. Bill said he was behind that MLK thing."

"No shit? *That's* why Hartmann was with him?"

"Looks that way. I think Bill's nervous about what might happen tomorrow. He and Matt think the group had something planned even bigger than MLK."

"Yikes, I don't like the sound of that. You think protestors or something? Doesn't make sense to me."

Kevin was quiet for a moment, turning over the tumblers. "I agree, it doesn't make sense, but if the FBI and the lead detective in Bellevue are concerned, then I guess I am too."

They finally hit the sack a little after midnight, not knowing what Saturday might bring.

The greens crew started preparing the course at four thirty. During the summer golf season, the greens were mowed seven days a week and cut even shorter for tournaments. Jesus was assigned holes twelve through fifteen once again. He hurriedly completed his chores in order to make time for his final act.

He'd need almost an hour to complete his plans, which had to be accomplished before first light. Along with his greens mower, trap rakes, and hole-cutting equipment, he carried a five-gallon bucket and a small paint brush in the equipment trailer. Also in the bed were long rubber gloves and a heavy sweatshirt.

After completing his greenkeeping activities, he donned the gloves and sweatshirt. He started on hole number twelve. He carried the five-gallon bucket over to the newly cut hole and removed the flagstick. Lifting the lid off the bucket and using his cell phone flashlight, he scooped up a small portion of the thick pasty material that resembled wallpaper paste. Using the paint brush, he coated the entirety of the plastic cup liner, then replaced the flagstick.

He continued this same operation on the rest of the holes he was responsible for. His next step was to coat the cups on the fourteen remaining holes, which would be more difficult. The responsibility for certain holes varied among the crew. Every week the holes were rotated so that no one person would maintain the same holes all the time.

This served to keep the crew interested as well as ensuring a uniform product. Jesus had been tasked with maintaining every hole at least several times. The order in which the holes were cut was the same no matter which crew member performed the operation. Almost always the greenkeeper started at the farthest hole from the maintenance complex, then worked back toward the shop.

With this in mind, Jesus easily completed coating the cups with his incredibly lethal creation on most of the holes without being noticed.

On this day, Santiago was still preoccupied with what he had seen the day before. Even though he had heard nothing of the arrests the previous evening, he still felt uncomfortable. Instead of starting on the fourth hole as he normally would have, he began on hole number one and worked his way farther from the maintenance building.

As Santiago approached his final green, now the fourth, he noticed one of the Workman utility vehicles approaching the third green. Rather than continue to the fourth, he pulled over into the rough, just to see if Keneally was checking up on him.

As he squinted to try to make out who it was, the figure took out the flagstick and started doing something to the hole. Santiago was fairly sure it was Jesus, but he held his position, trying to be certain.

Dawn was fast approaching and when Jesus stood to replace the flag, it was clear to Santiago who it was. Since both vehicles were running, there was little chance he could be heard. Mowers, blowers, and tractors had a way of cancelling each other out. Still, as a precaution, he kept a row of cedars and firs between him and his crew mate.

The young greenkeeper rushed to finish the fourth green. He had no idea what Jesus was up to, but based upon the previous day's events, he needed to tell someone.

"What the fuck?" Jesus had one more hole to coat, the fourth, but it was still being mowed by Santiago. That goddamn kid must have started late, or he didn't go in the usual order. Either way it was too light now for him to finish without being seen. Screw it, he figured seventeen out of eighteen was good enough. There would be so much going on, nobody would notice he had missed a hole.

Since every putt needed to be holed out, no gimmees, that meant whenever a ball was putted into the cup, it would be coated with the pasty goop containing the carfentanyl. Even though most golfers wore a glove on their dominant hand, it was generally removed for better feel when putting. As soon as the golfer retrieved his ball, his hand would be coated with enough of the opiate to either incapacitate an elephant or cause a massive drug overdose, killing within minutes.

Klein had had the idea of using the carfentanyl, but it was that asshole Hartmann who had thought up the idea of coating the cups with it. It made sense, too. There'd be no way to avoid the stuff if the ball was coated with it. By the time someone figured out what was going on, there would be bodies all over the golf course.

He thought it dicey that Klein and Hartmann would be manning the donation stand on the fourth tee, but that was their call. His only concern now was his final payment. He took off his gloves and sweatshirt and placed them in the pail along with what remained of the deadly paste. With his final payment he would be a rich man; there would be no need to expose himself any longer to the risks of selling drugs.

CHAPTER 22

Saturday morning at Kelsey Creek arrived with the full field of participants anxious to get going. The shotgun start had been delayed for some reason, probably something to do with the additional twenty-five FBI agents and Bellevue policemen now on the golf course.

The cops and agents had been instructed to wear golfing attire so as to blend in and not unduly worry the contestants. It was difficult to conceal many of their sidearms, however, and word was out that the police were on the property because of rumors of possible violence.

While the members and their guests milled around on the putting green and practice range, impatient to get things under way, there was no shortage of speculation about what the threat could be.

All of the club members knew of the recent attacks on two of their own, and most had heard of the killer's arrest. They rightly assumed that this had something to do with the recent troubles, although the probable existence of a powerfully deadly opiate somewhere on the property was known only to the law enforcement troops.

Because the O'Malleys arrived an hour before the original start of the tournament, it meant they had some time to kill. Kevin immediately sought out Bill to see if his plans for the day included being his partner on the golf course. As he descended the steps to the club entrance, he spotted his friend exiting the locker room with a croissant sticking out of his mouth.

"What, couldn't find any donuts? You look like shit."

"And I feel like shit, too. Got here at five thirty after an hour and a half in the sack. We managed to get a dozen officers here, at least for a few hours. Matt's done the same. Both my guys and his are scouring the place with the dogs; if there's anything here, they'll find it.

"If they come up clean, then we'll post a person on every hole when play gets going. As for me, partner, I'm going to attempt to play, at least until something happens. If it does, they'll notify me immediately via comms. They've cleared the clubhouse already of any opiates; we also had the explosives dogs here just to be on the safe side.

"We've set up a perimeter around the club property to make sure that anyone entering has a legitimate reason for doing so. No way we're gonna let a crowd of those racist assholes in."

"Geez, Bill, sounds like you've got all the bases covered. If you have to bag the golf, no problem. I understand. What did you mean, opiates?"

"I still may have to; depends. Maybe the show of force here will cause them to rethink whatever they had planned. Keep this to yourself, Kevin, but Matt told me that this Klein guy got his hands on one of the strongest opiates known to man. He thinks that whatever is going down has something to do with the stuff."

"Yikes, that doesn't sound good. I can't fathom what they would do with drugs, though. Maybe try to put them in the food?"

"We thought that, which is why we cleared the clubhouse. Right now, they're checking out the maintenance area just to be thorough."

While the two friends were chatting, a piercing bark sounded above the chatter of the hundred or so golfers milling about. At the same moment, a squawk came over the radio attached to Bill's belt, and he raised it to his ear.

"Got it, Mike. On my way.

"The dog's got something up by the maintenance building. I'll try to be back. Gotta go now." With that, the detective jumped into a golf cart and hurried off.

Maisy, the Shepherd, had just quieted down after receiving several treats for a job well done. As Bill pulled up outside the facility, the handler, Officer Mike Mullins, was speaking gently to the animal, telling her that she had been a good girl and done a good job.

"What do you have, Mike?"

"We checked out the inside and we thought she had something, but it wasn't definite. Then we were walking by the dumpster and she went crazy. My guess is you've got something in there that ain't just weed."

"Nice going, Mike. I'll get the hazmat crew over here to verify what we've found. If it's what I think it is, we don't want to go digging through what's in there."

After completing his mission, Jesus Martinez hustled over to the small pickup that had fulfilled his needs nicely but still helped him maintain his stereotype. This particular Mexican laborer, however, was going to be a rich motherfucker.

All there was left to do was to take the dinghy out to where Klein had anchored his boat and collect his final payment. So consumed had he been, mixing the deadly compound, then coating the interior of the cups on the greens, that he had heard nothing of the previous night's arrests.

The fifteen minutes it took to get to the Meydenbauer Bay Marina were spent envisioning what life would be like as a multimillionaire. Upon arrival, he noticed the tender for the larger vessel was still tied up to the *Purity*. It seemed as if Klein and Hartmann were still on board, which meant they would be late getting over to the golf course to witness the carnage.

Rather than call Klein, he opted to hitch a ride with a local young-ster puttering around the bay with a dilapidated five-horse outboard hung on a crusty ten-foot aluminum skiff. The kid was maybe thirteen years old and happy to pick up a fast twenty bucks.

As Martinez stepped aboard, bidding farewell to his taxi, he sensed the emptiness of the boat. He felt that there was no one on board, yet he could hear a woman's voice. As he stepped into the generous salon, he realized that the oversized TV was on some news channel, an attractive redhead prattling on about the fabulous stretch of summer weather.

Martinez called out for Klein, but there was no response. He tried to reconcile the dinghy being tied up with the boat being empty.

"And, just to recap the latest headlines, Bellevue police have an-nounced the arrest of Alex Hartmann, the alleged murderer of Jerry Johnson from a year ago." The TV screen had switched from the weather gal to the news anchor. "An associate with alleged ties to the white supremacist movement, a Robert Klein, has also been apprehended."

Suddenly Martinez's dreams of being a multimillionaire evaporated. *Goddamn, those stupid fucks went and got arrested.* Not only was there a growing concern about what the police would learn from those two, meaning he might now be a hunted man, but he was also out five million bucks.

Assuming time was of the essence, he began methodically searching the trawler. He figured Klein's was the larger of the two staterooms, so he began there. Other than a few hundred bucks, there was nothing. The other suite, probably Boyce's, yielded less than that.

He almost missed the small berth stuck in behind the galley, usually for a crew member, he guessed, and in this instance most likely Hartmann's. In his haste to get off the boat and away from the area, he threw the mattress aside to quickly explore the confined space. As he did so, he heard what sounded like a thousand BBs falling onto the teak flooring.

What the fuck …? Martinez was at first annoyed at the mess he'd made and then shocked at the realization that these were not BBs; they were goddamn diamonds. At least, they looked like diamonds. Beside the mattress lay a small blue velvet pouch.

He immediately picked up the little bag, which still held a number of the stones, and rapidly gathered up the rest of the diamonds that had been flung about. He was not a jeweler, nor did he know the worth of this treasure. What he did know was that Klein had given him less than thirty stones with a supposed value of half a million dollars. There had to be hundreds and hundreds of diamonds in the small pouch, which meant that he was once again a rich motherfucker.

Martinez wasted no time in getting away from the *Purity* using the RIB that served as the tender for the yacht. He hurriedly pulled into the nearest slip in the marina, threw a loop over the cleat, and jogged off to his pickup. Now he had to figure out how to get the hell out of the area.

CHAPTER 23

The last round of the Kelsey Creek Invitational was finally under way. The groups had gone to their assigned tees and were preparing for the shotgun start, now an hour later than scheduled. If the participants were put off by the cops dressed in golfing attire stationed at every tee box, they hid it well.

Kevin, along with Jeff Williams and his brother Bert, was assigned to the fourth tee. Bill Owens was still tied up with the situation at the greens crew facility.

At five minutes before eleven, one of the course maintenance vehicles raced up to the tee, depositing Bill and his clubs.

"We thought you were tied up."

"I was—I am—but I figured I could escort this group and play at the same time. The rest of the foursomes will be escorted as well."

Kevin was glad to see his partner, although he still was curious as to what was happening. "So, are we safe?"

"Both Matt and I feel pretty sure that with Klein and Hartmann's arrests, whatever they had planned is going to fizzle out. There's the whole thing about the carfentanyl, and there's traces in the dumpster, but we just can't see how they could disperse it over such a large area."

"If you're comfortable with things, then so am I."

"If I was comfortable, we wouldn't have thirty men out here. Let's just say I feel a little bit better about the situation. Ready for some golf?"

The boom went off exactly at eleven, and eighteen tee shots were hit simultaneously.

Bill, with hardly any sleep and with the tensions of the morning, barely got his tee shot airborne. The other three in the group all hit satisfactory shots. As they strode off the teeing ground, another crew vehicle came whizzing down the cart path, cutting them off. Santiago was at the wheel.

"Hey, Santiago, how are you? What's the rush?"

"Mr. Kevin, there's something I have to tell you."

"What is it?" Kevin couldn't imagine why this shy kid would interrupt him during the tournament. It had to be important.

"I saw the police last night. They took away the man that your dog attacked."

"Yes, they did. He was the man who killed Mr. Johnson."

Santiago's eyes got twice as big as he seemed to realize something important. "That man, he delivered something to Jesus, the new man on the crew."

"*Whoa!* Hold it, everybody; stop right now. Bill, come here, fast. Listen to this guy." Kevin had the feeling something really, really terrible was about to happen.

"Yes, he gave Jesus something and then it looked like he was telling him what to do."

"Is that all you saw?" Bill was now questioning.

"No, sir. This morning I saw Jesus after he finished his mowing. He was doing something to the cups on the greens, something with an orange bucket and a paintbrush."

Even though the entire foursome had now surrounded the work truck, no one spoke a word.

Just then, Bill's radio came to life. "Boss, boss ..."

"Mike, what is it?"

"That stuff in the dumpster, they found a bucket with some gloves and stuff in it."

"What else? Tell me fast."

"Boss, there was some pasty, goopy shit in the bottom of the bucket. Hazmat says there's very little of the stuff left, but what there is, is enough to kill a fucking army."

It dawned on Bill and Kevin at the same time.

"Mike, listen to me very carefully. Get to the pro shop and tell them to do everything they can, immediately, to stop play. Use the firecrackers, sirens, whatever, just do it. *Now!*

"Kevin, you go with Santiago. Stop everyone—par three holes first, fives last. Hurry!"

Bill put out a broadcast to the entire force on the grounds. "Listen up! The stuff is inside the cups on the greens. Stop everyone; stop the play! If anyone touches the stuff that's in the holes, they're dead. Go! Move!"

Just then a loud siren sounded. It was seldom used in the northwest, since it was an alert to stop play if there was a chance of a lightning strike. It squealed over loudspeakers located in strategic locations, a half dozen of them on the course.

Most of the field wasn't sure what was going on, whether to halt play or not. The law enforcement officers, after getting the blast from Bill, physically placed themselves in front of the greens to stop any chance of a player getting on.

The biggest challenge was on the par threes. Since it took only one shot to reach the putting surface, the groups on those holes were already heading for the greens.

Two of the par threes were close to the clubhouse, and the pro shop dispatched runners to get there and make sure play was stopped. The fifteenth hole, the shortest, was less of a challenge, mostly because the FBI agent assigned to that hole was an Ironman athlete. His sprint to the green as the foursome approached was the subject of Kelsey Creek lore for many years to come.

The eleventh hole proved to be the most problematic. By the time the siren had gone off, the group was already at the green. Two golfers had hit it in regulation, while the other two had missed and now needed to chip. The agent stationed on the tee was 200 yards from the green. The group wasn't sure what was happening with the siren, so they kept playing.

As the two who missed the green chipped up, they heard the agent on the tee yelling something, but he was downwind of them and too far away to be heard.

Mani Darzi was in the group and uncharacteristically had hit the green with his three wood. He was the first to putt from some thirty feet away and chose to leave the flagstick in while he stroked the putt. Mani was playing with his born-again brother-in-law at the behest of Yasmina. It was his penance, apparently, for using foul language again.

His putt came up two and a half feet short, but with no gimmees in the tournament, he needed to finish and putt it into the hole. As he reached over to pull the flag out, he wondered aloud, "What's this gooey shit all over the bottom of the stick?"

"I don't know, Mani. Just knock the putt in, will ya." His brother-in-law was focused on trying to win the event.

Mani stood over the short putt and stroked it in.

"Good one, pards. Let me get that for you."

As Mani's partner started to bend over, the entire group heard both Kevin and Santiago screaming at the top of their lungs as they roared up the hill to the green.

"Mani, STOP, STOP!"

Santiago was a big soccer fan and rarely missed a Sounders game at the loudest football stadium in the country. Much of the noise at the games was from miniature air horns that the patrons smuggled in. He had pulled one from his pocket and now held it up in the air with the button pressed down.

The foursome froze, even Mani's born-again brother-in-law, and that saved his life.

For the first time in its history, the invitational at Kelsey Creek Country Club was called off. Every green was sealed off with crime scene tape and either a special agent or a policeman was stationed there until a hazmat crew arrived to take over.

After huddling with Steele, Bill Owens deferred to the FBI lab and personnel to clean up the mess. It was also determined that the federal agency would process the items found in the dumpster to ID the person who had spread the deadly concoction.

The fingerprints found on the gloves were rushed through AFIS and a match was found. A Jesus Martinez found in the system had been arrested for drug dealing and was wanted for questioning regarding several drug-related killings.

A BOLO was issued for Martinez at once, across city, state, and federal agencies. Owens was confident they would get their man.

While there was genuine disappointment at not being able to complete the golfing portion of the tournament, the hundred or so contestants made the most of the generous supply of food and booze.

Moving the dinner from six o'clock up to early afternoon was a nightmare for the kitchen crew. The wait staff scheduled to be at work by four p.m. was called in immediately. Vince Walker was running about like his hair was on fire setting up tables, adjusting food displays, and waiting on members and guests.

The practice putting green, untouched by Martinez, was now the site of putting contests, betting games, jokes, and general sighs of relief as the full scope of the hate group's attack became known.

Mani's born-again brother-in-law was now fully engaged in attempting to convert his Muslim relative. Somehow the man was convinced his near-death experience had been made possible by his strong religious beliefs. The possibility that he had been saved from an excruciatingly painful death only because a young soccer fan had made use of an air horn had escaped his conscious thinking.

Mani excused himself to go find another glass of merlot.

"So, Kevin, do all your guests get to experience Armageddon or is it just your close friends?" Bill Owens had plenty to do, but since Matt Steele and his FBI cohort had fully taken things over, he had allowed himself a cold beer with his buddy.

"If it hadn't been for you as my guest, we couldn't have put the brakes on as fast as we did. Thank god you were here."

"I've got to make sure we coordinate things with the Feds with regard to the Martinez search, so I'll need to leave in a bit. Matt said the hate crime thing takes precedence, but he wanted some of my guys to give them a hand. Shelly's coming over with Jenne shortly, and it looks like I'm going to miss them. Do me a favor and take care of them, would you?"

"Geez, I don't know, Bill. You want me to escort the two smartest, best-looking women at the club around all day? I guess I could do it, but it won't be easy. By the way, someone told me you've been camping out with Shelly at her new digs. Any truth to that?" Kevin's cherubic face and the twinkle in his eye gave away any pretense of seriousness. He was really very happy for the both of them.

"Gotta go, pal; see ya." With a grin a mile wide, Detective Bill Owens was off to see about finding the man who might have murdered scores of people.

CHAPTER 24

Jesus Martinez figured he had a little time. Once the stupid golfers started dropping like flies, it would be a clusterfuck. There would be confusion and fear. Klein or Hartmann might rat him out, but he doubted it; they cared too much about their precious movement.

He sat in his truck, still parked at the marina, and took stock of his situation. He had a bag full of diamonds that were worth millions, probably, an old Toyota pickup, and the distinct possibility that very soon the law would be on his tail. They'd eventually ID him through his fingerprints and his workmates on the crew.

By then he would be wanted for mass murder, maybe even terrorism.

Hitting the freeways with his truck wasn't going to cut it; there *had* to be another way. He left the truck where it was and took the little blue velvet bag with him, back to the rigid inflatable boat he'd just left. The attached outboard was a forty horse that provided enough power to get the eleven-foot Zodiac upwards of thirty knots. He turned the powerful Merc over, untied the painter, and headed out into Lake Washington.

There were hundreds of islands in the Puget Sound where he could go; the problem was staying hidden long enough for the dragnet to ease up. An idea formed in his mind, one that might work, but also one that would require discipline and incredible discomfort.

It was early afternoon on a bright seventy-five-degree summer day.

Since he needed the cover of darkness to initiate his plan, he spent the afternoon motoring around the inlets of Hunts Point, Yarrow Point, and Medina, just another tourist inspecting the homes of the rich and famous. Prices on this "Gold Coast" ranged anywhere from several million to upwards of a hundred million.

As dusk descended, close to ten o'clock this time of year, he headed slowly across the lake to the Madison Park neighborhood. The home of quaint shops and trendy restaurants also sported several high-priced condo and apartment complexes, complete with their own docks.

Martinez took his time, searching for just the right opportunity. The three-story mixed-use complex had been built just south of the 520 bridge and presented exactly what he had in mind. A new dock with a half dozen slips, only two of them occupied, appeared in a small inlet on the south side of the property.

Listening to the roar of traffic on the bridge, even at this time of night, he waited until he was within fifty yards of the dock before he killed the outboard. He reached for his Kershaw Skyline knife, snapped it open, and began shredding the inflated portions of the boat.

The compartmentalized sections were a pain in the ass, making much more work for him than he would have liked. The Zodiac, pulled down by the heavy outboard, finally began its inexorable trip to the bottom of Lake Washington. Even though they were very close to the shore at this point, it was still thirty feet to the bottom—plenty deep enough to hide his ride for a long, long time.

Martinez was only a fair swimmer, but the fifty-yard journey was made easier after he donned the only life jacket in the boat. Making certain he still had his knife, his wad of cash from his former career, his sealed envelope of carfentanyl, and his blue velvet bag of diamonds, he pulled himself from the lake. After tossing the life jacket into a nearby dumpster, he began the trek down Madison Avenue in his soaking wet clothing, heading for the downtown area of the Emerald City.

After two weeks, the number of agents searching for Jesus Martinez was reduced by half. That left a sizable number of lawmen still assigned to the task; after all, the man was an alleged murderer, a former drug dealer, and an attempted murderer of scores of people because of their supposed acceptance of others of different religions and races.

The FBI was now in charge of all aspects of the search. Alex Hartmann had been charged with murder, attempted murder, and conspiracy to commit murder, all considered hate crimes. Klein was charged with being an accessory to murder for the MLK massacre as well as conspiracy to commit murder for the Kelsey Creek fiasco. Additionally, he was charged with sedition for fomenting violence for the sake of separation of the races.

Hartmann had confessed to his crimes for a plea deal, reducing his sentence from capital punishment to life imprisonment without parole. The reduction was the result of his informing on the Trump Island crew and the resulting arrest of the remaining members of the White List. Klein was awaiting trial for his crimes, his many millions effectively slowing the wheels of justice.

The weeks turned into months, then almost an entire year had passed. The trial of Robert Klein was finally getting under way. Most in the city of Seattle had moved on to the crime du jour. The members at Kelsey Creek and the better part of the City of Bellevue, though, still wanted to see the mastermind behind the almost-catastrophic disaster at the club punished severely.

"Matt, any news?"

Bill Owens had run into Steele at the courthouse for the Friday start of the Klein trial. Both were there to witness the opening salvo in the proceedings.

"Not since last month when we got together. You *do* realize if there was any news, you'd be among the first to know?"

"Yeah, sorry. I just cannot believe Martinez slipped away."

"We had the roads, the airports, the ferries, the borders, and the marinas covered. This was among the most heinous hate crimes ever conceived in this country, and the fucker who implements it gets away. Damn, that pisses me off."

"We know for certain he went back to the boat, though, right?"

"According to Hartmann, who incidentally spilled the beans on everything, it had to be him. Hartmann said he still had the diamonds he took from Jenne with him on the boat.

"When we went back to search the thing, we found a half dozen of the stones scattered around his berth. Martinez must have gone back there after he was done at the golf course. According to Hartmann, the guy was due a big payday from Klein.

"So not only does the attempted mass murderer get away, but he takes the goddamn diamonds with him. We needed them as evidence to put Chesnick away for a few more years. The serial numbers on those things would easily tie us to the customers he stole from. As it stands now, that asshole could be on the street next week."

"Does Shelly know?" Bill and Shelly were now living together, and marriage plans were being discussed.

"I haven't seen her. Bill, you should let her know."

"Geez, thanks, buddy. That'll be fun."

Steele grimaced a bit, then actually looked as though he felt for his friend. "Sorry, Bill, but as of now, that's the deal. Gotta get to court. Bye." As Steele headed for the courtroom, Owens trudged out of the door, contemplating the evening's conversation.

CHAPTER 25

The craziness of the previous year's invitational had finally started seeping away from the members' consciousness. The news of the near tragedy became national as well as international; the clubhouse had been inundated with news crews from around the world, and Kelsey Creek Country Club had become the most famous private club in the United States. Its policy of inclusivity became a model for all private clubs. Now, when a country club quietly hinted at its exclusivity, most prospective members turned away in search of a club with more diversity. The waiting list at the Creek was now five years long, and Vince Walker had more speaking engagements at the Club Managers Association than he could keep up with.

News stories and documentaries were being filmed on location so often that the members finally had to say "enough." Detective Owens had to ultimately refuse any further interviews, while Matt Steele preferred to keep a low profile. The O'Malleys were featured prominently in many news features and even appeared with Al Roker on the *Today Show*. They only agreed to do the show if Emma was part of the interview. She was.

Santiago became an instant star. The camera loved his infectious smile, and his heavily accented English endeared him to both the Anglo and Hispanic communities. A children's book was being written about his heroic efforts to save many lives, and it was rumored that Netflix was producing a full-length feature film based upon the events. Fame be damned, though; he wanted to remain on the crew.

The White House occupant attempted to have the main players visit him in the Oval Office, where he would present them with the Medal of Freedom. Bill was too busy working, Matt wanted no part of it, and both the O'Malleys and Santiago refused the invitation, saying the president had not done enough to foster harmony with people from all walks of life, regardless of color or position.

The invitational was a month away, and the members were looking forward to a much less eventful time. Mani and his brother-in-law were teamed up again this year. It seemed that the near-death experience his wife's brother had experienced had somehow elevated the fellow's tolerance level. He'd even been seen skimming through the Quran.

Jeff was going to play with his brother once again, while Kevin and Bill would try to complete the entire thirty-six-hole event this year. The O'Malleys had scheduled dinner with Shelly and Bill this Friday evening and were seated at their table, awaiting the lovebirds.

"Uh oh, Jenne, I'm not sure I like the look on Shelly's face. You think they had a fight?"

"I doubt it. I've never seen two people get along as well as they do. Must be something else."

"Hey, you guys, welcome." Kevin stood to give Shelly a hug and shake hands with Bill. "Everything okay?" Even Bill had a subdued look on his face.

"We're just fine. We did get some disturbing news today, though," Bill offered as he glanced at Shelly, attempting to force a smile.

"What news?" asked Jenne.

"The news that my fucking asshole ex-husband is getting out of jail next week. *That* news." Shelly's profanity-laced exclamation drew a few glances in the Grill Room. When the patrons saw that she was with the O'Malleys, they just smiled and turned away. Kevin and Jenne had had so much publicity over the past ten months that they had become the face of the club. They could do no wrong.

"Geez, Shelly, really sorry to hear that. How come so early?"

Bill attempted to explain. "He was given five years at his first trial, Jenne, but then they appealed. Because the diamonds were never recovered, his attorneys argued lack of evidence, then pushed for time served, and the judge awarded it."

"Well, that sucks. Tell you what, Shell, have a seat, grab a mojito, and let's talk about your new home, your wonderful stud horse here, and all the good things that have happened to you this past year. Who gives a shit if Bernie's on the street? I can't imagine he'll bother with you; you're divorced now." Kevin's summation seemed to settle Shelly, and they all sat down and began to relax. A hint of a genuine smile even crossed her face.

"You're right about everything, Kevin. Ever since I met you two, my life has gotten better. I'm free of that dooshkabob, thanks to Jenne I have a beautiful home, and thanks to this guy I'm in love. I *should* be happy. Fuck Bernie."

Kevin had to admit some of the colorful stuff this woman came up with was refreshing. "Let's toast your future. To the both of you, before Bill's face gets any redder."

The balance of the evening was spent enjoying each other's company, great food, good wine, and the frequent genuine acknowledgments by many of the other patrons.

Jesus stretched out on the triple-layered cardboard box he'd stolen the previous night. This new residence, a small clearing in a copse of trees just west of I-5 and south of I-90, would have to do for today.

He was wearing most of the same clothing he had worn on the night he landed in Madison Park. It was filthy, smelly, and threadbare. His dark beard was several inches long and covered much of his gaunt, weather-beaten, insect-bitten face. He had spent some rough days as a youngster when first coming to the US, but the past ten months had sapped his entire reserve of patience and energy.

Living as a homeless person on the streets of Seattle was a brutal proposition; the damp, rainy winter had almost done him in. Spending most of his life in Southern California had not prepared him for winter in the northwest. As fall turned to winter, he came down with the flu and spent the entire month of December huddled under the 520 overpass near Capitol Hill.

He had cash for clothing but couldn't be seen spending it or wearing anything new. Since he found most of his brethren to be either addicted to something or mentally ill, he preferred to be alone. Living on scraps from dumpsters and the occasional warm bowl of soup from one of the missions had contributed to his twenty-pound weight loss, which aided his efforts to hide his identity.

While he may have murdered a few drug peddlers and attempted to murder dozens more for money, he didn't consider himself to be a violent man. Those things were just business. When it was necessary to assault another homeless person for food, clothing, or shelter, he actually felt bad about it. Not bad enough to stop him from cracking a skull or stabbing a guy, but a tiny bit bad just the same.

Being attacked by another homeless person was always a possibility, but after the community became aware of his ruthlessness, no one considered it. His cash, carfentanyl, and blue bag of diamonds would remain safe.

His greatest luxury was his burner cell phone. He had paid someone to buy it from a local convenience store. It wasn't that he had anyone to call; he did not. Jesus used it solely to get Grub Hub to deliver food to him when he grew tired of foraging or starving.

He chuckled at the prevailing thinking that the homeless *wanted* to live on the street. Because he felt it was the only way to avoid being caught, he had opted to do so. That people *chose* this street life was a fucking joke. It had been the most miserable ten months of his entire life. He was *always* tired, *always* cold, *always* hungry, and *always* filthy.

He was ready to be done with his chosen retreat from humanity; he just needed to figure a few things out. His cash wasn't going to last forever, and he needed to find some way to fence the diamonds. He was pretty sure that some homeless guy walking into a jewelry store might seem suspicious; hell, even trying a pawn shop would seem suspicious.

He wasn't sure how he felt about the attack on that country club being thwarted. He was a little pissed that all his hard work was for naught, but the thought of aiding those white supremacists rankled him as well. From the papers he'd seen—there were always papers in the homeless camps; it was what most of them lined their coats with to keep warm—both Klein and that dipshit Hartmann were now in jail. He felt good about that.

Bernie Chesnick walked out of the Cedar Creek Corrections Center under clear sunny skies on a Tuesday morning. This particular facility was not for killers or rapists, but it was still prison. Much like at the country club Bernie used to belong to, however, the inmates avoided him like the plague.

There were accountants, petty thieves, embezzlers, and a few drug dealers incarcerated at the facility. Still, the combination of Bernie's abrasive, narcissistic personality and his annoyingly bombastic articulation quickly made him a prisoner to be avoided.

Since even the rest of the prisoners shunned him, it proved to be the equivalent of ten months in solitary confinement. For 300 days Bernie spent every waking hour with Bernie. With as much time as he had to contemplate his wrongdoings and the hurt he had caused people, it seemed logical that some incremental progress in empathetic socialization would ensue. But no; progress was avoided.

Bernie reentered the civilized world much the same as when he had left it. The single improvement that prison had foisted on him was his voice. Apparently, with all that time alone in his cell, he began talking to himself. As a result, even *he* got tired of his annoying voice. Now when he spoke, it was with a subdued, almost church-like whisper. Even the guards had to lean in to hear him.

His voice modifications aside, he was still a waste of a human being. He was pissed at his wife for divorcing him, closing his stores, and selling off his real estate. He had neglected to get a prenup when he married the bitch, so that meant she got half their assets. The divorce agreement they had signed called for her to not only get the house and the balance of her share of the community property in cash, but it also awarded her a very healthy alimony allowance.

If he hadn't been so consumed with his trial, he would have paid more attention to the goddamn thing. Course, back then he had still held out hope that Hartmann would come up with the diamonds. Now that the jewels were gone, his focus was riveted on the woman who had dismantled his empire. That the absence of the stones was the *reason* for his early release failed to register.

The restitution required of him would deplete a good deal of what remained of the divorce settlement. Fortunately, without the diamonds, it would be difficult to track down most of the customers he had screwed over. When Shelly had liquidated things, she had made a point of saving all the receipts and paperwork from the stores that were managed by the lawbreakers. This at least helped track down some of the unfortunates who had been swindled.

Because Cedar Creek was a minimum-security prison, he was allowed phone calls and a PC, which allowed him to stay in touch with most of his crooked former managers. Sure, he was pissed at them for rolling over on him, but maybe now that he was out, his relationship with them might prove profitable; it was the jewelry business, after all.

Bernie hadn't exactly figured out what his future would look like, but he was certain of what would take place over the next week or so. He planned on paying a visit to his ex-wife. He was sure he could convince her to cough up enough cash to get him started again.

Kevin, mostly because of his part in avoiding a catastrophe the previous year, was the head of the invitational tournament committee. Naturally, he put Mani and Jeff on the team with him, as well as Jenne and Shelly to help with the food, entertainment, and volunteer assignments.

The membership had high hopes for an outstanding event this year, especially considering the mid-tournament cancellation of the last one. As head of the committee, Kevin was going to make sure of it. With six weeks to go, the tournament was full and an additional ten teams were on a waiting list.

Things at work were settling down after a very busy period. The log home on Orcas Island was wrapping up, and Shelly's house was finally completely furnished. There had also been a startling number of new opportunities after the publicity from the White List attack. He and Jenne were extraordinarily careful about which projects they took on and which ones would not be a good fit.

He still managed to play on Wednesdays and Saturdays, but that was about it. Jenne and Shelly managed to play a couple of times a week as well.

Dinner was planned at Shelly's the following night. The group included the entire "A" Train along with Bill; of course, he was living there. The occasion was to celebrate the final completion of the Thornton residence. Shelly had ditched the Chesnick name shortly after Bernie's conviction.

Shelly spent the entire morning preparing for the evening's festivities. The menu included seared scallops on a bed of lemon risotto and a side of grilled asparagus spears. She had asked Bill to extend an invitation to Matt Steele and his date and to remember to pick up the wines she had requested.

The final seating group, a very modern collection from A. Rudin, had been delivered the previous week. She was adjusting the position of one of the chairs when the doorbell rang. She went to the door.

"Well, hello there, Shelly. How *are* you?" At first, she was shocked. The appearance was that of Bernie, minus a few pounds, but the voice was not his.

"Why are you here? What happened to your voice, and what do you want? I'm busy getting ready for a dinner party."

"Geez, Shell, I thought you'd be happy to see your ex-husband."

"I'm not. Now get the fuck out of here."

"Come on, now. Is that any way to greet the guy you were married to for ten years?"

"Bernie, we're divorced. This is my house. I'd like you to leave and never come back. Just so you know, my boyfriend is the head detective with the Bellevue Police, so don't fuck with me."

Bernie appeared to have second thoughts at the mention of the detective. "I don't want any trouble, Shelly. I just came by to see if maybe we could work something out on the finances. Maybe we could supplement my share. The alimony I have to shell out from what little I have left is killing me too."

Bernie's new and improved vocal technique seemed to throw his ex-wife off kilter. Shelly looked as though she was considering something but then seemed to come to a decision.

"Sorry, Bernie, but no. You broke the law. You're a goddamn crook; you still have enough money to start over. As for the alimony, I expect you won't have to pay that much longer. I'm getting married in the fall."

The declaration of impending nuptials seemed to be the tipping point for the ex-jeweler. "Getting married? My little fucking house cleaning, life-wrecking cunt of a wife is gonna marry a goddamn cop?

Well, isn't that just fucking perfect!" With that, Bernie walked out and slammed the door.

Shaken by the verbal assault, Shelly called Bill Owens as soon as the door slammed. Unable to reach her fiancé, she called her best friend.

"Jenne, sorry to bother you, but I have to talk to you. Bernie was here and we had a confrontation. He wanted money, but I told him no. Then when I said I was getting married, he went apeshit and started calling me names. Then he slammed the door and left."

"Are you afraid he'll come back and do something?"

"I really don't think so, but he was more upset than I've ever seen him."

"Tell you what, you're probably busy getting ready for tonight. How about I come over and help? We can talk about it."

"I'd really appreciate that, Jenne. Thank you so much."

With that, Shelly disconnected and sat down to wait for her friend.

CHAPTER 26

Jesus had finally had enough. After ten months it appeared as though most of the furor surrounding the Kelsey Creek attack had abated. At least, the three-day-old papers he came across no longer had the stories on the front page; if anything, an update would surface every other week or so.

Of the ten-thousand-dollar wad of bills he started with, he still had almost nine. It would have to be enough until he could figure out some way to fence the diamonds.

A trip to a SODO thrift store netted him a pair of slacks, two dress shirts, a blue blazer, a three-pack of underwear, some socks, and a pair of black shoes that almost fit. He also picked up a used electric razor and a pair of scissors. They were used to seeing the downtrodden in the store, but rarely a homeless person with ready cash.

After locating a sleazebag hourly motel, he took a room for the remainder of the day. The first complete shower in ten months lasted until the hot water ran out, and then began the trimming. First the beard was hacked back until it was a stylish goatee with a slim mustache.

Next, he trimmed his hair to a fashionable length, long enough to comb straight back. With his coal-black eyes and newly groomed look, he resembled a cast member in one of the old Spaghetti Westerns. Along with the weight he had lost, his new look and business attire would make him difficult to identify. Just another businessman in the city.

Fitting in with the rest of civilization, he hoofed it down to Pioneer Square to one of the many corner Starbucks. He relaxed in a just-vacated booth and perused the discarded newspaper while sipping his latte.

On the third page, above the fold, was a story about Bernie Chesnick, the diamond thief, and his recent release. According to the story, Hartmann had stolen the diamonds from Jenne O'Malley after Chesnick's wife had given them to her for safekeeping.

Jesus was amused at the shit show it had turned into. The story continued on about Hartmann's subsequent arrest and mentioned that to this day, the diamonds were still missing, hence Chesnick's early release. There was little else of note save for the mention of the crook now living somewhere in Bellevue and a quote from his attorney proclaiming his client's wrongful prosecution.

Jesus folded the paper and began a leisurely stroll up First Avenue toward the center of the city. He felt reasonably safe with his new look as he continued to formulate a plan for the disposal of the diamonds.

The dinner party celebrating Shelly's new home started off under the cloud of Bernie's visit. Jenne did her best to calm her down, as did Bill when he returned later in the afternoon. By the time the rest of the guests had arrived, she was back to her old self, but relating the story to everyone caused her to retreat.

"Listen, Shelly, if that guy even comes near you again, call me. I'm sure Bill can get a restraining order against him, but *I* can bring the FBI down on him. No offense, Bill." Matt was irritated at the thought of Bernie harassing Shelly.

"None taken, Matt. I understand completely. Are you guys still trying to locate the diamonds?"

"We are. We're pretty confident Martinez took them when he went back to the boat. His fingerprints were all over the berth where we found the stones he missed. We can't figure out where he went. By now there should have been a sighting or something. Maybe he'd try to fence them and we'd get a call, but no, nothing."

Kevin was interested, as was the rest of the group. "So, do you think he slipped the country? Maybe Canada?"

"If he did, he had to teleport himself. We had everything covered. This was one of the top five terrorist attacks this country has seen. Everybody was on this, and I mean *everybody.*"

"Well, somehow he got away. I'm not sure the attack was all bad, though."

Kevin was surprised at this from Mani. "What are you saying Mani? What good could possibly have come from it?"

Mani's little grin and sparkling eyes told everyone he had something up his sleeve. "Well, shit, it got Yasmina's brother reading the Quran; that's what I'm talkin' about."

Even after a nasty look from his wife, there were chuckles all around, and with that, the party got going in earnest. There were house tours to do; there was wine to be poured. When the entire "A" Train got together, there were always good times. Matt and his date were treated as if they were regulars, and Bill and Shelly by this time *were* regulars.

The evening broke up just after midnight, with Bill making sure that all those driving were not unduly under the influence. As it turned out, two of the attendees' cars were left at the house to be collected in the morning.

"Shelly, beautiful job on the dinner. Your house looks fabulous."

"Of course, it does, Jenne. I had the best design team in the country helping me."

"It makes no difference; if the client isn't willing to be a team member, the best designer in the world can't deliver. It was you who made this happen. You should be very proud." It wasn't the first time Kevin had heard his wife say this, and as usual, she was correct.

"Bill, you're a lucky man, and Shell, you're lucky too. Thanks for a great evening." Kevin shook their hands and hugged them before he and Jenne left the Thornton residence.

"Is this Bernie Chesnick?"

"Who wants to know?"

"I guess you could say the guy who now owns all the diamonds you suckered those poor folks out of."

Bernie paused for a moment, trying to make sense of the call. "I thought Hartmann had them." There had been no mention of the diamonds after the arrest of the White List terrorists.

"Well, I guess he did. As you know, that fellow is in for life. He wouldn't have much use for them anyway. I now have the good fortune of holding a little blue velvet bag with millions of dollars' worth of diamonds in it."

"What do you want and how did you get my number?"

"I called your attorney and told him you'd really, really want to talk to me. I have a proposal I'd like to offer you."

"Why? If you've really got them, what do you need me for?"

"I need you to fence the stones for me. For a healthy cut. I'm guessing you still have some connections in the business, and I'm also guessing you could use a few extra million."

The silence suggested that it was taking some time for Bernie to process his thoughts. "How do you see this working?"

Why don't we get together and chat about that? Tell me where you are staying. I'll come to you."

"I'm at the extended stay place over on 116th Avenue Northeast. Suite 304."

"It'll take me an hour or so. See you then."

Bernie ended the call, stretched out on his bed, and stared at the ceiling.

Feeling clean for the first time in almost a year, Jesus actually enjoyed the bus ride across Lake Washington. The Cascades still had a few patches of snow from the winter, and Mount Rainier was majestically solid white from its 14,000-plus-foot peak down to the timber line.

He walked the half mile from the bus depot across the 405 freeway, then down 116th to the three-story budget hotel. Bernie answered the knock at the door and seemed surprised at the tidy-looking Hispanic fellow waiting to come in.

As the two appraised each other, Bernie motioned for Jesus to be seated at the cheap desk in a straight-backed chair. "Hi, Bernie. You can call me Joseph." Jesus didn't see the sense in using his real name.

"How about I call you Jesus Martinez? Isn't that your name?"

"I see you've done your homework. Since you have, you must know that I've killed a few people and attempted to kill many more. If I were you, I'd be very careful about using my real name."

Bernie was a loudmouth and full of bluster, but to his knowledge, he'd never been in the same room as a murderer. The look on his face displayed his nervousness. "Sure, okay, whatever, Joseph. What did you have in mind?"

"I'm assuming you still have connections in the jewelry business. Correct?"

"Some, yes. Go on."

"How were you planning on fencing the diamonds if you got away?"

Bernie's chubby face was becoming red with anxiety. "I know a few people that are a little shady. I was planning on selling a few at a time, below wholesale. There are probably half a dozen or so former associates that are back in the business who wouldn't mind making four hundred percent profit on some quality loose stones."

"I've heard that these things have serial numbers on them. That true?"

"It is." If Bernie was surprised at Jesus's knowledge of the industry, he didn't let on.

"So, if you offload them to these *associates*, how do they get around that?"

Bernie's obnoxiousness was now on display. "Don't be obtuse. All they need to do is *show* them the number and then print out a fake GIA certificate. The suckers actually think everything's on the up and up."

Jesus had learned to be cruel, especially when it suited him in the drug business. His lightning-quick hands shot across the narrow desk and grabbed the former jeweler by the throat. As he stood up, he lifted Bernie and pinned him to the wall.

"Just so we understand each other, fuckwad, I couldn't give two shits if you're alive or dead when our arrangement is completed. If I think you're being condescending or just being an asshole, which apparently, you're quite capable of, I will cut you." With that he reached into his pocket, grabbed his Kershaw Skyline, and snapped it open. "Do you understand?"

Bernie's face had gone from red to white. His eyes were now focused on the three-inch razor-sharp blade. "Yeah … yes. I'm sorry. I didn't mean to; I just got carried away. What do you want me to do?"

Jesus released his grip but maintained his intense glare. As he snapped his blade shut, he said, "You're going to contact your associates and tell them they're going to get an incredible deal on some excellent merchandise. Sell them the diamonds at fifty percent of wholesale; I don't care. Even at that, there should be twenty-five or thirty million dollars' worth of diamonds here."

"They won't be able to take them all at once. There are too many. It could be three or four months to unload all of them." Bernie had lost some of his more annoying tendencies."

"You're going to tell them it's a quantity discount. I want ten million dollars in cash, and I want it in a month."

Bernie's nerves were once again surfacing. "I don't know, Mar— er, Joseph. I don't think it's possible."

"Make it work. If I get my ten million in four weeks, you can have the rest of the diamonds. Do whatever you want with them. I don't care. Just don't *think* of fucking with me. You know you'll regret it." Jesus knew the fat fuck was calculating how much money he'd be left with, and, judging by the look on his face, he was going to move heaven and earth to make it happen.

"I think I can maybe do it, Joseph. Leave me a handful of stones and I'll get on it right away."

Jesus pulled the blue velvet bag from his blazer pocket and poured a small quantity of the glittering stones into Bernie's hand. "I'll be in touch. Call me if you need more."

With that, Jesus pocketed the blue bag and left a stunned Bernie Chesnick in his room to contemplate his future. Even if he didn't come up with the ten million, it would still be a bigger payday than what Klein had promised.

CHAPTER 27

With only two weeks until the invitational, Kevin had everything under control; or rather, Jenne and Shelly did. As the tournament chairman, he was supposedly responsible for the entire event. In reality, the head pro handled the golf tournament portion and the head chef took care of the hospitality issues.

The two women did the difficult work of signing up volunteers and deciding on menus, while Kevin decided on when the invitation letters went out. Basically, the only time the chairman *ever* did anything was in the unfortunate but unlikely event of someone cheating. If that occurred, it would be up to the chairman to handle the disqualification, although that had only happened once in the last fifteen years.

"Vince, everything looking good for the big event?" Kevin had just walked into the locker room after finishing his Wednesday afternoon round.

"Of course, Kevin. No snags just yet, and I don't expect any."

"Hell of a difference from last year, eh?"

"You can say that again. That was one scary event. I gotta tell you, though, with all the publicity we've had, our waiting list is longer than ever, even after boosting the initiation fee."

"Well, let's not let it get up there too high. Remember we're inclusive, not the other way around."

"Oh, sure, I know. We're still below the other clubs. It'll be nice to be able to get some new equipment for the course, though. Did you hear Shelly and Bill have reserved the club for their reception in mid-October?"

"That's terrific, Vince. I didn't know they had set a date. Remind me to give him a hard time."

"Of course. You know, next year you'll have to find another guest. Bill will be a member then."

"Yeah, well, I'll worry about that then."

Kevin was meeting Jenne and Shelly and her fiancé for dinner. He couldn't wait to see how they reacted to his knowledge of their tying the knot.

After meeting Jenne in the bar, Kevin ordered a bottle of Moet to be poured as soon as Shelly and Bill arrived. Jenne was thrilled at the news; she considered Shelly almost like a sister at this point.

"Hi, you two. Congratulations on the upcoming event." Kevin greeted Bill and Shelly as they entered the bar. He intentionally said it loudly enough to let the other members in on it, also to see the two of them blush a little.

"Okay, big mouth, how did you know?"

"I ran into Vince; he spilled the beans. Did you tell him to keep it a secret?"

"No, not really. Hell, we just made the reservation yesterday. Doesn't take long around here, does it?"

"Course not. It's a private club; no secrets, remember?"

Bill smiled warmly, more at Shelly than at the O'Malleys. "Yes. I should have known. We're planning on a reception here, but we're actually going to get married the week before. It's going to be very private, just the Justice and the two witnesses at Shelly's place."

"Our place, Bill, our place." Shelly left no doubt that she was all in with the relationship.

"That sounds wonderful, Bill. We wish you the very best." Jenne's sincerity was the perfect offset to her husband's constant needling.

"We want you and Kevin to be the witnesses. Will you?"

"Of course we will. Thanks for including us."

"Wait, don't I have a say in this?" Kevin just couldn't leave it alone.

"No, shithead, you don't. Now grab your glass and let's toast these guys."

Kevin, genuinely happy for his friends, proceeded to make a heartfelt toast. The entire bar grew quiet during the offering, clinked glasses after the salute, and clapped loudly for the soon-to-be-wed.

Chesnick had been a very busy man. He had unloaded the diamonds Martinez had given him and asked for another handful to move. Several of his former managers had found gainful employment and were in positions to move the merchandise.

Ginny Paterno had found a job as head buyer for a three-store chain in the Boston area. The arrest and plea bargain were still on her record, but apparently this was not a negative when searching for new employment within the industry. It seemed, in fact, that these were attractive talents when looking to fill a position of procurement in the jewelry business.

Paterno was eager to show her new boss how profitable she could be and had no qualms about falsifying GIA certificates. She alone had purchased close to a million dollars' worth of the stolen gems and wanted more.

Martinez found another, slightly less sleazy, motel that would take cash with no questions asked. He'd already received just over a million from Chesnick, and now the ex-con wanted a new supply to fence.

With his new wealth, he managed to find an expert forger who provided a driver's license, social security number, and fake credit cards. Martinez, now Joseph Bender, was able to open up a checking account at one of the B of A local branches. He convinced the young manager that he was new in town and needed to lease a safe deposit box as well. It was in this deposit box that Martinez stored his newfound cash, the diamonds, and the small plastic envelope of carfentanyl. The flophouse motel was fine for sleeping, less good for keeping valuables.

Chesnick and Martinez had been in phone contact several times during the past two weeks, and Chesnick had dropped off the cash at the motel, neatly packaged in a cheap briefcase. This second meeting, once again at the Extended Stay Hotel in Bellevue, was much more civilized than the first.

"Joseph, nice to see you again." It seemed Chesnick had remembered the lessons from their last meeting.

"Yes, Chesnick. You've done well so far moving the merchandise. I'm having second thoughts about a few things, however."

Chesnick's face now displayed great concern and not a small amount of fear. "I'm doing what you told me."

"Yes, you are, and very well." Chesnick seemed to relax some. "My problem is that all this cash is a pain in the ass. I can't just go lugging around suitcases full of the stuff. If my plan is to live in another country where I'll be safe from the FBI, I'll have to find some way to get my money there."

Ever the opportunist, Chesnick sensed an opening. "That's why the diamonds are so easy; they take up very little space and are much easier to smuggle into other countries."

Martinez nodded, obviously aware of this fact. "Agreed. The diamonds are easier to smuggle in, but they still need to be fenced once they are there."

"I have many contacts. Suppose I was to also move to that same other country. Diamonds are very simple to ship via UPS or FedEx. My associates could pay us in whatever currency that country uses or Bitcoin or something else. There is nothing left for me here anyway, since my fucking wife dissolved my business."

"I'm not sure I want to associate with you after I leave here. In fact, I *know* I don't."

"You won't have to. It can be the same arrangement as here— business only."

Martinez's look of concentration suggested he was mulling over the prospect of a continued relationship with this distasteful person. "Let me think about it. In the meantime, I have enough cash for now. Let's not convert any more of the diamonds. Tell your people there will be opportunities in a few months."

Martinez stood to leave the room. Chesnick jumped up.

"Joseph, I have a question for you on another subject."

"Yes?"

"All those people you tried to kill at Kelsey Creek."

"What about them?"

"Well, not really about *them*." Chesnick seemed about to step out on a plank suspended above a very deep ocean. "That stuff you were going to kill them with … do you know where I can get some?"

The look on Martinez's face was a combination of curiosity and even amusement. "Why?"

"If or when I leave here, I want my wife dead. She's the one who caused me this grief, and now she's living in luxury, all thanks to me. I was thinking if there was still some of that stuff around, I could find a way to use it, and before the cops could figure it out, I'd be gone. It would be much less messy too."

"So, you want to kill your wife?" Martinez was smiling now. "Have you ever killed anyone?"

"No."

"But you think you could do it?"

"I really fucking hate her. Yes, I'm certain I could. Besides, I'd find a way, with that stuff, so she'd croak when I wasn't there."

"Bernie, you're a surprising man. I'll get back to you."

Costa Rica. Martinez had heard about a number of Americans retiring there. It was rumored to be inexpensive and beautiful. Maybe that would be worth taking a look at. He was thinking he'd been lucky to make it this far without getting caught, and he wasn't going to tempt fate much longer.

Chesnick was a dipshit, but he *did* have connections. He wasn't sure he wanted to spend much time near the guy, however. Martinez decided the diamonds were far easier to transport than paper money, and the million or so in cash he already had would tide him over for some time.

As long as he kept the jewels, he felt safe from Chesnick trying anything silly. He was confident, too, that the jeweler was afraid of him. He stifled a chuckle, thinking maybe he would give him that last envelope of carfentanyl. It might be entertaining seeing him try to kill his wife.

Another week passed before he visited Bernie again with his proposal. "Here's what we'll do, Bernie. I'm going to buy a used car from one of those con artists out on Aurora. Then I'm going to load up my money and head south. I'll find a way to get across the border with it into Mexico. I still know some people there.

"I will take the rest of the diamonds too. If you are interested in getting some of them back and want to do some fencing, you can contact me on my cell. You can either move down there or not; your call."

"What about my money?"

"If you want *some* money, then you can help me fence the stones when you get there."

"Suppose you just take them and leave and I can't reach you?"

"Bernie, you're much better at selling these than I am. That's what you have going for you. I'm leaving in three days. Oh, and here—be very fucking careful with this stuff." He tossed the plastic envelope onto the desk. Bernie looked at it, stunned.

"Is that …?"

"Yes, it is. How are you going to use it?"

"I thought maybe I could put some on her steering wheel or something. She drives that new SLC convertible and usually keeps the top down when it's nice. I think I could do it at the golf club."

"It's almost like sugar inside that envelope. You'll need to mix it with something to coat the wheel—maybe use cold cream or Vaseline or something. And when you do, wear gloves, long sleeves, and a respirator. That shit is lethal."

Bernie was looking like maybe this was too complicated. "Is it hard to do?"

"You mean kill someone?"

"No, I mean is it hard to mix the stuff up?"

"Bernie, you get a bowl, put the goopy stuff in it, and then pour the carfentanyl in and stir. Does that sound difficult?" Jesus was losing patience with his protégé.

"Okay, got it."

"You're on your own now, Bernie. Call me when you're ready to do business again." Jesus turned and left, leaving Bernie still staring at the small plastic envelope.

CHAPTER 28

Santiago Hernandez had experienced a whirlwind year. The publicity surrounding his heroic effort to save many lives had plastered his likeness on so many TV screens that he was instantly recognizable. While still a happy member of the greens crew at Kelsey Creek, he had resorted to a large straw hat and sunglasses whenever he was in a public setting.

At first the screaming girls and autograph seekers were flattering and welcome. Lately, though, he just wanted to be left alone. His financial worries were much less concerning now that he was being paid as a consultant on the new Netflix movie. His publicity tour would net him more money than he had ever seen, and the children's book looked to be a bestseller.

Still, he enjoyed maintaining the golf course and he was good at it. His boss liked him, the members *loved* him, and his crew mates treated him like just one of the gang. Closing in on his sixteenth birthday and with the afternoon off, he was headed to Bellevue Square on the bus. His mother's birthday was on Saturday, and now that he had a little money, he could get her something special.

The bus had made its final stop at 116th before heading to the depot. Santiago was seated midway down the bus, on the aisle side. When he saw the Hispanic businessman get on and remain standing until the next stop, he felt a chill.

The man was skinnier than he remembered, and he had a beard and long hair. Santiago had worked alongside him for several months. This was the man who had put the poison in the putting green cups. It was Jesus.

Santiago knew that the police were trying to find this man. He still had Kevin's phone number from when he had brought the detective to see him. He called it now.

"Mr. Kevin, it's Santiago."

"Hi, Santiago. I told you it's Kevin—no Mr. And why are you whispering?"

"Okay, Kevin. The man who did the poison is here on the bus with me."

"What, are you sure?"

"Yes, very sure. He looks different, but I know this man. It is him."

"Okay, tell me what he's wearing and what he looks like now. Be very quiet about it. Can he hear or see you?"

"No. I am farther back in the bus and I have my disguise on." Santiago proceeded to describe Jesus's appearance to Kevin.

"Now listen to me, Santiago. Don't follow him and don't let him see you. If you can, see what bus he transfers to, but make certain he doesn't see you. Got it?"

"Yes, Kevin. I will. You will call me back?"

"Yes, either I will or Bill Owens or Matt Steele. Now, *be* careful."

Kevin had been standing next to Bill the entire time he was on the phone. They were getting ready to play a practice round for the upcoming tournament when Santiago had called.

"Don't tell me, it's Martinez."

"It is. He's on the bus with Santiago. They'll be at the final stop in a couple of minutes."

Without a word, Bill got Matt Steele on the phone.

"Matt, Martinez is getting off a bus at the transfer station in Bellevue in a minute or two. Can you get someone over there?"

"Not that fast. Do you have any uniforms over there?"

"None that I want messing with this guy. How soon can you mobilize?"

"Probably fifteen minutes or so, soonest. Can you find out the bus he transfers to?

"I'll get back to you. Please hurry." It was the FBI's ballgame now, but Bill had been in the middle of this since day one. He would not let go this time.

"Kev, can you get Santiago on the phone again?"

"Let me see. I just don't want that kid getting hurt."

Kevin's call was answered on the first ring. "Kevin, I can see him. I'm standing behind the newsstand. It looks like he is getting in line for another bus."

"Can you make out the number or see where it's going?"

"Si. The bus says downtown Seattle. It is number 328. He is getting on now."

"That's great, Santiago. Don't do anything else. You've been a very big help."

"Thank you, Kevin. I'll go to the mall and do my shopping." With that, the youngster headed over to Bell Square to find a gift for his mom. Perhaps later he would realize the import of his information.

Jesus Martinez, aka Joseph Bender, hopped on the bus for the short trip to the Bellevue transfer station. He had walked this short leg of the trip in the past, but he was tired. He was glad he would be leaving the country soon.

He was also glad that he wouldn't have to endure any more meetings with Chesnick. That the putz would find a way to fuck up murdering his wife was something he felt was inevitable.

Jesus had plenty of cash and millions in diamonds. When he got to where he was going, he'd find a way to fence the stones even if it meant getting twenty cents on the dollar. First to the bank to return the diamonds to the safety box, then to shop for a car. He was sick of taking the bus.

After transferring to the express coach, he settled down for the thirty-minute trip across Lake Washington via the I-90 bridge. He was looking forward to leaving this part of the world.

His ride finally pulled up to the Pioneer Square station, located in the southern end of the massive bus tunnel. There were several other busses coming and going, as well as a number of pedestrians waiting for theirs to arrive.

As Jesus took the two steps down to the curb, a young woman and an older gentleman seemed to walk into him. He looked up in surprise as they immediately pulled his arms behind his back and slipped thick zip ties over his hands. Another man walked up and faced him. "Jesus Martinez, my name is Special Agent Matt Steele. You are under arrest for domestic terrorism, murder, and attempted murder. You're coming with us."

He had spent ten months in the hellhole of the homeless. He had suffered more than any other time in his life, and now, three short days before he left this place, he was being arrested. The only image that kept him from total despair was that of Bernie Chesnick, wannabe murderer. Maybe someone would let him know how *that* turned out.

CHAPTER 29

"It seems like whenever we plan on playing in this tournament, the shit hits the fan." Kevin was chatting with Bill Owens while standing on the practice green after passing along the information to the FBI. They were supposed to tee off in twenty minutes.

"I'd give anything to be there when Matt arrests that guy, but it's really his show. I have complete confidence in him."

"I sure hope this closes the door on this case. It's been a long slog with some very bad folks."

"I agree, Kevin. I—" Bill's phone buzzed in mid-sentence.

"Hey, Matt, talk to me … that's great news! Congratulations." A moment or two went by, then, "Yes, we'll be sure to do that."

"Tell me they got him."

"They got him. They finally got the bastard. Seems like he was living as a homeless person on the streets for the last year, in plain sight."

"Unbelievable. How about the diamonds and any of those drugs the guy had?"

"Matt said they found enough diamonds on him to be worth millions. He also said that Santiago gave a perfect description to you. They nailed him right as he stepped off the bus, no complications. He said make sure you tell him that he couldn't have done it otherwise."

"Somehow I think that kid's long-term future won't be on the greens crew. He's very smart and full of personality. I hate to think what would have happened if not for him."

"You know, Kevin, it looks like we're finally going to be able to complete this event this year. I'm sure there are criminal elements in play somewhere in the city, but nothing like what we've been through.

Let's go kick some ass." The two friends headed up the short rise to the first tee, both looking forward to a stress-free tournament at last.

Shelly had picked up Jenne from the office to spend a few hours shopping at Nordstrom's. With the upcoming wedding still months away, there was ample time for roaming the mall. Her motto, though, was *you can never start too soon*, and she swore by it.

Jenne was happy just to be along for the ride. Yes, there was the occasional sale item that caught her eye, but mostly she enjoyed the hunt. Somewhere lurking was the perfect pair of shoes, the absolute one and only dress that would work, and the purse that was "to die for." These items needed only to be discovered, and these were the two women to do it.

The plan was to spend most of the afternoon searching for the holy grail of specialness, or maybe the best bargain of all time. After the hunt, they were meeting Kevin and Bill at the Creek for an early dinner.

Bernie was sick of his suite at the goddamn Extended Stay Motel. After his divorce settlement plus the restitution he had to pay, he only had forty or fifty thousand bucks to his name.

If he had had to pay all the people he'd stolen from, he'd be millions in the hole. Thank god they hadn't recovered most of the diamonds. That bitch of a wife was sitting in the lap of luxury with the money *he* had earned. She had sold all the real estate and bought out his leases.

When he was sitting on top of millions in stolen jewels, he hadn't given any thought to her. Now that he was damn near broke, all he could think about was her and her fucking new boyfriend, the dick who had helped bring him down.

Martinez was gone with the jewels and the money, but Chesnick had managed to sneak half a dozen of the flawless stones from the last batch he'd fenced through his former managers. At least those would net him some cash.

He would think about following the killer to wherever he was going, but only if he wasn't able to come up with a better plan. Not only didn't he like Martinez, he was afraid of him.

First things first, he thought. *Gotta get rid of that bitch.* He figured that if he used the carfentanyl, the cops would think it was the same guy who had hit the golf course last year. He tried to remember how he was supposed to mix it with something—something goopy.

He found some lotion in his shaving kit, but it proved too thin; it would in no way stick to anything. After a trip to the drug store and then Home Depot for safety equipment, he settled down to concoct the deadly weapon.

At first, he considered cold cream, but it proved too viscous. All the potions he had purchased were much too thin and watery, and the Vaseline petroleum jelly, although thick enough, appeared as though it would liquify under the heat of the sun.

Losing patience with his selection of ingredients, he had a sudden brainstorm. Something that was *really* sticky and pasty, but he only considered it because it had been recently used. Toothpaste!

The tube of Colgate Optic White appeared in his crosshairs. The only problem was that it was white. He'd just have to make sure to coat the underside of the steering wheel with it.

He donned the rubber gloves and the painter's respirator and poured the contents of the plastic envelope into one of the hotel water glasses. The one-ounce portion looked harmless enough; it was really hard to believe that it was that potent. He tried to remember what Martinez had said about how to mix the stuff, but he had only been half listening to the guy.

Next he squirted the entire tube of toothpaste into the glass and, with a fork left over from his takeout last night, did his best to mix the two ingredients. After what he felt was sufficient stirring, he placed the provided sanitary cap over the top of the glass.

Since he was a past club member, he was well aware of the format of the invitational. The Wednesday before the actual event was always the practice round, and *almost* always the spouses met up afterwards for a bite to eat.

There was a good chance his former fucking wife would be there with her fancy fucking convertible. Just the thought of her spasming in death gave him a partial woody. He figured his forced abstinence from strange pussy was not without side effects.

CHAPTER 30

For a year Emma had led an uneventful life. There was that time she was on TV when everyone made such a fuss over her, but that was long ago. The routine was what she really loved; knowing where to go, what to expect, who to see.

There were her playdates with Rosie once a week that were really fun. Chasing each other, wrestling, smelling, and, yes, barking; those were great times. Rosie's mom and dad were really nice to her; they gave her lots of treats. She liked them a lot, but she didn't *love* them. She only loved *her* mom and dad, her pack mates.

She loved where her pack lived too, in the woods. There were so many smells to experience! There were rabbits to chase, coyotes to bark and howl at, even bear cubs to chase, but her mom got angry when she did that.

Whenever the FedEx or the UPS truck came, she got nervous and really started barking. They were strangers to her, and an unknown person was always something to be wary of. If her mom or dad said it was okay, then she stopped, but she was still vigilant. If *anything* seemed like a threat to her pack, she would watch it until it went away. That was her job, and she did it well.

Going to work with her mom and dad was fun too. She got to ride in the truck and spend the day with Valerie and Ilene. She had gone to work this morning with her mom and dad, and then her dad took her to Rosie's. She was already tired from chasing Rosie around the yard and was resting in the shade of the big maple tree.

Rosie's yard had a big fence around it that was old and falling apart in places. Her mom and dad were normally outside with them while they were playing, but now that they were tired and resting, her parents were in the house. Emma's eyes were drooping as she started to doze, when she instantly alerted at some motion at the base of the fence.

The tiny ball of cotton suggested a bunny was there, then the smell instantly confirmed it. Tired or not, she loved chasing them, and now was no exception. The rabbit bolted under the decayed section of fence while Emma crashed through the rotten wood.

She chased it down the sidewalk, around the corner, and down a gravel walkway. By the time the bunny had vanished into a thicket of blackberry bushes, Emma found herself in the middle of Kelsey Creek Farm. She came here lots of times with her parents for walks and to visit the animals. They had goats and pigs and horses here for youngsters to see, and they all smelled wonderful.

Emma knew where she was, and she knew that the golf course where her mom and dad played was right next to the park. She started trotting toward the golf course, hoping to see a member of her pack. She'd rather see them than Rosie now anyway.

After scoring several once-in-a-lifetime bargains, Jenne and Shelly motored toward the club. Shelly's AMG SLC 43 was a beautiful car. She had purchased the candy-apple-red roadster several months ago, and Jenne thought it suited her well.

Her friend had come a long way from having to live with that asshole, Bernie, to ending up with a wonderful partner who really cared about her. Fate was a funny thing, she thought. First a murder at the club, then the stolen diamonds, then the terrorist attack, and the guy in the middle of it all was Bill Owens. If not for Shelly's being married to Bernie, the prick, she would never have met Bill.

Since they had come to work in Kevin's truck, Jenne accepted the taxi service from Shelly. Taking two vehicles back home after dinner was to be avoided; that way there was always a designated driver.

It was four o'clock on a beautiful sunny afternoon when they pulled into the club parking lot. Both lower levels were full because of the tournament, so they parked in the upper lot, a good 150 yards from the entrance. With the security alarm activated, it was no problem leaving the top down.

Bernie Chesnick parked his eight-year-old Acura in the small parking lot of the Kelsey Creek Farm. The huge white barn that housed the animals was up the hill on his right as he followed one of the bark-strewn paths that meandered throughout the 150-acre property.

This favorite site for walkers, joggers, and animal lovers bordered the entire south boundary of the Kelsey Creek Country Club. Most of the boundary line was inaccessible due to heavy brush, creeks, and wetlands, but there was a connecting trail at the far east end of the farm.

A significant elevation change, negotiated by 163 railroad tie steps, left Bernie panting and winded as he finally reached the summit. From there it was another 1,500 yards to the upper parking lot of the country club. Bernie had placed the glass containing his deadly toothpaste into one of the plastic laundry bags that hung in his hotel closet and sealed it tightly. He had carried it like a grenade with its pin pulled for the entire journey.

He approached the rarely used upper lot carefully, making sure he was shielded by the trees from the clubhouse. Shelly's car was easy to spot—bright red exterior, saddle interior, a very beautiful vehicle. Too bad he had to defile the hand-stitched leather-wrapped steering wheel. Bernie carefully untied the laundry bag and removed the hotel glass with the cardboard cover still in place.

He congratulated himself on remembering to bring the rubber gloves along, but somehow, he had forgotten something to use to coat the steering wheel. A quick search yielded a broken branch, about three feet long, from one of the nearby trees. He figured the bitch had turned her alarm on, so it was important not to lean on the vehicle or even touch it.

Chesnick stripped the needles from the branch, removed the cover, and stuck the branch into the goop. The mixture smelled of peppermint and was pasty and sticky as hell. He proceeded awkwardly to scrape small blobs of the stuff onto the back side of the steering wheel.

After he had used all but a small portion of it, still stuck to the bottom of the glass, he set it aside. Next, using the same branch, he scraped the blobs as smoothly as he could to coat a good portion of the back of the wheel.

His arms were aching after leaning over the door for so long. He had messed up a few areas, but hopefully she wouldn't see it when she returned. He placed the almost-empty glass back into the laundry bag and flung the stick deep into the blackberry bushes. He removed his gloves and as he prepared to make his way back to the farm, he heard a low, menacing growl.

CHAPTER 31

Emma was in no hurry. The smells here on the farm were many and varied. Lots of new things, never before smelled, were here and many old smells from when she had last visited this place.

She had been trotting on the worn path for a few minutes when a whiff of her mom floated by. She dropped her nose to the ground but got nothing. Only when she held it up high could she grab the scent.

The next time she caught it, there was another familiar smell. Her mom's friend was there too. This was great news; she could surprise them, and they would ooohh and aaahh and tell her what a good girl she was.

As she passed the last grouping of trees, the scent became much stronger, along with another familiar smell, like the stuff in the tube in the bathroom. She entered the end of the parking lot nearest the trees and saw her mom's friend's car. She could smell the leather in it too.

Something was wrong, though. There was a man leaning over the car and she didn't know his smell. Through thousands of years of evolved instinct, her breed was uncanny in sensing danger, and she sensed it now.

It wasn't immediate danger like when the man who came to their house had threatened her mom, but she sensed something amiss, nonetheless. She uttered a low, menacing growl to let the man know that she was there and that he shouldn't be near anything that smelled like her mom.

He turned and looked at her, first surprised, then afraid. He started running. There was a white plastic bag in his hand. When someone she knew ran from her, she knew it was a game, so she chased after them. When someone who shouldn't be near a place where her mom had been runs away, she knew to chase him away so he wouldn't pose a threat.

The man was clumsy and slow. After only a few strides, she caught up with him and bared her teeth with another growl, just to make sure he left the area. He was really afraid now and turned, swinging the bag, trying to hurt her. This *was* a bad man.

He missed with the first swing but connected with the second and hit her on the head with a glancing blow. It only hurt a little, but it made a funny noise like one time when she hit her mom's wine glass with her tail and it broke. She had got into trouble for that.

The man was out of breath and stood staring at her, still holding his bag. She sat, stared, and growled.

He looked inside his bag and as he did, a round piece of something fell out of a hole near the bottom of the bag where he'd hit her with it. He quickly caught it, then he did a strange thing. He looked at his hand and screamed as he dropped the thing on the ground.

Emma was now just sitting, her head screwed sideways, attempting to figure out what was happening. The man wasn't running anymore, and he no longer seemed afraid. He just stared at her for a minute, then grabbed at the neck of his shirt and fell over, shuddering violently as he hit the ground.

The peppermint smell was strong here and something else too. She sat several yards from the man and started barking.

Jenne had just sat down with Shelly and ordered a glass of wine from the bar when her cell phone buzzed. It was taboo to talk on the cell while in the public areas of the club, so after seeing who the caller was, she excused herself and quickly moved to the outside patio.

"Hi, Gail, what's up? Everything okay?" Gail was Rosie's mom and also a good friend.

"Jenne, I'm so sorry. I hate to tell you this, but Emma was chasing something and busted through the fence. The last time I saw her, she was headed over to Kelsey Creek Farm."

"She's been over there a lot, Gail. I'm sure she'll be fine. I'll go look now. I'll call you when we find her."

"Please do, Jenne. I'm really sorry."

Jenne went into the bar and told Shelly what the problem was.

"So, let's go find her. We can go in the back way through the upper lot." Shelly was always willing to pitch in.

While they were leaving the club, Bill and Kevin were just coming in from their practice round. After Jenne told them what was happening, it was decided that the men would join them; it *was* a big farm.

As they headed up the hill, they could hear Emma barking very loudly. "That's Emma. I'd know her bark anywhere. She must have walked here on the east trail. She sounds like something's wrong, though." Jenne began calling her, with no success.

"C'mon, let's see what the big racket is all about." Kevin and Bill were double timing it up the hill.

As they passed Shelly's new car, they saw the German Shepherd sitting some distance down the path. Several paces from her they could see something large lying on the trail.

"Whoa, guys, hold up right here. Jenne, see if you can get Emma over here." Bill Owens instantly turned into the professional that he was.

Jenne, in a calm voice, coaxed her dog away from what they could now see was a body.

"You three stay here. I'm gonna go take a look." Bill walked deliberately over to the body as Emma passed him, trotting dutifully over to Jenne.

After checking for a pulse, he stood back up and walked in a wide circle around the body. He quickly called the station to get the crime scene techs over. It seemed they were always coming out to Kelsey Creek Country Club. He picked up a long stick and poked at something on the ground and then, still with the stick, lifted part of the white plastic laundry bag and peeked inside.

Bill got back on the phone as he slowly walked back to his friends. "Better get the hazmat folks out here too, Joey. I'm thinking I know what happened." He disconnected and looked over at his soon-to-be wife.

"Shell, that's Bernie over there. I can't say for sure, but it looks like he OD'd on something. It could be the same stuff they tried to use on everyone last year."

Shelly appeared stunned by the news. "Holy shit! I really detested the guy, but I didn't want him dead. Could you tell what happened?"

Both Kevin and Jenne were paying very close attention as well. Emma was doing her best to stay quiet and out of the way.

"I can't say for sure—lots of unknowns. It looks like his hand was cut by some glass. He had some white stuff on it that *looked* like toothpaste. I can't imagine what he was doing here or why. I *can* tell you that if that stuff is what I think it is, he died very quickly."

"Geez, Bill, it seems like this place is a shit magnet. I sure hope this is the end of things." Kevin voiced what the others were undoubtedly thinking.

"It's gonna be a dog and pony show over here in a few minutes, guys. You should probably head back to the bar; I bet they'll let their hero dog in there too. Shelly, I'm sorry about you having to see this. I think you'd better move your car down to the lower lot. We'll have some big vehicles arriving soon."

All agreed. Bill stayed to protect the scene, the O'Malleys headed down to the bar, and Shelly climbed into her brand-new car. After getting a peck on the cheek from her fiancé, she reached over and pressed the start button as she grabbed the steering wheel with her left hand.

CHAPTER 32

"Ugh, what is this shit? It smells like fucking toothpaste."

Bill, distracted for a split second by the arrival of the support troops, suddenly realized what had happened. All the pieces tumbled into place.

He reached into the red sports car and yanked Shelly out by her shoulders. Her left hand held a smear of Colgate Optic White on three fingers.

Shelly's eyes began to flutter as he laid her on the asphalt, ripped her sweater off, and scraped her fingers clean.

He turned to the arriving techs, "Narcan, now, fast!"

The officer in the lead dropped his bags and quickly opened one. He reached in and tossed the spray bottle to Bill, who, in one motion, twisted off the cap and gave each of Shelly's nostrils a generous spray of the drug.

She was still breathing as Bill carried her to a patrol car. He yelled over his shoulder to consider the Mercedes a crime scene as well and not to touch anything. With lights and sirens blasting, he raced her to the hospital.

One of the officers stationed at the crime scene walked down to the bar after receiving a call from Detective Owens, now at Overlake Hospital. He walked over to the O'Malleys' table, the only one with a German Shepherd lying beside it, and, at Owens's direction, filled them in on what had happened.

Jenne had tears in her eyes. "God, Kevin, I can't believe it. That stupid fuck actually tried to murder his ex-wife. C'mon, let's go see Bill at the hospital." After a quick call and a trip to see Gail, who was more than happy to mind Emma after her escape, they hurried off to the Medical Center.

They arrived at the ER and were told to go to a small waiting room, where they found a pale, worried-looking detective sipping shitty machine coffee. Jenne rushed over to give him a hug as Kevin patted him on the back.

"One of your guys told us what happened. We're in shock. Have the docs said anything?"

"About a half hour ago they said her pulse was very weak but that she was still breathing. He said the Narcan might have tipped the scales in our favor. That's all I know."

Just then the door opened, and a young woman entered and looked directly at Bill. "I am Doctor Safa Chandra. Are you the fiancé?"

"Yes, I am."

"And these people?"

"We are her very close friends. How is she?" Jenne seemed about to lose it.

The young Indian doctor looked at the three of them and took a deep breath.

"She is going to be fine. For some reason the opiate—it was very powerful—only contacted her skin in one tiny place. Still, if it had not been for the Narcan, she would be dead. She is very lucky. We'll keep her tonight for observation, and she can go home in the morning."

"Can we see her?" Jenne's eyes were tearing up as she tightened her lips in an effort to stave off the waterworks.

"Yes, but only for a moment."

As the three friends entered the room, Shelly's eyes fluttered open. "Hey, Bill. Hey, you guys." Her voice was drowsy and her smile weak, but she was very much alive.

"You gave us a hell of a scare, honey. They say you're gonna be fine, though, and you can go home tomorrow." Bill was giving her hand a squeeze as he spoke.

Jenne was holding her other hand. "Don't you ever do that to me again, got it?" she said with a tender smile.

"I got it, I got it." The words were slightly slurred, but the smile was genuine.

The O'Malleys said their goodbyes and promised to hook up with Bill the next morning. He still had a big night ahead of him.

CHAPTER 33

Thursday was a day off for the tournament contestants. With the practice round on Wednesday and the tournament proper on Friday and Saturday, it was a welcome respite.

Bill had taken Shelly home from the hospital and had invited the O'Malleys over for coffee at eleven o'clock.

The four friends were seated in Shelly's new seating group and all looked over at a very tired Bill Owens to bring them up to speed on yesterday's events.

"The techs and the hazmat crew were at the scene until two this morning. The drug *was* carfentanyl. Here's what we think went down. Apparently, Bernie was fencing the diamonds for Martinez."

"Huh, what?" Kevin seemed lost already.

"I talked to Matt Steele last night and he filled me in on a few things. Martinez had some forged IDs with him when they picked him up; they found a safety deposit box key on him as well. It was an easy deal to find the bank and the box, and when they opened it, they found over a million in cash, a few diamonds, and Maisy, the drug dog, found a trace of opiate in there.

"We think Martinez—he's not talking, by the way—fenced a bunch of the stones through Bernie, and we think Bernie got the opiate from Martinez.

"We're pretty certain about all this because we found a few loose diamonds at Chesnick's hotel room that were most likely from Martinez. Right now, Matt has a crew rounding up some of Bernie's old associates to have a little chat with them."

"Yikes, it's getting complicated. How come Bernie died and my pal here made it through?" Jenne was engrossed in the story; she

212

wanted all the details and she was very happy her friend was still here. Shelly stole her a glance and a wink.

Bill's phone buzzed before he could continue. As he looked at the caller ID, he told them, "It's Matt. Give me a sec."

"Okay, talk to me … really, come on … no shit? Oh man, that helps clear up a few things. Thanks, Matt.

"Well, Jenne, that information just checked all the boxes for me. What we found was that the glass that pierced Bernie's hand was the round bottom of a hotel glass that had broken in the laundry bag. I'm guessing he swung it at something, maybe Emma if she was after him, and broke it. The sharp edges sliced the plastic bag and the glass fell out. Bernie either touched it or tried to catch it and it cut his hand.

"Matt just told me that Martinez did say something. He said, 'Did that fucking nimrod Chesnick manage to off his wife or did he fuck it up?'

"He said he figured Bernie wasn't paying attention when he told him how to mix the stuff. When Matt told him Bernie was no longer with us, Martinez got a big kick out of it.

"The lab crew found that the concentration of carfentanyl in the broken bottom of the glass was ten times stronger than the stuff on Shell's steering wheel. They were able to figure out that Chesnick dumped the opiate in the glass, then squirted the toothpaste over the top of it. Because of the consistency of the toothpaste, the stuff didn't mix very well.

"Martinez made a point of telling him to add the opiate last, not first. I guess if he's gonna spend the rest of his life in prison, it's good he has that memory to humor him."

"So, the combination of the smaller concentration of carfentanyl in the toothpaste on my steering wheel and the quick squirt of the Narcan saved my life, right?" They were the first words Shelly had spoken since they had all sat down.

"That's pretty much it, Shell," confirmed Bill.

"So, I owe my life to a dolt of an ex-husband and the quick actions and intelligence of my future husband. Cool." She stood and came over to Bill to hug him.

Kevin and Bill were on the first tee at Kelsey Creek Country Club for the opening round of the tournament on Friday morning. Jeff Williams and his brother were their playing partners, while Shelly and Jenne had gone to their assigned hole to sit and chat and maybe look up if a hole-in-one occurred.

Jeff was aware, as was everyone else in the club, of Chesnick's demise and the Wednesday evening crime scene in the upper parking lot.

"So, you two," he said, looking at Kevin and his partner, "do you think there's any fucking way we can get through this event without mass murder or people getting clubbed with wedges or poisoned in their cars? I mean, really, do you?"

Kevin reached over to his partner and put his arm around his shoulder. "Jeff, my boy, that's a high bar you set. I think *this* year, though, we just might make it."